REDEEMER

A JOHN MILTON NOVEL

MARK DAWSON

PROLOGUE

Andreas Lima had enjoyed his week away. London in the spring was always a pleasant place to visit, and this particular trip had been lavish, even by his own recent standards. Lima had been to London on business, and, as the company he had gone to visit was paying for his trip, he had been treated to the very best hospitality. He had stayed in a suite at the Dorchester, reclining with Arabs and Russians amid the most opulent surroundings. Dinner had been at Alain Ducasse and The Araki, the Japanese restaurant in New Burlington Street that had only just been awarded its third Michelin star. There had been women, too, young beauties who appeared at his side at the bar after dinner and paid him an inordinate amount of attention given that he was not the most attractive of men, nor as young as he once was.

Lima was no fool. The entire trip, and all of the entertainment—the women included—had been paid for out of the largesse of the multinational corporation that was bidding for the deep-water drilling rights to the Campos and Santos basins. His employer was Petróleo Brasil

Nacional, and it had been awarded three of the six drilling blocks that had been put up for auction by the Brazilian government. PBN was looking for a partner to help exploit the most challenging block, and the corporation's executives, including Lima, had been flown around the world to a series of beauty pageants. There had been visits to Texas to see a large American multinational, a week in St Kitts at a Dutch company's expense, and a jaunt to Paris with a French conglomerate. The host of the London trip was extremely keen to make a good impression, judging by the amount of effort that had been expended to woo Lima and his colleagues.

Returning to Rio, and the mundane realities of making his way through security at Galeão and then the crowds of other passengers going about their business, was something of a comedown. He had flown first class in both directions and had been insulated from the ignominies of poor service, cramped space and the foibles of other passengers, but now those pleasures were quickly fading away into the background. The queue for immigration was slow, and, even though he had been able to disembark first, he had already been waiting for twenty minutes. He had promised to return to the office for the monthly meeting of the executive division, and now it looked as if he was going to be late.

The queue shuffled forward until, finally, Lima was at the front. He waited for the woman at the booth to be processed, and then, summoned by a curt gesture from the official, he came forward.

"Passport," the woman said.

Lima opened the document at his photograph and slid it through the gap at the bottom of the booth's Perspex screen. The woman looked at the picture and back up at Lima's face. He waited for her, tapping his foot with an impatience that he was unable to hide. There was no reason that she would know that he held a senior role in the biggest oil and gas operation in South America, that he had a chauffeured Mercedes waiting for him outside, and that he had more money in his wallet than she would make in a month. There was no reason why she should know any of that, but, even though he knew it was irrational, it was all Lima could do to prevent himself from rapping his knuckles on the screen and asking her to hurry up.

Finally, she slid the passport back through the slot.

"*Bem-vindo, senhor* Lima."

Lima acknowledged her with a curt dip of his head and made his way through the passage into the arrivals lounge beyond.

He descended the escalator into the shabby hall. Two barriers had been erected, and the passengers were being funnelled between them. Lima looked for the chauffeur who would drive him back into the city. He wheeled his case around a slow-moving family and searched along the signs held aloft by the waiting drivers for his own name.

He saw it, caught the driver's eye, and indicated with a flick of his hand that he would meet him where the barriers ended. He pulled around another slow-moving passenger and quickened his pace, keen to get into the car and away.

"*Senhor* Lima?"

He stopped. A man dressed in a police uniform had stepped out to block his way.

"Yes?"

"You're under arrest."

"What? What for?"

"On suspicion of fraud, extortion and embezzlement. Come with me, please."

The officer reached for him, but Lima pulled his arm

away and stepped back. "This is a mistake," he said. "Do you know who I am?"

"I do, sir, and I'm afraid that it's not a mistake. You're under arrest. It would be better for you if you came with me without protesting. I could cuff you, but I'm sure you'd rather I didn't."

Lima was blinded by the sudden flashes of light from both sides of the barriers. There were photographers there; they had been waiting for him, waiting for the moment when he was put under arrest. They had been tipped off.

Lima felt sick. He knew exactly what was happening: this was the classic strategy of Felipe Saverin, the judge from Curitiba who was conducting the high-profile corruption investigation that had been such big news over the course of the past month. It had been in the papers and on the nightly news, but Lima had been careful and had been as confident as he could possibly be that he was insulated from Saverin's attention.

But now this...

Saverin had made it his policy to tip off the press before he made arrests. He wanted to load the shame onto those men and women he suspected, capturing their lowest moments in an attempt to convict them in the court of public opinion before they were even brought to trial. He brought them down, trashed their reputations, ruined them so that they would be more amenable to the deals he would offer them if they were only prepared to finger someone higher up the food chain.

And that was a problem for Lima. There were so few above him.

He had always known, however, that there was a possibility of this, so even though he had pushed it to the back of his mind, he had prepared a contingency. There was a man, hidden among the shacks and shanties that made up the slums of Rocinha, who would be able to help him. Saverin thought that he was insulated by the authority of his office, but he was wrong. The man whom Andreas Lima had already decided to contact would pay no heed to any of that. He would find the judge's weaknesses and exploit them.

There was no doubt in Lima's mind: Saverin had made a terrible mistake, and now he was going to have to pay.

PART I

THE FIRST DAY

1

J ohn Milton looked out of the window of the 747 as it emerged beneath the black thunderhead that the pilot had warned them had settled over the city. The plane banked, and Milton could see the land beneath them: the jagged spires of mountains, the brown rock garlanded with lush green vegetation, and, laid out on their flanks like a vast chequerboard, the *favelas* that comprised most of Rio de Janeiro. The plane banked in the opposite direction, and the porthole window tipped away from the city to show the underside of the angry storm clouds above. The pilot announced that they would be on the ground in ten minutes and told the cabin crew to take their seats.

Milton had slept during the seven-hour flight from Panama City, and he felt a little sluggish. He reached down to the mesh pocket that was fixed to the seatback and took out his phone, popped a sweet into his mouth to help equalise the air pressure, pressed his earbuds into his ears, and scrolled through his playlist until he found his Guns N' Roses playlist and swiped down until he found 'Paradise

City.' The music started to play, muffling the noise of the engines as the jet lined up for landing.

Milton watched out of the window again and saw the statue of Christ the Redeemer, His arms spread wide, welcoming new arrivals to the teeming metropolis over which He watched.

Milton closed his eyes and concentrated on the music.

THERE WAS a shortage of open booths at immigration, and Milton had to wait in line. He had expected the airport to be busy. Rock in Rio opened tomorrow with several days of concerts that would bring thousands of people to the city. Coming here to experience the festival had been on Milton's bucket list for years, and despite his usual dourness, he found that he was excited at the prospect. The airport had been decorated to welcome tourists who had come to enjoy the week-long event, with banners draped from the ceiling that displayed photographs of the artists taking part. Guns N' Roses were headlining the first night, but hundreds of other performers had been scheduled to appear across the seven days. Samba music could be heard from the other side of the immigration booths, and the irritable official who chivvied the queue onwards had been made to wear a feathered carnival headdress. It was an incongruous sight.

Milton was called to the window. He handed his passport to the officer and waited as the man looked down at his photograph and then up to his face.

"*Senhor* Smith?"

"That's right."

"What is your business in Brazil?"

"Pleasure," Milton said. "The music festival."

"Where are you staying?"

"With a friend."

The man looked down at the passport again as if weighing up this new piece of information, and then flipped through the document to an empty page and stamped it. He pushed the passport back through the slot, muttered something in Portuguese that Milton did not understand, and then beckoned the woman in the queue behind Milton to make her way forward.

Milton hiked his rucksack onto his shoulder and made his way between the two booths.

Shawn Drake was at the front of the barrier in the arrivals lounge. He was wearing shorts and a Guns N' Roses T-shirt, and his clothes and hair were wet from the rain that Milton had seen through the windows as he had disembarked from the jet. Drake's face broke into a broad smile as he saw Milton.

"John!" he called out, waving an arm.

Milton raised his own hand in acknowledgement and made his way to the end of the barrier. Drake met him there. He wrapped his arms around Milton, embraced him and clapped him roughly on his back. The two of them had much in common, but Milton's reserve stood in stark contrast to Drake's fondness for shows of affection. Milton had never been one for that; it had been true when they had known each other before, and the intervening years had led to him withdrawing even more. Drake either ignored or failed to notice the discomfort that Milton couldn't entirely hide; he maintained the embrace for a beat too long before finally letting go.

"You're soaked," Milton said.

"It's pissing down," Drake said.

"Welcome to Rio."

"Stop moaning," Drake said. "It passes. Forecast is great for the rest of the week. This way. My car's in the lot."

Drake led the way to the exit. The airport was thronged with people, and the noise, echoing down from the high roof overhead, was intense enough to make Milton a little uncomfortable.

"It's good to see you," Milton said.

Drake grinned at him. "How long's it been? Twenty years?"

"And the rest."

Milton had been reunited with Drake on an army forum that he occasionally visited. They had exchanged a few private messages and, when Drake had mentioned that he was living in Rio, Milton had said—without really considering what Drake might say—that he was thinking about visiting the city for the festival. Drake had immediately responded with an invitation to come and stay with him and the suggestion that he could show Milton what the event was really like, away from the sanitised commercial version that the city sold to tempt foreigners. Milton did not like to rely on the hospitality of others, but he had always been fond of Drake, and his offer was tempting. After thinking about it for a day or two, he had accepted.

"Nice T-shirt," Milton said.

Drake looked down at his chest and the shirt that sported a logo of twin pistols girdled by a thorny rose stem. "Still got mine from the first time I saw them," he said. "Doesn't fit now. Bought this on eBay."

"We're not as young as we used to be."

"That's the truth," Drake said with a rueful smile.

"What are you talking about?" Milton said. "You look good."

Drake beamed. "That's Rio. Great weather, fantastic

beaches... fantastic women." He grinned. "Have you been here before? You didn't say."

"Once," Milton said. "Must be ten years ago."

"After the Regiment?"

"That's right."

Drake didn't ask what Milton had been doing after he had left the SAS. Milton knew the question would come and was ready with a suitable answer. He wasn't about to tell him the truth.

"The city's changed," Drake said. "You wouldn't recognise it. The Olympics and the World Cup made a big difference. Forced the government to clean it up."

Drake nudged his way through a line of people waiting to check in, seemingly oblivious to the angry muttering of the people he left in his wake. That was something that Milton remembered about him: Drake had a big personality, full to overflowing with *joie de vivre*, but he was sometimes enthusiastic to the point where he was not aware of the effect he had on others. There was a puppyish bounce about him that needed a little endurance every now and again. Milton had forgotten that in the intervening years since he had last seen him, and he reminded himself now that he might need to be patient.

He had found a few more lost memories bobbing up to the surface during his long flight: one, in particular, was clear. He remembered the two of them in a bar in Hereford during their training for the Regiment. They had been talking to another soldier. The third man had become so annoyed at his inability to get a word in edgewise that he had thrown his drink in Drake's face. They had all been drunk, and, in the inevitable brawl that followed, Milton had been pushed into a table, spilling the drinks that were stood there into the laps of two local farmhands. All five men had been arrested and spent the night in the drunk tank at the police station in Bath Street.

It was half seven by the time Drake and Milton broke out of the crowd and pushed through the double doors. Thunder boomed and the rain came down so hard that it splashed against the asphalt with a steady hiss. It was ridiculously hot despite the rain. A sign in the arrivals lounge had noted that the temperature was in the nineties, but it had been air-conditioned inside. Now, though, it felt as if Milton had been dunked into a bucket of hot water.

"Warm?" Drake said with a grin.

"Just a little."

The taxi drivers sounded their horns impatiently as they tried to slide their cars in and out of spaces that were almost too small for them. Passengers whistled and shouted to attract their attention, and Milton saw an argument brewing between one family who were waiting in line and another who had, seemingly, jumped to the front. Drake plotted a course around them, and Milton followed, leaving the sound of their argument in their wake.

"My car's over there," Drake said, pointing to a garage on the other side of the access road.

A gap in the traffic appeared, and Drake jogged through it, leaving Milton to wait a moment for his own chance to cross. Finally, he hurried across the road as the driver of an approaching black town car held his hand on the horn to complain that he had been forced to slow down. The rain lashed against him and, despite only being out of shelter for a few seconds, he was quickly soaked.

2

The rain hammered against the tin roof of the building and drummed against the window, filling the room with a noise that was impossible to escape. Paulo de Almeida went to the window and looked out: their apartment was on the top floor of the three-storey building that had been constructed halfway up the Hill, and, from there, he could look all the way down to Gávea and São Conrado and the grand buildings that accommodated those with more money than the *cariocas* who were forced to live in the *favela*. The rain became heavier, and, within the space of a minute, the view narrowed so that he could only just see the building on the other side of the steeply ascending road that led to the top of the Hill.

Paulo had lived in Rocinha all of his life, and he was familiar with these springtime downpours. The storm clouds would collect north of Rio and then, gathering strength as they swooped to the south, they would be funnelled by the Andes and sent straight to the centre and south of the country before being swept out to sea. The slum was not built to withstand extremes of weather, and there had been one particularly bad storm when Paulo had been a boy where a mudslide from the top of the Hill had swept down and swamped the rickety structures that had been established on its flanks. Several dozen people had been killed, either crushed beneath the weight of the lumber that had been torn up and sent down the slopes on the back of the mud, or drowned.

This storm, while not forecast to be dangerous, would still cause no end of inconvenience and unpleasantness. The drains were little better than medieval, with open sewers that ran down the centres of alleys and passages that would soon be filled up with run-off so that their effluent was spilled out and sent into the street. The stinking mounds of garbage would be scattered and sent down the Hill. Paulo often wondered, when he lay awake at night, whether the bodies of the men and women who had crossed the gang before being taken to the top of the Hill to be killed and dismembered would be disturbed, too, and washed back to their families in bits.

He turned from the window. Their bedroom was tiny, with little more than a mattress and their daughter's small bed. It was painted a light shade of green, but there was a problem with damp, and the plaster was peeling away in scabrous patches. His wife, Rafaela, had tried to lighten the room with colourful rugs and throws, and she had fixed a series of devotional pictures of St George on one of the walls. There was a small hallway where they kept their shoes, this communal room, and then a screened-off area that they used as the bathroom with a bucket and a single tap that delivered an unreliable supply of cold water. The apartment was little more than six metres square, not nearly enough for two adults and a child. Natural light was a luxury for many inhabitants of the Hill, and they had none save the tiny slit of a window in their bedroom. The lack of privacy had been the source of the recent arguments that had made living here a trial. But what were they going to do? They had no money for anything else, and every spare *real* that they had was being saved for their daughter's treatment.

Rafaela was kneeling by the small mattress and murmuring to the child curled under the thin sheet. Their young daughter, Eloá, was crying softly.

"How is she?" he asked quietly.

"Can't sleep. There's too much noise."

"It's the damn roof," Paulo said, gesturing up at the ceiling. "If it was something other than tin, we wouldn't hear it so much."

"There's no sense complaining about something we can't change," Rafaela said, her voice tired.

"It'll stop soon. It always does."

Paulo looked at his wife. She didn't just sound tired; the fatigue was in her bones. He felt the same. Eloá hadn't slept through the night for three or four months—the time had become difficult to distinguish—and, since they all shared the same tiny bedroom, if their daughter was awake, then they were, too.

She had been a good sleeper for the first five years of her life. It was only recently that things had changed. They had noticed the weight loss first of all. Paulo and Rafaela had always made sure that Eloá ate first, and the little girl had always been a happy, well-nourished child. But, over the course of a few weeks, she had lost several pounds and her cheeks—once so plump that Paulo found it almost impossible not to kiss them—had hollowed out. She had started to cry more and then had begun vomiting every morning as soon as she awoke. Rafaela said that she thought that the girl was bruising more easily, and then she had found the small pea-sized lump in the armpit beneath the child's right shoulder. They had no money for the doctor, and, while Paulo was trying to arrange for a small loan from his employer, Marcos, the lump had grown from a pea to the size of a golf ball. They had taken the girl to the emergency room at one of the local hospitals and, there, after two days of questions and tests and, finally, a biopsy of the mass, the diagnosis that had crushed the life out of their little family had been grimly delivered.

Paulo tried to put it out of his mind. He needed to be reminded of why he was doing what he was doing, but he couldn't afford for his thoughts to be clouded by it. He stepped across the room and collected his jacket from the futon.

"Where are you going?"

"I told you," he said. "I have to go out."

"You're racing tonight?"

"I have to, baby."

"But the rain—they'll call it off. It'll be too dangerous."

"No, they won't. And we need the money. I have to go."

Rafaela got up, too tired to stand without putting her hand down on the side of the chair and pushing herself upright. Paulo went to her and touched her face. "Do you trust me?" he asked her.

"Of course."

"I'm going to make it all better," he said. "I swear it."

"Be careful."

"I will."

He kissed her on the lips, took his keys from the hook that he had driven into the wall next to the door, and left the room.

3

Rocinha had spread across one of the steep hills that provided Rio with its undulating landscape. No one could remember where or how it had started, but, in the decades since the first slum-dwellers had decided that they would put down roots on the Hill, the *favela* had crawled in all directions until the entire Hill had been swamped by it. The slum was a mile or two across and the same from the summit to the foot, and the government had estimated that around one hundred thousand men, women and children called it their home. The slum might have been one of the poorest areas of the city, but, even here, there was stratification: the very poorest lived in flimsy shelters with no electricity or toilet facilities; others, like Paulo, had a little more, but to describe anything here as comfortable would have been facetious.

The Hill had become more than just a shanty; it had stores, several banks, a recognised bus route and its own TV station. The buildings had been painted in a multitude of colours and, from the gilded streets of Leblon and São Conrado, they speckled the lush green of the mountain's vegetation to form the distinctive patchwork that both shamed and identified the city that had allowed it to grow up there. The *cariocas* who lived in the *favelas* called them the Hills. The middle-class areas below were known as the Asphalt.

Paulo's apartment was halfway up this particular Hill, and the garage where he worked was at the bottom. It was on the main road, Estrada da Gávea, and comprised a space that was big enough for three cars, with a small office next door. The owner was a grizzled old *carioca* called Marcos; he had known Paulo's father before he had been sent to jail, and had offered Paulo a job as soon as he had turned thirteen. He had started by sweeping the floor, but, as the years went by, he had watched and learned, and now he was the best mechanic in the shop.

Paulo took his cycle and freewheeled all the way, putting down his feet to regulate his speed in the absence of working brakes. He reached Estrada da Gávea and looked down to see the lights of the slum sparkling all the way to the ocean. It was a simple thing to distinguish between the Asphalt and the Hills: the former was brightly lit, but where Paulo was, powered by a mixture of legitimate and illegitimate low-voltage cabling, it was dim and gloomy. He was drenched within moments, but quickly put the discomfort out of his mind.

The rain continued to hammer down, and as he wheeled down the road to the bottom of the Hill, he saw a thatch of cables that siphoned power from the grid short out in a bright conflagration that scattered yellow and orange sparks onto the sodden ground beneath them. The fizz and spit of the electricity was loud, but it quickly faded away to be replaced by the ever-present thunder of the rain, the angry barking of dogs, and, high above, the screech of the monkeys in the rainforest.

Paulo passed the last bus stop that served the slum, swung around the corner, and looked down the last stretch of slope to the margin that separated the *favela* from the more affluent streets of Gávea below. He rolled to a stop next to the garage. It was next to a smoke shop, one of the illicit establishments originally named for the marijuana that had once been enjoyed there, but now offering cocaine, crack and heroin instead. He got off the bike and wheeled it to the rusted iron door, then waited for a drunken couple to stagger past. He dropped to his knees and pushed the tip of the key into the padlock that fastened the door to the brackets that had been sunk into the concrete lintel. He heaved up, the heavy door catching against runners that never seemed to have enough oil, jerking it first left and then right until he was able to slide it up above his head.

Marcos let Paulo use the space to work on his car. The Subaru Impreza was there now, parked on the runners that suspended it above the inspection pit. The space was tight, and Paulo turned side on and shuffled along the gap between the driver's side and the wall, opening the door and forcing himself through the narrow gap and into the cabin of the car. He closed the door and sat there quietly for a moment, feeling the firmness of the racing bucket against his spine and smelling the fresh oil that he had changed last week.

The car was an early edition of the Impreza. Paulo's father had bought the car when Paulo was still a boy. It was second-hand, but it had still cost him fourteen thousand *reais*. Paulo was no fool; his father must have used the money he had made through his criminal exploits. Inheriting the Impreza had made Paulo deeply uneasy, but if he could use the car to improve the lot of his family, then it was a compromise he could live with.

Paulo had needed to modify the car to make it competitive enough to race, and he had fitted it with a Hydra stand-alone ECU, 850cc injectors and an 18G turbo. None of the modifications had been cheap, and he had borrowed the money to fund the work from a loan shark on the Hill. Until his priorities had suddenly changed, Paulo had been paying off the debt with his winnings.

He ran his fingers through his wet hair, swiped the moisture from his eyes, and turned the key in the ignition. The engine grumbled to life; he fed the gas, revving the engine, feeling the vibrations through the bucket seat and hearing the gravel-throated roar louder than the rattles of thunder outside. He put the car into reverse, dabbed the accelerator, and rolled off the runners and out onto the street.

Outside, he put the Impreza in neutral, then stepped out into the rain once more, rolled his cycle inside the shop, heaved the garage door down again, and locked it. He slid back into the vinyl seat, wiped the water out of his eyes again, and, as he reached down for the gearshift, he heard the distinctive chatter of an automatic weapon somewhere higher up the Hill. It wasn't an unusual sound for Rocinha, and he disregarded it at once. He put the car into first and turned the wheel.

4

D rake led the way through the garage to the short-stay area and stopped in front of a white Porsche 718 Boxster. He blipped the lock and went around to open the driver's side door. Milton opened the passenger door and lowered himself into the seat. The car was obviously new, and the seats still had the smell of fresh leather.

Milton put his bag on his lap and closed the door. "Nice car."

"Thanks," Drake said, obviously pleased with Milton's opinion.

"You're doing well."

"Can't complain," Drake said as he fired up the engine and reversed out of the parking space.

"I don't even know what you do."

"I didn't say?" Drake said.

"You said security."

Drake nodded. "I've got a company," he said. "Close protection, safety assessments, that kind of thing."

"Par for the course," Milton said. "I've lost track of the

number of men from the Regiment who end up doing the same thing."

"Better than being a mercenary," Drake said. "There's a few we were with who ended up like that. Remember Clinton?"

"Vaguely," Milton said, although he didn't.

"Took a job in Sierra Leone. Got shot last year. Left two kids behind. Fuck that. That's not going to happen to me."

Drake edged the car into a line of traffic queuing to leave the garage via a barrier up ahead.

"And it's that much safer here?" Milton asked him.

"Safer than Sierra Leone? There are areas you don't want to go to, but this isn't Freetown. As long as you do your homework and treat it professionally, it's a piece of piss."

They reached the barrier, and Drake lowered the window so that he could insert his ticket into the slot. The machine chattered and buzzed, and the barrier was lifted. Drake rolled through and onto the road beyond. He turned to the south and followed Estrada do Galeão.

"You ever thought about getting into that line of work?" Drake asked Milton.

"Not really my thing these days. Getting older."

"So, what do you do?"

"I'm a cook," he said.

"*What?*" Drake exclaimed. "Fuck off. You're never a cook."

"I'm afraid I am. Nothing special—it's not like I'm Gordon Ramsay—but it pays the bills. I work for a bit and then I travel. I wander around until the money is gone, and then I find a job again. It's perfect for me. No commitments. Nothing to tie me down."

Drake started to sing 'The Wanderer' before hammering his hand on the horn as a transit bus pulled out and forced him to swerve around it. He yelled out something in Portuguese, and the driver responded by raising his middle finger. He accelerated away from the bus and slotted back into the same lane again. "You always were weird like that," Drake said, shining Milton a grin across the cabin. He started to sing the Dion song again as if he hadn't just been interrupted.

"You got anything else?" Milton asked.

Drake took his phone from his pocket, linked it to the car's stereo, and pressed play. Slash's distinctive intro to 'Sweet Child O' Mine' started to play.

"Better?"

"Much," Milton said.

They raced across the bridge that linked Galeão with Ramos and then merged onto the multi-laned Via Expressa Presidente João Goulart.

"You ever get married?" Drake asked him over the start of Axl Rose's vocals.

"I was once," Milton said. "A long time ago. Not anymore. I'm not the relationship type."

"Girlfriend?"

"No."

"Seriously? Anything I need to know?"

"I doubt it," Milton said, knowing very well that now he was going to have to put up with speculation as to why he was on his own.

"Well," Drake said, "we'll soon get that fixed. This is Rio, Milton. Wait until you see the women." He shone another grin, this one more like a leer.

Milton allowed himself a rueful smile and looked out of the window as they raced along. Drake had often been a little too laddish for Milton's tastes; he had forgotten that about him, and now, as the Boxster touched seventy on a road that was surely limited to a speed below that, he could see that it wasn't something that he had grown out of. It didn't matter. He was friendly and accommodating, and his heart was in the right place. And Milton hadn't committed to staying with him for more than the couple of days he had scheduled to enjoy the festival. If he found him to be too annoying, he would just make his excuses and leave. He wanted to strike out deeper into the interior, away from the cities, and it would be a simple enough thing to bring his plans forward a little. He put his reservations to one side and chided himself. He was here to enjoy the music and, what was more, it wasn't as if he had many other friends. He would try to relax and enjoy himself. A bit of company would be good for him. He had been on his own for too long.

They sped south through Caju and then São Cristóvão, the road rising and continuing by way of a flyover, a scruffy industrial zone passing beneath them with the cranes of the port lined up like sentries to their left. Drake was in the outside lane, the Porsche effortlessly flying along, when Milton heard the roar of a powerful engine approaching them quickly from behind.

Drake looked into the mirror and muttered, "What the fuck..." as a midnight blue Subaru Impreza roared by them in the inside lane. If they were doing seventy, then the Subaru must have been doing a least a hundred; it curved back into the outside lane and raced by the truck ahead of them as if it wasn't even there.

"Street racers," Drake grumbled. "They've been racing on the coast road the last couple of months. The police said they were going to crack down, but they just change the route and nothing gets done."

Milton watched the red of the Subaru's taillights as it arrowed onto a slipway and disappeared off to the left.

Drake changed down and pumped the accelerator. "Think I could take him?" he asked with another grin.

"Just get me back to your place in one piece," Milton said.

5

———

Paulo turned the Subaru off the rain-slicked main road and rolled up to the gate of the derelict garage. The sign on the wall of the old building said Terminal Rodo - Edifício Garage M. It had once been used as a place where visitors to this part of the town could leave their cars, but it had been shut for several years since a newer replacement had been built during the preparations for the World Cup and the Olympics.

Paulo flicked on the headlamps and followed their glow into the guts of the building. It wasn't really necessary; he could hear the sound of the PAs that would provide the soundtrack for the *baile funk* that would take place during and after the racing. The equipment was portable, brought to the venue in the back of an anonymous panel van and easily removed in the unlikely event that the police were able to find them and coordinate an operation to shut them down in the limited amount of time between the start of the night's activities and their conclusion.

Paulo turned a corner, and the garage opened out into a wide space. He saw fifty or sixty people gathered around half a dozen cars. He rolled up to them, slipping the transmission into neutral and revving the powerful engine. Men and women turned to watch his approach and one of the other cars—a 1996 Mitsubishi Lancer Evolution—switched on its high beams, making Paulo squint.

He switched off the engine and stepped outside. He was excited at the prospect of the evening's racing and had spent the last few days working on the car. The Impreza was notorious for a delicate transmission, and this one had also suffered from various exhaust leaks, a blown turbo and a cracked seal that had led to a loss of pressure in one of the cylinders. Paulo was an excellent mechanic, however, and had been able to keep it in tip-top condition. His winnings had allowed him to save a little, together with making the regular payments to the loan shark, Palito.

Things had changed since Eloá's diagnosis. Now, Paulo was forced to cut back on the money that he spent on the car and had put everything else toward the thirty thousand *reais* that they needed to find for Eloá's treatment at the specialist children's hospital in Lagoa. Paulo hadn't paid Palito for a month, and he had been avoiding the places where their paths might cross. But Palito came to the racing, and Paulo had expected to see him tonight. He was relieved to see that there was no sign of him. He didn't know what he would say, and he had been avoiding any consideration of it in the vain hope that the problem might go away if he ignored it.

A man separated himself from the crowd that had gathered around the Evo, and walked in Paulo's direction. It was Aldo. He was big, over six feet tall and with a muscular frame that was liberally decorated with tattoos from the six months that he had spent in Bangu for assaulting the traffic cop who had pulled him over a couple of years ago.

"Hey," Aldo called out over the drumming of the rain as he approached. "How you doing?"

"I'm good," Paulo said.

Aldo bumped fists with him and then walked around the car, running his fingers over the bodywork. "You sure I can't buy this off you? Offer still stands."

"She's not for sale," Paulo said firmly. Aldo always asked that, and Paulo always said no. He had meant it, too, until recently. He knew that he would be able to get ten thousand for it, maybe a little bit more if he dug his heels in, but that was only a third of what he still needed to find for Eloá's treatment. He could sell it, but then he would have no way to earn the twenty thousand that he would still need. He figured that he needed to win five more races. That ought to be good for twenty-five grand, with another ten for the car making thirty-five. He could take thirty to the hospital for the doctors and the drugs and pay off some of what he owed Palito with the balance.

He just had to keep on winning.

Aldo was around the back of the car now. Paulo had never lost to him, and Aldo liked to pretend that it was the car, and not the driver, that was responsible. Paulo let him think that, although he knew that he was much faster. It didn't serve him to rub that in, though.

Aldo made it all the way around the Subaru and rapped his knuckles on the hood, just above the distinctive bug-eye headlights. "You change your mind, you let me know."

"I will."

"You know you ain't gonna beat me tonight, though, right? I don't care how nice your wheels are. There ain't any way they gonna be faster than mine."

He gestured across the open concrete space to the Evo. It had been given an aggressive red paint job, and the scoop on the hood suggested that Aldo had been working on the engine.

"Five hundred horses," he said proudly.

"Doesn't matter if you're scared to use it."

"I ain't scared," he said with a grin, but Paulo could tell that he had gotten under his skin. "You ready?"

"Sure," Paulo said. "We're going first? I'm going to take all your money."

"Speaking of money," Aldo said, nodding in the direction behind Paulo. "Looks like someone wants to speak to you about that."

Paulo turned. It was Palito.

P alito was not slender, as his nickname—Toothpick —might have suggested. He was a large man, a big six-footer, and overweight with it. He was wearing an oversized New York Knicks singlet that was stretched around his belly. His arms were flabby, with every spare inch taken up with lurid tattoos and gang tags that proclaimed his allegiance to ADA, the Amigos dos Amigos gang. There was a running joke among locals that Palito's loyalty depended upon who was offering him the best terms, and that he had covered up previous tattoos signalling his devotion to Red Command and Third Command, the other gangs who vied with ADA for power in the *favela*. No one made that joke when Palito was around, at least not after the head of the last person to bring it up had been found at the side of the road at the top of Rua Um.

He lumbered up to Paulo. He had come with two of his crew, but both men—tooled up with pistols that they made no effort to hide—stayed on the other side of the garage, next to Palito's Lexus. It was a calculated snub. Palito was signalling that he did not consider Paulo to be a threat.

He bared his teeth and grinned, exposing gold caps. "Where you been hiding?"

"I'm not hiding anywhere," Paulo said.

"But I ain't seen you since last month. You know what I think about that, right? I mean, I'm sure we spoke about that when you came to ask me for the money. I forget to tell you?"

"No," Paulo said. "You told me."

"So, given you know what happens to those who try to avoid paying me what they owe—"

"I'm not trying to avoid paying you."

Palito stepped up until he was right in Paulo's face. "Given you know what happens," he started again, "why is it that you've missed the last two payments? You need to explain that to me, kid, because, right now, it looks like you're trying to make me look like a fool."

Paulo's heart raced. Palito had told him all about the consequences of missing payments, but it had been unnecessary; his brutality toward defaulters was legendary throughout Rocinha. There were stories of beatings, of bones broken with metal bars, and fingernails pulled out with pliers. Paulo would have preferred to do business with practically anyone else, but his choices were limited. One of the other consequences of Palito's reputation was that no one else would risk going into business with one of his competitors. He owned the market in Paulo's part of the *favela*, and bad things had happened to loan sharks who had tried to muscle into his territory. His jealousy was not limited to his rivals; there were stories of beatings for potential clients who had eschewed his services in favour of lenders in other parts of the city.

"I'll have your money," Paulo said.

"When?"

"Tonight," he said.

Palito put out a fat hand.

"After the race," Paulo said. "I'll cover the payments I've missed and the next two."

"How much to enter the race?"

"A thousand," Paulo said, aware that that would be enough to pay off the money that Palito wanted.

The fat man pursed his lips and paused, seemingly weighing up the offer. "Payment's gone up," he said. "Interest on top of the interest."

"Fine," Paulo said. "You'll get what I owe."

Palito grinned at him again, his gold caps sparkling in the artificial light. "What if you lose?"

"I won't," Paulo said.

Palito turned and looked at the Impreza. "If you lose, I'll take that."

Paulo knew that he had no choice. "Fine."

Palito grinned again. "Good luck."

7

The starting point of the race was beneath an overhead sign that identified the bus lane on the Avenue Rodrigues Alves. The route followed the coast for half of its length, heading east and then south so that they passed through the neighbourhoods of Santo Cristo, Centro, Glória and Botafogo, before they cut due south to Copacabana, Ipanema and the three-quarter mark at Leblon. They turned north there, for a straight burn-out through Lagoa and Humaitá and then the final stretch along Avenue Paulo de Frontin to the start-finish line.

There were four cars in the first race. Paulo had his Subaru, and Aldo was driving the tricked-out Mitsubishi that he had shown off inside the garage. A teenager called Rafael was at the wheel of a lurid green Nissan Skyline with an all-black hood and spoiler, and a woman called Kat was racing a Toyota Supra that sat so low to the road that it looked as if the underside would scrape against it the moment they set off. The four of them lined up side by side. Paulo was on the inside, with Rafael next to him. There was a raised kerb that separated their two lanes from the two lanes to their left; Aldo was next to the kerb on the other side and Kat was outside him.

Paulo reached down into his pocket and took out the rosary beads that his mother had given him half a lifetime ago. He held them to his mouth and kissed them and then hung them over the stem of the rear-view mirror. He reached into his pocket again and took out the picture of Eloá. It was his favourite picture of her: she was playing on a swing boat on the beach in Leblon, the sun shining bright and her smile shining brighter still. He had a little sticky-tack on the dashboard and he pressed the picture against it, holding it in place. He kissed his forefinger and index finger and touched them against her lips.

He pressed down on the clutch and fed the car just enough gas to rumble the engine. He could smell the faint odour of the exhaust, and that, combined with an under-lying note from the fresh oil, made him feel at home. He knew the car inside out: the distance between the wheel and the gearshift, the slender gap between the brake and the accelerator.

He took out his watch and checked the time: nine fifty-nine.

The flag girl strutted onto the raised kerb between Rafael and Aldo and raised her hands above her head.

Paulo pushed down a little more with his foot, revving the engine. The four cars strained like chained dogs, and their engines filled the night with their hungry whines.

The flag girl threw her hands down.

Paulo lifted off with his left foot at the same time as he stomped down with his right. Paulo knew his car perfectly and knew exactly how to set off without spinning the wheels. The car lurched for a moment before the rubber bit on the pocked asphalt, and then he darted ahead with enough force to press him back into his seat.

The girl was gone in a flash, and, as he glanced up in his mirror, he saw a quick glimpse of her as she disappeared into the distance. He could feel the vibration of the engine in his seat, and the noise was so loud that he could feel it in the middle of his gut. He shifted up and then up again and again, stomping down on the clutch and driving the gearshift down and then up and then down again with sharp, practised, forceful stabs.

The first mile was dead straight and practically a drag race until they reached the Aquarium. The road cut through an industrial district, and it was almost empty at this time of the evening. All of them were able to drive flat out without having to worry about traffic getting in the way. Paulo focussed on the road ahead, the derelict warehouses and factories on either side of him passing by in a blur. Rafael kept pace with him and then started to pull ahead. The Skyline was faster than the Subaru, but Paulo was the better driver; he let the kid get ahead and ducked in behind him, slipstreaming him as they reached a hundred miles an hour and kept climbing. He looked to his left and saw, amid the flash of the colourful graffiti on the walls of the buildings, that Aldo and Kat were alongside each other. The raised kerb was still to his left, preventing him from changing lanes, but he didn't care about that. He was happy to stay where he was. He knew the course. He knew his best chance was in biding his time.

The bus lane merged with the rest of the road, and the raised kerb disappeared. The four cars formed up: Rafael took the lead in the Skyline, followed by Kat in the Supra, Aldo in the Evo, and Paulo at the back. The engines buzzed like locusts, and backfire flamed out of the Skyline's exhausts. The warehouses disappeared to be replaced by gleaming metal and glass buildings and the cranes of the harbour east of them. The road started to bend to the right, swallowed by the two-mile-long tunnel of Prefeito Marcello Alencar. The road's three lanes became enclosed by sheer concrete walls and lit by two rows of harsh lamps that were suspended by metal rods from the ceiling. The road banked as it turned to the right, and Paulo allowed the car to drift down to the bottom. The noise of the four straining engines was deafening, echoed and amplified by the enclosed space. Paulo looked to his left, up the banked turn; Aldo was next to him, and, for a moment, their eyes locked.

They raced out of the tunnel and into the neon-stained night. They were on Avenue Alfred Agache, heading south toward the Museum of Modern Art and Glória. Paulo was still at the back of the pack, with perhaps a hundred metres separating him from Rafael at the front. He glanced ahead: the Supra started to jerk left and right, its fishtail becoming more and more pronounced as Kat failed to bring it under control. Paulo saw the flap of torn rubber from the rear right wheel and knew that she had had a blowout. The back end swung all the way around to the side and the front lost traction, the car whirling around into a full spin. The car slid over the central reservation, narrowly missing a tree, and spun out onto a grass run-off that separated the road from the city's second airport. The grass was replaced by gravel, and the scree brought the Supra to a stop, a parabola of loose chippings spraying into the air as the car beached.

He turned his attention back to the road. One down, he thought. Two to go.

8

They had raced through Flamengo and Botafogo, along the gilded ribbon of Copacabana, and now they were tracing the road west through similarly rich Ipanema. The traffic was busier here, and now they had to slow down in order to pick a path through the slower-moving vehicles. Rafael was still in the lead, with Aldo close on his tail; Paulo had held onto them both as they blazed their way south, knowing that he would be able to reel them in now that his driving ability was more important than the straight-line performance of their cars.

They raced along Avenue Vieira Souto with the ocean to their left and the gleaming high-rises to their right. Paulo drew closer to Aldo and Rafael, swinging out into the east-bound lane and picking a path through the sudden oncoming rush of traffic. He swung the wheel left and right, swerving between a taxi and a minibus, then slid around a second taxi, over the kerb and into the cycle lane and then onto the sidewalk. He stomped down on the gas and felt the acceleration press him back into his seat. He raced ahead, eating up the distance between the Subaru and its quarry, wrestling the wheel hard left to swerve off the sidewalk and back onto the road just in time to swoop around the tables from a restaurant that had been allowed to encroach onto the path.

The engine roared, a constant backdrop against the regular outraged blaring of horns. Paulo looked left and saw Rafael and Aldo suddenly fall behind a slow-moving clot of traffic. The Skyline ran out of road, and Rafael had no option but to slam on the brakes and stop; Aldo had the space to react and launched the Lancer over the kerb and into Paulo's lane.

Two down. It was just him and Aldo now.

Paulo hammered the accelerator, and Aldo reacted, edging ahead. They burned through Ipanema and Vidigal, with Aldo ahead but nothing really between them.

Paulo readied himself as they approached the hard right turn where Avenue Niemeyer switched back through ninety degrees as it raced toward the Royal Tulip hotel and then picked its way up the flank of the rugged ground leading to the Hill and up to Rocinha.

He nudged up closer to the Mitsubishi, trying to give Aldo the impression that he was going to take him on the inside. Aldo had to defend the move, and he turned the wheel and swung his car over, shutting the door. Paulo drifted back, hoping that Aldo might think he would wait for a chance to go by him again, but then, as they roared onto a stretch of narrow road where the speed of the corner made overtaking almost impossible, he yanked the wheel to the right and swung inside the Evo. Aldo saw him make the move and tried to cut him off; the Evo swung right, too, its back end almost clipping against the front wing of the Subaru. Paulo stomped on the brake. His feints had distracted Aldo, and he was taking the right-hander ahead much too quickly. He had no choice but to brake; the Lancer lost its speed and Paulo yanked up on the handbrake, sending the car into a controlled power slide that sent it gliding around the corner through the space that Aldo had just been forced to vacate.

The two cars turned together: the Lancer on the outside, the Subaru on the inside. Paulo could feel the traction on the inside right tyre, the whole car seeming to pivot around it as the rear end swung around. He was going too fast, too, but the rear end touched the Mitsubishi, and the bump held the car in the turn. And it added a little extra momentum to the Lancer that made it impossible for Aldo to control.

The Mitsubishi's wheels screeched as Aldo braked, bringing the car under control just before it could slam into the concrete facing of the structure on the outside of the turn. Aldo had to slow almost to a halt; Paulo whooped as he came out of the turn and buried the pedal, racing away up the hill in first place, the Evo surely too far back now for Aldo to be able to catch him.

He gripped the wheel and let the thrill of the adrenaline buzz through him. He looked down at the picture of Eloá on the dash. His advantage allowed him the luxury of thinking about how much he stood to win, and the difference in her life that he would now be able to make.

He was on the final part of the course. There was no sense in pushing too hard, so he dabbed the brake in an attempt to bleed a little speed off. The pedal felt wrong. It was soft—almost spongy—and it travelled farther down than it should have. He tried again and, this time, the pedal went all the way down to the floor without slowing the car at all. He glanced down at the speedometer and saw that he was doing eighty; he knew the road ahead and knew that there was a hairpin right-hander that he would not be able to take unless he was able to cut his speed all the way down.

He downshifted to fourth and then third, the engine protesting loudly as the revs increased. He pumped the brake pedal up and down, again and again and again, trying to build up brake fluid pressure. Nothing happened; the brakes were completely gone.

The hairpin was coming up fast. The terrain was hilly, and he knew that there was a sheer face of rock to the left of the turn. He would crash into it unless he was able to slow down. The road climbed a little, enough to slow the car to sixty, and then Paulo saw the guardrail on the right-hand side. There was a twenty-foot drop on the other side and the rail looked flimsy, but he didn't have any other option if he wanted to avoid wiping himself out against the rock. He turned the wheel to the right and steered into the rail, scraping against it gently and then, once he was confident that it would hold, turning a little more aggressively so that the car ground against the metal more firmly. Sparks flew up, a cascade that alighted on the windshield before vanishing just as quickly as it had appeared.

The friction slowed the car and, as the hairpin approached, Paulo was able to drift over to the other side and then turn in, taking the apex once again. He was still going too fast to manage the turn completely, and the car veered across the road until the fender crunched into the bare rock. The hood lodged against an outcrop and the rear end spun out; the car skidded through a hundred and eighty degrees, its momentum finally arrested as the opposite side crunched into the rock.

The Impreza was left facing back down the road. Paulo slammed his hands against the wheel as, below him—but climbing fast—he saw the lights of a car moving at speed.

The lights followed the bend as it ascended and, after disappearing behind an outcrop for a moment, they emerged in a blaze of light on the road that led to the hairpin. It was the Lancer. Aldo sounded the horn as he took the turn, putting his arm out of the open window and extending his middle finger. He gunned the engine as soon as he was around the bend and hit the horn again—once, twice, three times—and then disappeared up the road and out of sight.

Paulo slumped forward, his forehead resting against the wheel.

This was not the way he had seen the night finishing.

9

Paulo called Marcos and told him what had happened. His boss was at home and had grumbled about being disturbed just as he was about to watch the latest episode of *Supermax*, but then he must have heard the desperation in Paulo's voice. He told him to stay where he was, and that he would come out in the truck and pick him up.

Paulo got out of the car. It was late and the road was quiet. Two cars had already gone by, but, as he looked back down into the valley, there was no sign of anyone else approaching. He took his phone out of his pocket, switched on the flashlight, and slid underneath the front of the Impreza. He pushed, sliding on his back until he was underneath the car, and then turned the flashlight onto the mechanics. He followed the brake lines from the hood, checking the driver's side rear wheel first. The line was steel to start with, and, as he had expected, it looked fine. He traced it back, running his finger along it until the steel line was replaced with rubber.

The line had been cut. It was impossible to miss. It was a

neat incision, clearly deliberate. He knew that it could not be something that could be attributed to wear and tear; he had checked the lines that afternoon, and they had all been just as he had expected. Fluid was dripping out of the line now, viscous globs that stained his fingertips as he probed the incision.

He slid across so that he could check the opposite wheel and saw the same thing: a neat, intentional slice that had been made in the rubber between the steel line and the wheel cylinder. More fluid was running out of the cut, falling to puddle on the asphalt.

He lay there for a moment longer, just staring at the damage that had been done. It was a skilful job; the lines had not been cut all the way through, not quite enough for him to have noticed it earlier on in the race but more than enough to cause the brakes to fail if he pumped them too hard. He thought about the route: most of the early going was flat out, and the only significant turn until he reached this hairpin was the switchback on Avenue Niemeyer where he had lost Aldo.

He thought back to the start of the evening. His attention had been distracted during his talk with Palito. He had turned away from the car, and that might have been enough time for someone to slide underneath with a blade and go to work.

He scrambled out from underneath the car and stood. The road was still quiet and, perhaps emboldened by the peace, an owl hooted loudly and swooped by low overhead. Paulo went around to the front of the car. The fender had been mangled beneath the outcrop, with large holes torn in the metal. He didn't even want to think about the damage that must have been done to the suspension. He started to price how much it would cost to fix, but then stopped himself: that was irrelevant now. He didn't have the money to afford replacement parts and, worse than that, Palito was going to want to get paid.

He slumped back against the hood. No money meant no treatment for Eloá. He had failed her, Rafaela, and himself. He closed his eyes against the tears that had started to form, but it was no good. They ran down his cheeks as he bowed his head and waited for Marcos to come and pick him up.

10

Drake drove Milton through Santo Cristo until they reached Santa Teresa. It was an exclusive neighbourhood, a collection of high-end villas and apartments on a hilltop that stood between Rio's centre and the sandy crescent of beach that fronted Copacabana and Ipanema. It was different in atmosphere to the other districts that they had passed through; this was more like a village, with narrow, winding streets that were lined with elegant mansions, many of which had been converted to accommodate boutique hotels, cocktail bars and, as they neared the summit, restaurants offering romantic vistas of the bay beyond. He slowed by the side of a particularly impressive building—more modern than the other properties that they had passed—and reversed off the road and into a private garage.

Milton got out of the car and jogged up a flight of stairs to follow Drake to the front door. They paused under a porch and looked around. The property was large and had been built on the edge of the forest on a part of the hill that was particularly secluded. It benefited from an elevated position, and it had a million-dollar view: Milton gazed out at Sugarloaf Mountain, Guanabara Bay, and the sparkling lights of the skyscrapers that studded the central parts of the city.

"Very nice," Milton said.

"Like I said, business has been good."

"Is it yours?"

"Rented," he said, then pointed to an unfinished villa on the other side of the road. "Looking at that one, though. The developer went bust. I reckon I can get that for a steal."

Milton looked over at the property. It would be as impressive as this one when it was finished.

Drake reached for the door handle. "Come inside," he said. "There's someone I want you to meet."

Milton put his hand on Drake's elbow. "There's one thing," he said. "I don't use my own name. I'd rather you kept that between the two of us."

Drake regarded him curiously. "This to do with what you did after the Regiment?"

"Yes. And don't ask me to talk about that, because I can't."

"So what do I call you?"

"John Smith."

Drake chuckled. "Very imaginative."

"Humour me."

"Of course," he said. "John Smith it is."

Milton followed Drake inside. They passed into a large living room with expansive windows and stepped through open French doors onto a patio with a vaulted concrete pergola. The patio was generously provisioned with outdoor furniture, and a woman was resting on a bamboo armchair, her long legs propped up against the edge of a glass table.

"I'm home, baby."

The woman turned at the sound of Drake's voice. Milton could see at once that she was an uncommon beauty. She stood, and her long dark hair, parted in the centre, fell down to the middle of her back. Her eyes were framed with eyeliner, her lashes were dark and full, and her lips were painted a subtle red.

"This is Sophia," he said to Milton. "Sophia, this is John"—Drake caught himself—"Smith."

The woman closed the distance between them and, instead of taking the hand that Milton offered, she brushed it aside and leaned in to kiss him on both cheeks. Her scent was heady and strong; she smelled of citrus.

She stepped away from him and smiled. "Shawn has been looking forward to you coming all week," she said to Milton, reaching up to touch him on the shoulder. "He doesn't have many visitors."

"What are you talking about?" Drake protested, although Milton could see that he enjoyed Sophia's gentle teasing.

"How long have you been in Rio, baby?" she asked him.

"A year."

"A year and a half," she corrected. "And how many visitors have you had?"

"My mother," he replied with a grin.

She turned to Milton and shrugged. "You see?"

"It's a long way from home," Drake protested again.

"But Rio has the beaches and the weather and football —and still they do not come."

"I think what she's trying to say is that I'm not very popular."

"I'm saying that I'm glad John has taken pity on you."

There was an obvious spark between the two of them; Milton could see it and found it rather charming. Milton remembered an awkwardness to Drake that was amplified whenever he was around women. The recruits had often gone out in Hereford during their training; it had been easy to identify them as soldiers, and as always, there were local women who went out with the aim of snaring a soldier for themselves. Milton had always been too shy to be a ladies' man, and he had found comfort in the fact that, even though Drake talked a good game, he was even worse than him. It was odd given Drake's obvious good looks and the fact that it was evident to everyone—bar him, perhaps— that he was regarded as a prize by the women who tried to catch his eye. The relaxed banter between Drake and Sophia was something Milton would not have credited to the man that he remembered.

Sophia laid a hand on Milton's arm again. "What about you, John?" she said. "What do you do?"

"I'm a cook," he said.

"So he says," Drake said. "I don't believe it. He was always terrible at cooking."

"I've had a lot of time to practice."

"Shawn," she chided, waving a hand in mock exaspera- tion. "What kind of places do you work?"

"Nothing special," he said, thinking of the taximan's shelter where he had worked for the longest stretch of time since leaving the Group. "I'll usually find somewhere to work for five or six months, and then I'll use the money to go travelling."

"You're not married?"

"No," he said.

"No girl?"

"Not at the moment."

She cocked an eyebrow in an exaggerated show of surprise. Milton could see why Drake had fallen for her. She was good looking, but she had a sultriness that was extraordinarily attractive. He found himself wondering how old she was, and guessed that she must have been at least fifteen years Drake's junior. His friend had aged well, his good looks a little more refined now that he had more lines on his face, yet Milton concluded that he was still batting well above his average when it came to his new girlfriend.

"So you've come for the festival?"

"Yes," Milton said. "It's been on my list for years."

"It's good this year, no?" she said. "You come with me and Shawn—I show you what it is like for locals, not tourists."

"Perfect," Milton said, yawning.

"Tired?"

"It was a long flight," Milton said.

Drake looked at his watch. "It's still early. I thought we could go out for a drink?"

Milton had been worrying about that. He remembered Drake as a big drinker, like most of the soldiers he had served with over the years, and he knew that Drake would want to go out and hit the bars with him. Milton had spent an hour of the flight flicking through the Big Book of Alcoholics Anonymous in an effort to find the fortitude that he knew he would need to resist the temptation. He was confident that he would be able to say no to Drake, but he wasn't looking forward to the badgering that he knew he could expect, and then the ribbing about being a lightweight that would follow.

"I'm pretty tired," Milton said.

"A couple of drinks? There's this bar I know, not far from here. You'll love it."

"Not tonight," he said. "I can barely keep my eyes open. And tomorrow's going to be a busy day."

"What happened to you?" Drake said. "You were always the last man standing."

"Like I said," Milton offered. "Getting older."

Drake didn't press. "All right," he said. "Maybe it's best to save our strength for tomorrow. The beer will taste like piss at the festival, but at least there'll be plenty of it. Come on— I'll show you to your room."

11

P aulo walked up the Hill to his uncle Felipe's bar. It was the only place that he knew in Rocinha where he could get a drink without any money. Although Felipe made frequent references to the size of the tab that Paulo had been allowed to run up, he had never made any serious attempt to collect it.

The bar was a cheap dive, and Paulo knew that it was only kept going because it was a convenient business through which the profits of some of the neighbourhood's more unsavoury operators could be washed. It was not much bigger than the front room of the house in which Paulo had grown up, with a makeshift bar at one side of the room and six mismatched stools set out next to it. The walls were decorated with photographs of soccer players: there were pictures of Ronaldo and Ronaldinho, with one poster showing the statue of Christ with the head of Neymar photoshopped onto it. The wooden bar had been scarified by the graffiti of the listless regulars, and, at one end, a glass cloche had been lowered over a plate of stale pastries that had probably been there for two days already.

Paulo approached the bar. "Hello, Uncle."

"What's the matter with you?" Felipe said. "You look like shit."

"Money troubles." He let the sentence drift away and shrugged sheepishly.

"You and all the rest of us."

"This is worse."

"Were you racing tonight?"

Paulo nodded. "Someone cut my brakes. I crashed it."

"Cut your brakes?" Felipe frowned and put his shoulders back, giving an impression of outrage that Paulo knew was false. Felipe was too selfish to do anything to help; his indignation was for show. "You know who did it?"

"I know," Paulo said. "But it doesn't matter. I couldn't prove it."

"You want a drink?"

Paulo nodded. Felipe had hung a bottle of *cachaça* on the wall. He took a dirty glass, rubbed it with a dishcloth that he wore tucked into his belt, and held it underneath the optic so that he could pour out a miserly shot. He put the glass down on the bar. Paulo sat down, took it and sank it in one hit. He put the glass back, but, instead of refilling it with another shot, Felipe turned away and started to grumble about football to the fat man to Paulo's left. He would give him another drink later, but he would make sure that Paulo knew that it would be going on his tab and that, because he still hadn't called the debt in, Paulo still owed him. Felipe had always been the lesser brother, and Paulo suspected that having his sibling's son rely on his patronage was his way of improving his self-image. Paulo didn't care; it meant that he could drink for free, and, when he had no money and nowhere else to go, his uncle's attitude was a price he was prepared to pay.

"Look at that," the fat man said, pointing to the TV on the wall. "They got another one."

Paulo turned. The TV was tuned to a news channel, and the presenter was talking about the PBN scandal. Paulo had been following along with each new development as avidly as everyone else in the country. It was the biggest story anyone could remember. Everyone knew that corruption was a problem in Brazil. It had always been that way, but the police investigation into PBN had been stunning in how deeply it had already cut into the state. The thoroughness with which the case had proceeded was surprising, but perhaps more remarkable than that was how powerless the politicians had been to do anything to stop it. The government had been elected on a promise to tackle corruption, and, now that they had established the enquiry and given it the powers that it needed to do the job, there seemed to be nothing that they could do to call it off. It was like a car with no brakes sitting at the top of a hill; one little push had set it in motion, but now it was rolling so fast and with so much momentum that it could not be slowed down. It would crash through everything and anything that was in its way.

The channel cut to footage of a man in a suit with his hands cuffed in front of him. Paulo recognised the arrivals lounge at the airport. Paulo had never been there before, but he had seen the Brazilian team returning from the World Cup last year.

"Who is it?" Paulo said.

"You don't recognise him?"

"I wouldn't have asked if I did."

Felipe tapped him on the shoulder and handed him another shot. "It's Lima."

The fat man nodded. "He took bribes from a company

that wants to drill the oilfields. They said it was millions. *Millions*. Guys like that, they never get caught."

Felipe laughed, a barking sound that always caused the regulars to turn around in shock until they remembered what it was. "Except now they do."

Another man came into the shot behind the man in cuffs. Paulo knew who *this* man was—everyone did. It was Saverin, the judge who was running the anti-corruption investigation from Curitiba. The others in the bar raised their glasses; one man applauded, until, realising that no one else had followed his example, he let the clapping awkwardly fade away. Paulo had seen the fuss that had been made of Saverin, who had become something of a celebrity. He had seen graffiti on walls and banners draped from bridges declaring 'God save Saverin.' The protestors who took to the streets against corruption did so wearing masks of the handsome judge and held up placards suggesting that he should run for president. At the last carnival, Saverin had been lauded with a five-metre-high doll and a samba tribute song. He was more famous than the businessmen and politicians that he brought down.

Felipe came out from around the bar and took the empty stool next to Paulo.

"Cheer up," he said.

"What am I going to do?"

"How much do you need?"

"A lot."

"For Eloá?"

Paulo nodded.

"I wish I could help," he said, and, again, Paulo knew that he had said it for the benefit of the others who might be listening to their conversation. Felipe made a lot of being a family man, and he wouldn't want anyone to think that he would leave his nephew in financial difficulty, especially when his grandniece was involved. "Could you get another job?"

Paulo snorted. "Do you know how much the treatment costs?"

"You don't have any savings?"

He shook his head. "I'm broke."

"Then there's only one thing left to do."

"What?"

"Speak to Garanhão."

"Are you *crazy?*"

"You asked me for ideas. That's all I've got."

"I can't," he said. "If Rafaela knew I went to ask him..."

"But she wants the treatment for Eloá, too."

"Of course she does."

"Then maybe she'd understand. Desperate times, desperate—"

"I'm not sure I'd ever be *that* desperate," Paulo cut in. "Jesus. What would my father say?"

"He's not around to offer you any advice," Felipe said, the subtext being that he *was* around and that Paulo should be grateful for that.

"I know that," Paulo said.

"Look," Felipe went on, "I know a guy who knows a guy. I could get you a meeting with him."

"Thanks," Paulo said, but shook his head to turn the offer down.

Felipe shrugged. "You want another?"

He nodded that he did. He had the taste for *cachaça* now. He wanted to forget his problems.

PART II

THE SECOND DAY

12

Milton woke at six, put on his running gear, and went out before the temperature could rise any higher. He ran through Santa Teresa, descending the hill that overlooked the city's harbour. The neighbourhood looked very different in the daylight, and Milton passed elegantly faded plantation mansions arrayed along the cobblestoned streets. He took Rua Monte Alegre to Rua Frei Caneca, then headed for the Carioca Aqueduct and the Lapa Arches. He followed the path around the Catedral Metropolitana de São Sebastião and then started to climb the hill toward the house.

He showered and changed and then made his way out to the veranda, where Sophia was waiting for him.

"Sleep well?" she asked him.

"Yes," Milton said. "Thanks."

There was a tray with a jug of coffee, fresh bread, cheese and cold cuts and a bowl of fruit. Sophia poured him a cup of black coffee, and Milton took a hunk of bread and cheese and ate it.

"Where's Drake?"

"Something to do with work," she said. "He got a phone call this morning. I think one of the men who works for him has a problem. It's nothing. He'll be back soon."

They stayed out on the veranda together for half an hour, and then Milton helped Sophia clear away the breakfast things. She said that she had to run an errand, but that she would be back at eleven so that they could make their way to the festival site. Milton waited until he heard her leave, then collected his Big Book from his pack and took it back out to the veranda. He hadn't been to a meeting for a month, and he was feeling a little more vulnerable than he would have liked. He opened the book and read.

"When I am willing to do the right thing, I am rewarded with an inner peace no amount of liquor could ever provide. When I am unwilling to do the right thing, I become restless, irritable, and discontent. It is always my choice."

It was exactly what Milton needed to hear. Alcohol had been the solution to his problems for as long as he could remember. Recovery had taught him that it did not provide all the things that it promised. The beauty of recovery was that Milton had learned that inner peace did not come from external sources, but that it came from within. The way that he could find it was by doing the right thing, which was always his choice. He had chosen to help others and, in so doing, atone for the things that he had done in his life. He could not make recompense to many of the men and women that he had sinned against, because, often, those sins had led to their deaths.

He put the book down and closed his eyes, enjoying the warmth of the sunshine on his face. The book reminded him that he was fortunate to be in recovery, with the luxury of choices to be made. He would undoubtedly have been dead without it. Reading the book was no substitute for a meeting, but it was a solace to remind himself that he wasn't alone, that the way he felt wasn't unusual, and that there was a solution that worked for him.

13

Sophia and Milton took a taxi to the staging post where buses to the festival were picking up passengers. Drake met them there, waving three tickets in his hand.

"Everything okay?" Milton asked him.

Drake waved a hand dismissively. "Work shit," he said. "I'll deal with it later. You ready?"

Milton grinned. "I've been looking forward to this for a long time."

Drake had spared no expense. He had bought three first-class tickets, and that meant that they were able to ride an air-conditioned executive coach out to the festival site at Cidade do Rock. They were deposited at an arrival terminal with a series of bars and several stages where local bands were playing. Fans, mostly clad in classic band tees, burst through the gates in a stampede of excitement, shoulder-barging performers dressed as Marvel comic-book heroes on their way in. Some of them stopped to kiss the ground before streaming inside. Milton found their enthusiasm contagious and noticed that he had goosebumps on his arms and down his back. The majority of the band tees were for Guns N' Roses, and Milton ascribed most of the excitement to the prospect of seeing them play. The band had been back together on an on-again, off-again basis, but the reviews of the warm-up shows prior to their headlining slot tonight were so ecstatic that even the fans most jaded to Axl Rose's unpredictability had seemingly allowed themselves to be swept up in the promise of what the night might bring.

Drake diverted toward the first bar.

"What are you having?" he said.

"I'll have a beer," Sophia said.

"John?"

"Just a water for me," Milton said.

"What?" Drake said with mock outrage. "You'll have a vodka with me."

Milton felt a flicker of temptation and then the usual response to that: panic. "No," he said. "Water is fine."

"What are you on about?"

"There's something I have to tell you," Milton said. "I don't drink."

"Bullshit," Drake said.

Milton spread his hands in a gesture of helplessness. "I don't."

Drake was about to say something else and then stopped; he must have noticed the way that Milton was holding his eye, his straight face, the lack of any suggestion that this might be a joke. "Seriously?"

"I had a problem with it," Milton explained. "I was drinking too much, and it was getting me into trouble. In the end, I couldn't do it anymore. So I stopped."

Drake looked dumbfounded. "When?"

"I haven't touched it for months."

"You might have told me," he said. "Half the fun of coming here is getting smashed."

"I don't need to drink to have a good time, Drake."

Drake was about to retort, but Sophia silenced him by laying her hand on his. Milton was grateful. He wasn't ashamed of his alcoholism and had learned to treat it as an illness like any other. He had no control over his compulsion, nor did he bear any blame for it. Not everyone understood what it meant, and, although Milton had explained it enough times, he found that he was grateful that he didn't have to do that now. He didn't doubt that Drake would bring it up later, but at least it wouldn't spoil the rest of the day.

Drake went to the bar.

"Good for you," Sophia said when Drake was out of earshot. "My father had a problem with drink, but he didn't know how to stop. He died. His liver."

"I'm sorry," Milton said.

"It was a long time ago," she said. "I think Shawn drinks too much sometimes. But you try to tell him that..." She let the sentence fade out.

Drake returned with two vodkas, two pints of lager and a plastic bottle of iced water in a cardboard carrier. He gave a vodka and a pint to Sophia and the water to Milton. He held up the vodka and touched the plastic beaker to Sophia's.

"Cheers," he said, rolling his eyes with mock disdain as he touched his beaker to Milton's pint of water.

14

Marcos had brought the car back to the garage last night, and it had already been moved over one of the inspection pits by the time that Paulo arrived for work. He had known that the car was finished, but that fact was made even clearer in the grim light of day. It would have been possible to repair it, but it would have been a big job. The hood was buckled, the fender was crushed, and the windshield had a big crack right down the middle. The suspension looked as if it was shot, two wheels were buckled, and the brakes would need to be repaired. That was just what he could see without getting underneath. But Paulo had no appetite for doing that; what would be the point? He didn't have the money for new parts nor any way of getting it.

"Hey," Marcos said, taking a cigarette out of his mouth, squeezing the tip between wet fingers and sliding it behind his ear. He nodded at the car. "What you think?"

Paulo shrugged. "Fucked."

"No way you can fix her up?"

"Just looking at what needs to be replaced? That's five or

six thousand right there. And that's without looking properly. You got five or six lying around that I could have?"

It was a bitter joke, and Marcos rewarded it with a sour chuckle. "I'm sorry, Paulo."

He sighed. "Forget it."

"What you want me to do with it?"

Paulo couldn't ask Marcos to keep it in the garage; there was no space for it. And there didn't seem to be much point in paying for it to be stored somewhere else if there was no prospect of getting it fixed.

"How much you reckon it'll get for scrap?"

"I know a guy in Vidigal. Normally, you'd pay him to come and take it away. Maybe I can get a free pickup. I don't think you'll get cash—not from him or anyone else."

Paulo sighed again. What was the point of struggling against the inevitable? He knew that Marcos was right. The car had been his best hope of making money for his daughter; now the best outcome was not to be charged for having it taken away.

"Could you give him a call?" he said.

Marcos nodded, put his cigarette back into his mouth again and lit it. "We've got a busy day," he said, pointing to a blue Renault Megane that was waiting outside. "Got a new exhaust to fit. You want to get it inside?"

Paulo nodded and went to the office to find the keys. It was going to be a long day with nothing to look forward to at the end of it.

15

Milton found that he was having the most enjoyable day that he could remember for months. To his surprise and relief, Drake had not tried to persuade him to take a drink. Milton suspected that Sophia had spoken to him while Milton was queuing for the toilets, because, save the occasional eye roll as Milton returned from the bar with another bottle of water, nothing else was said.

The atmosphere between the three of them was pleasant, too. Milton found that he settled into Drake's company more easily than he had expected, and was pleased to find that the conversation flowed naturally as they shared memories and anecdotes from their time in the Regiment. Sophia was good company, too. She was patient as they regaled each other with stories that had nothing to do with her, but, when they were finished, she more than held her own in the banter that passed between them. Drake and Sophia drank regularly, but not excessively, despite the former's bragging about how much he was going to put away, and, even though they grew steadily drunker as the afternoon went on, they were convivial drinkers and not argumentative. Milton was relieved.

The festival, too, was everything that Milton had hoped it would be. The crowd was vast, with two hundred thousand people slated to attend each day, but the infrastructure of the Olympic Park was excellent, and it was easier to move between the stages than the muddy bogs that had blighted the Glastonbury festival on the occasions that Milton had visited. They made their way between the various stages and enjoyed sets by Alice Cooper, The Kills, and Sepultura, and, as dusk descended, they watched Tears for Fears play their backlist on the Palco Mundo stage. They followed the crowd toward the main stage, stopping for thirty minutes to enjoy the dance-rock of CSS, the Paulistanos ending their set with a joyful rendition of 'Let's Make Love' that ended with a forest of upraised arms saluting them as they took their bows.

They were sitting down near one of the speaker stacks as they waited for Guns N' Roses to come to the stage. There wasn't much space, and Sophia was close enough that Milton brushed his knee against hers as he turned to watch a jet burning a trail across the sky on its final approach to the airport. She looked at him and held his gaze; Milton felt a buzz in his gut. She was pretty, certainly, but there was something else that was extraordinarily attractive about her: confidence, perhaps, an insouciance born of the effect that she had on other people.

Drake had been talking on his phone for the last five minutes. Milton couldn't make out the conversation over the excited babble of the crowd, but he could tell that Drake was frustrated and then angry.

"Is he okay?" Milton mouthed to Sophia.

"The problem from earlier," she replied quietly, with a shake of her head. "He's having some trouble."

"What is it?"

"He told me earlier," she said. "He's got a job tomorrow afternoon, but one of the guys has let him down. I don't know the details. Shawn can tell you about it."

Milton turned his attention back to the stage. One of the attractions that the organisers had arranged was a zip line that ran right over the top of it. Intrepid festival-goers could climb a tower to the right of the stage, attach themselves to a harness, and then slide over the heads of the crowd. Milton and Sophia watched as a man raced across the wire, his arms raised high above his head.

Drake put his phone away and came back to them.

"Everything okay?" Sophia asked him.

He said that it was, the words followed by a thin smile that Milton could see had been forced.

"It's been a great day," Milton said in an attempt to brighten his mood. "Thank you."

"The best is yet to come," Sophia said.

Their distraction appeared to have served its purpose, and when Drake smiled again, it was much more natural. "You seen them before?" Drake asked.

"A long, long time ago," Milton said. "Monsters of Rock. 1988, I think."

"You *are* old," Sophia said with a grin. Milton realised that he didn't know how old she was; she was in her mid-twenties, he guessed, but certainly much younger than Drake. He wondered again how he had managed to land a girl like her.

"Where did you two meet?" he asked them.

"Clubbing," Drake said.

"You go to clubs?"

"Just because you've given up doesn't mean we all have to," Drake retorted. "I'm not ready for slippers and a pipe."

Milton ignored the jibe and turned back to the young woman. There was something about her that he couldn't quite wrap his head around. She didn't come across as a gold-digger, and although Drake was good looking, he was much older than her. Perhaps she genuinely liked Drake; Milton knew that he was looking at things with his own world-weary preconceptions, but he still wanted to know more.

"What do you do?" he asked her.

"I'm training to be a lawyer. I take the national bar examination next year. If I pass that, then I can start work—I'm an intern at a firm in the city, and they said that they have a job for me if I can pass."

"She's amazing," Drake said with obvious pride. "She was brought up in Rocinha."

He paused, as if waiting for Milton to react.

"Rocinha?" Milton said.

"One of the *favelas*."

"Shawn," Sophia chided mildly, "where I was born doesn't mean a thing. I'm nothing special."

"Doesn't mean that I can't be proud of you."

She looked at Milton with a half-smile on her lips. "You think he's patronising me?"

"No," Milton replied. "I doubt he'd dare."

Drake roared with laughter and raised his half-empty bottle of Sol. "Correct," he said. "I would not."

Sophia laughed too, and the moment—if, indeed, it had even been a moment—passed. She held up her own bottle so that they could all share a toast.

"To old friends," Drake said.

"And new," added Sophia, smiling at Milton as she did so.

Milton touched his plastic bottle against theirs, feeling the same usual twinge of discomfort that his contained water and not alcohol.

16

Paulo worked late, replacing the chipped windscreen on a Peugeot that had been brought in five minutes before they were due to shut up shop for the night. The owner had a fleet of taxis and was one of Marcos's best customers, and it was important that he was kept happy. Marcos said that he had to go out, but Paulo had offered to do it in exchange for a couple of hours of extra overtime. The windscreen was more difficult to remove than he had expected and, when he was checking the car over, he discovered that two of the tyres were so worn that they had to be replaced, too.

By the time Paulo was finally finished, it was nine o'clock, and he had missed the chance to see Eloá before she went to sleep. He switched off the lights, pulled down the roller door, and locked up. He turned just as a man stepped out of the shadows ahead of him and moved across to block his way ahead. He was wearing shorts and flip-flops, and his face was obscured by the cap that he wore low down on his head. Paulo took a sidestep to his right; the man matched it. Paulo apologised and took a sidestep to the left; the man matched it again. Paulo's stomach fell. This had to be a joke. He was going to get mugged, tonight, after everything that had already happened? It would be funny if it wasn't so tragic.

"I haven't got anything," he said. "I'm broke. You're wasting your time."

"It's not about that," the man said.

Paulo didn't see the two men who stepped out of the alley behind him, but he heard their footsteps as they closed in. He spun around; the man to the right of the pair was big and fat, with a gold tooth that glittered as it caught the glow of a light that shone through a nearby window. Paulo recognised him at once.

Palito.

"What do you want?" he said, taking a step back.

"You didn't come back after the race," Palito said.

"I crashed. Someone cut my brakes."

"Shame," Palito said. "Doesn't change anything. I want what's mine. The car?"

"I told you," Paulo said. "I crashed. It's a wreck. You can have it if you want."

"I want my money."

"I don't have it," he said.

He repeated it slowly, loading each word with menace: "I... want... my... money."

"I'm broke."

Palito stepped closer, and Paulo stepped back. This time, though, his retreat was blocked. The man with the cap had closed right up tight behind him and, as Paulo tried to move away, he bumped into him. The man grabbed Paulo, wrapping his arms around him so that Paulo's arms were pinned against his torso.

Palito stepped right up, bunched his right fist, and

jabbed Paulo in the face. Paulo's head cracked back, and he tasted blood in his mouth. Palito drew back his fist again and drilled Paulo a second time and then a third. Paulo tried to bring his arms up to defend himself, but the man with the cap held him steady. Palito swung a left hook that jammed into the side of Paulo's head, and then followed it up with another volley of quick right-handed jabs. The three men were laughing; Paulo heard their gleeful cackling over the ringing that filled his head. His vision swam, each fresh blow detonating explosions of pain.

"Hey!"

The man with the cap released Paulo, and he fell to the cobbles.

Paulo looked up to see Marcos. He was brandishing a tyre iron.

Palito crouched down and took a fistful of Paulo's shirt. He leaned in close. "My money," he said, spitting into Paulo's face. "Give me my money or I'll kill you."

Palito shoved him, and Paulo fell to the side, his face bouncing off the cobbles and sloshing through a puddle of dark, brackish run-off that had gathered there. He blinked his swollen eyelids and, in a moment of clarity, saw the feet of his three accosters disappear into the gloom of the alley, sent on their way with a bellowed threat from Marcos.

"Paulo," Marcos said. He felt hands slide beneath his arms, and he was pulled up off the ground. "Paulo, can you hear me?"

He managed a feeble groan in response.

"Who were they?"

"Doesn't matter," Paulo mumbled.

"That was Palito."

He didn't answer.

"Do you owe him money?"

Paulo spat out blood.

"Jesus," Marcos said. "He's an animal. You borrowed money from him? What were you thinking?"

"It's for Eloá," Paulo mumbled. "I didn't have a choice."

"Come on," Marcos said. "I'll get you home."

17

The stage was enormous. It comprised a series of large white blocks and loomed over everything around it. The blocks served as the canvas for a series of psychedelic light projections that flickered to and fro in time with the music that played out over the PA. There was a long platform that stretched out into the crowd and a tall riser for the drum kit that was now being checked over.

Sophia said that she would go to the bar to get more drinks before the start of the performance. Milton and Drake stayed where they were, but, as Milton was about to thank Drake for the day, Drake's cellphone rang again. He apologised for taking it, put it to his ear, and turned away so that Milton couldn't overhear the conversation. It lasted no more than thirty seconds, and, when he put the phone away and turned back to the stage, his expression was grim.

"Are you okay?" Milton asked.

"Sure," he said, but it was evident that he was distracted. "Why?"

"You've got a face like thunder. Bad news?"

He laughed bitterly. "That obvious?"

Milton nodded. "What is it?"

"The business," he said, sitting down on the grass. "It's fucked."

"You said you were doing well. The Porsche—"

"Rented," Drake said, waving that away as if it was so obvious that a child should have realised.

"And the house?"

"I can barely afford the payments."

"You said—"

"I know what I said," Drake snapped and then, catching himself, he added, "Sorry. Lot of stress."

"So get rid of the car and move somewhere else."

He sighed and gazed over to the stage. "Can't do that."

"Why not?"

"Because of her," Drake said, gesturing toward Sophia. She was picking a path through the seated crowd, three drinks in her hands.

"She doesn't know?"

"No," he said. "She thinks I'm successful. If I tell her what things are like..." He let the sentence trail away.

"You have to tell her," Milton said. "You can't have a relationship based on a lie. She'll find out."

"Wait a minute—*you're* lecturing *me* about women now?"

"No," Milton said, aware that Drake's mood was on a knife edge. "I'm saying that she strikes me as the kind of woman who's more than smart enough to figure it out for herself. And that you might want to get out in front of it— she might not be as bothered as you think."

"Can't risk it," he mumbled.

Milton looked over to make sure that Sophia wasn't too close. She had paused on the way back to them and was engaged in conversation with a couple that she evidently knew.

"The business," Milton pressed. "Is there something in particular?"

Drake emptied his bottle and dropped it next to its predecessor. "It's one of my guys," he said. "I can't get hold of him."

"Why's that a problem?"

"Because I have a job tomorrow," he said dismissively, as if Milton had just asked a particularly foolish question. "There's this one client I have. A judge—Felipe Saverin. It's not so much the money I get from him, it's the connections he can make for me. He's important."

"Why does he need you?"

"He's running an anti-corruption case and making a lot of enemies. Judges have been hit here before. It's not uncommon. They get federal agents to protect them, but he's paranoid; he keeps the feds for himself but pays me to provide extra cover for his wife and daughter. I promised him a team whenever they left the house. The only problem is I *specifically* told him that we'd need a four-man team to do the job properly, and, because I said that, he made sure that I put it in the contract."

"And now you only have three?"

"Me and two others." He nodded glumly. "We could keep them safe with three, but the wife is sharp and she'd notice. And that's going to make me look bad."

"So get someone else."

Drake scoffed. "Find someone I can trust the day before a job? The gangs have men everywhere—I'd have to vet every candidate before I could even begin to consider them, and I don't have time."

"Then tell them that they have to stay home tomorrow."

He shook his head. "Can't do that either. The little girl has a recital. She's been excited about it for weeks—she tells me every time I see her. I can't call him now and tell him that she's going to have to miss it. I might as well tear the contract up myself."

Milton folded his arms and gazed back to the stage. Roadies were finishing up with the preparation and, as Drake stared glumly up at them, the drum tech stomped on the kick drum, each beat throbbing in the air around them.

"It's an easy job?" Milton said, raising his voice a little to be heard over the beat.

"Cakewalk," Drake said. "Pick them up from their apartment, take them to her school, keep an eye on them there, take them home again."

"So I'll stand in."

"Don't be daft," Drake scoffed.

"Why not?"

"You said it yourself, Milton—you're a cook."

"I keep in shape."

"Come on, John."

Milton deadpanned. "I could still take you."

"The *fuck* you could," Drake said.

Milton looked over and winked.

"What about the drinking?"

"What about it?"

"You said you had a problem."

"I do," Milton said patiently. "That's why I don't drink anymore. I'll promise you one thing: I'll be sharper and clearer-eyed than you will be in the morning."

"Maybe."

"I'm serious," Milton said. "You're in a spot. Let me help."

Drake sighed and shook his head. Milton had made his offer, but he wasn't going to press. He couldn't tell Drake just how qualified he was for this kind of work. His friend had no idea about Group Fifteen, and Milton was not about to tell him about it, but he had conducted close protection assignments during his government employment in places that made Rio look like a walk in the park. And, during those times when Milton had been poacher rather than gamekeeper, he had tested and ultimately breached the security of high-value targets around the world. That kind of experience did not fade away; a simple job like this, protecting a mother and her child, would be easy.

"I'd have to tell Saverin," Drake said. "He'd probably want to meet you, too. He's paranoid. You wouldn't believe how paranoid he is."

"Fine. I'm happy to do it if it'll help you out. Least I can do."

Milton saw that Sophia was on her way over again. "She's coming back," he said.

The crowd screamed as the lights on the vast stage went out. It was dusk, and they could make out the shadows of the band as they took up their positions.

Sophia handed a fresh beer to Drake and another bottle of water to Milton. Drake's mood had rapidly improved, and he grinned widely as he raised his bottle for a toast.

"To old friends," he said.

Milton touched his bottle to Drake's and then to Sophia's.

"Old friends."

The kick drum boomed again, and then a single chord thrummed out from the speaker stack. Cellphones were held aloft, a thousand screens glowing like fireflies.

"Rio!" the emcee boomed. "Thanks for coming. Please welcome, from Hollywood, Guns N' Roses!"

PART III

THE THIRD DAY

18

Milton woke at six and went out for another early morning run, following the same route as yesterday. He settled into the rhythm of his steps and allowed his thoughts to drift back to the night before.

The concert had been amazing, even better than he could have hoped for. The band had gone on stage at eleven and played all their hits plus a reworking of Pink Floyd's 'Wish You Were Here' and a cover of Derek and the Dominos' 'Layla' that segued perfectly into 'November Rain.' Drake and Sophia had accelerated their drinking and had been thoroughly drunk by the time the final encore was finished and the lights came back up. Milton had navigated their way through the crowd to the bus terminal and led them from the stop back to the house in Santa Teresa. It was very late by the time they finally returned, and Drake had persuaded Sophia to stay up to drink a bottle of wine with him. Milton had tried to dissuade him, reminding him that he had work later that day, but Drake had dismissed his concern with a theatrical flourish of his hand and a reminder that it was a simple job and that it wasn't until midday; he had plenty of time to sleep off his hangover. Milton had heard the two of them talking as he lay on the bed and willed himself to sleep.

It had bothered him then and it bothered him as he ran: Drake had work, and it was not the kind of work where you would roll into an office after a few hours' sleep and a bellyful of alcohol without consequences. Close protection was dangerous work that required clear thinking and fast reactions. Milton had started coming to work drunk toward the end of his time with the Group, but he had been good at hiding it. If Control had noticed, then he had never commented upon it. But Milton had known, and it had been one of the reasons—together with the towering guilt that he could no longer ignore—that had forced him to quit both the bottle and his employment.

He returned to the house and let himself in, pausing to run a glass of cold water and then sinking it in one draught. He could hear the sound of stirring in the bedroom that Drake shared with Sophia. He made his way past the door to his own room, where he changed out of his sodden gear and put himself under a cool shower for ten minutes. He stood in front of the mirror as he dried himself down, looking absently at the tattoos on his arms, the IX on his breast to signify the ninth step of the Fellowship and, across his back, the angel wings that he had drunkenly commissioned during a lost night years earlier.

Times had changed since then.

MILTON HAD TRAVELLED LIGHT, with just a change of underwear and a second plain black T-shirt in his pack. He dressed in the T-shirt and his jeans and pulled on the Red Wing boots that he had found in a thrift store in Brighton Beach.

Sophia and Drake were waiting for him in the kitchen.

"Morning, John," Sophia said. "How did you sleep?"

"Very well," Milton said.

"You know what I said to you when you told me to stop drinking?" Drake said.

"He thought it was a big joke last night," Sophia added.

"But not now?" Milton asked.

Drake chuckled. "Abstinence is much more attractive now than it was then."

"Are you going to be okay to work?"

"I'm fine," he said, waving away Milton's concern. "A cup of coffee and *pão francês*—that's all I need." He indicated the pot of coffee. "You want a cup?"

"Thanks," Milton said.

The coffee was strong and served with warm milk, and the *pão francês*—French bread—was toasted and came with cuts of cold ham, mortadella, a cheese from Minas Gerais called *queijo prato*, and slices of mozzarella that was processed and nearer to a mild cheddar than the Italian equivalent. Drake took his plate and went out onto the veranda; Milton followed him.

"You heard from your guy?" Milton said.

"No," he said. "He's completely AWOL."

"Any reason to be worried about it?"

"No," Drake said. "He's not the most reliable man I've ever met. He drinks too much and disappears. Not the first time."

Drake delivered the withering verdict with a lack of self-awareness that Milton recognised all too well.

"You still want me to help?" Milton asked him.

"You still okay to do it?"

"Of course." Milton sipped his coffee and watched as a kiskadee landed on the back of an empty chair, eyeing up the crumbs on Drake's plate. "Tell me more about the client."

Drake shooed the bird away and sat down. "What do you know about PBN?"

"Nothing."

"You don't read the papers?"

Milton shrugged. "I try to avoid them as much as I can."

"Petróleo Brasil Nacional—biggest oil and gas corporation in South America. The top executives are all corrupt. I mean, Jesus, the whole *country* is rotten, but this is as bad as it gets. You've got government officials colluding with people in business to overpay on contracts. Construction was the first one that went bad. All those new World Cup stadiums? You have a cartel fixing it so bids went in way above the real value of the work they were tendering for. Government takes the lowest bid, and the winning business skims off the top and passes that back to the politicians and the other executives in the cartel. The politicians get millions of *reais*, and then they send some of it back as bribes, put some of it toward their re-election campaigns, and pocket whatever's left."

"And no one noticed?"

"Like I said—Brazil's rotten to the core. Not the country so much, but the government and institutions. Corruption's a way of life. The government just opened up drilling rights to fields off the coast. Trillions of *reais* worth of oil. Same thing is happening, but in reverse—PBN pays over the market value; the corrupt officials get paid and then send some of it back. But that's Brazil—everyone is involved, one way or another. Business, government, everyone. But if one domino goes down..." He let the words drift away.

"And has one gone down?"

Drake pressed two codeine tablets out of a blister pack and washed them down with the last of his coffee. "There was an election last year. They all promised to go after corruption. The democrats got in and gave the judiciary the power to go after anyone who had their snout in the trough —businessmen, politicians, *anyone*. And they kept it quarantined from Rio. The judges are from Curitiba, down in the south. It's not like Rio down there; the people are much more..." He struggled for the word.

"Law-abiding?" Milton suggested.

"Less corrupt," Drake qualified. "There were demonstrations against corruption before the World Cup. The president couldn't ignore it after the campaign he ran, and certainly not with football about to start, so he fast-tracked reforms that made it easier to prosecute fraud. And, for the first time, the judges were allowed to offer plea bargains. It's a whole new ball game for them now. New tactics. They start at the bottom, round up the small fish, and offer them deals so they can keep going up the chain."

"And it's worked?"

Drake nodded his head. "And one of the judges is my client."

"Saverin," Milton said, remembering the name from last night.

"That's right—Felipe Saverin. Him and his family—wife and kid. He's decent. Serious. No bullshit, hence my problem."

"You ever had any problems with him before?"

"Problems?"

"With his security?"

"No. It's been easy. That's why I—"

"Don't mind me coming along," Milton finished for him.

"You said that, not me."

Milton smiled. "But still—he must have enemies. He wouldn't need you otherwise."

"Of course he does," Drake said. "They all do. A private plane with a flight log from São Paulo to Rio crashed into the sea last month. It was a new Hawker-Beechcraft twin-prop, fresh off the line, and the pilot was in good health. They came down in the ocean near Paraty. Four people on board—all killed. Civil aircraft come down all the time in Brazil, but this one was different. One of the passengers was a judge called Garcia. He was working the case with Saverin. Scared the shit out of him. There are a lot of people who'd pay good money for him to be out of the way."

Milton stood. "You said he'd want to meet me."

"He does," Drake said. "I called him to confirm they wanted us this afternoon, and I told him I might have a new man on the team. He wants you to come in with me when we pick them up."

19

The first thing that Paulo was aware of as he awoke the next morning was a pounding headache. It was brutal: a thudding, jarring jackhammer that sent out constant throbs of pain. He lay in bed with his eyes closed. He remembered working late and what had happened after he had left: Palito and his thugs. They had threatened and beaten him.

He opened his eyes and immediately wished that he hadn't; the light stabbed into his brain, and he squeezed them tight again.

"You're awake."

It was Rafaela. He felt her hand on his brow.

"Hello," he said weakly.

The mattress shifted as she sat down next to him. "How do you feel?"

"Not great," he admitted, cautiously opening his eyes again. "How do I look?"

She reached over to the overturned wooden crate she used for a bedside table and took a mirror from her make-up bag. She held it over Paulo's face so that he could look into it.

"*Puta que pariu!*" he cursed.

"Marcos said you were mugged."

"Did he bring me home?"

"Yes," she said. "You woke Eloá."

"*Merda*," he muttered. "Sorry."

"What happened?"

"Three guys," he said. "They jumped me."

"Marcos said it was outside the garage."

"I was just coming home."

"Do you know who did it?"

He shook his head; the motion drew a fresh throb of pain and, for a moment, he thought he was going to throw up. He didn't like lying to his wife, but he couldn't see the sense in frightening her any more than she already was. Palito had made it plain that last night wouldn't be the end of it; what good was there in giving Rafaela something else to worry about, especially when there was nothing that she could do to help?

"You're sure?"

"I told you," he snapped, regretting his tone of voice at once.

She ignored it. "Did they take anything?"

"I don't have anything to take."

He put his arm down on the mattress and tried to push himself into a sitting position. The effort was dizzying. Rafaela put her arm behind him and held him until his strength had returned.

"What time is it?" he asked.

"Ten."

"Where's Eloá?"

"With my mother. I didn't want her to see you like this."

He nodded. She had been right to send the girl away. He marshalled his strength, swung his legs off the bed, and put his feet on the floor. He leaned forward and pushed; Rafaela helped him get to his feet and held him again as he mustered his balance.

"I need to get to work," he said.

"Today? Looking like that?"

"I can't afford to take time off."

"Don't forget the appointment."

That was right: Eloá had an appointment at the hospital at midday, and Paulo had made it his policy to go to all of them. "I hadn't forgotten," he said, although it had slipped his mind. "I'll tell Marcos I'll work late again to make up for it."

"Good," she said, resting her hand against his cheek. "Are you sure you're okay?"

"I'll be fine. Just need to clean myself up."

RAFAELA CHECKED that he was okay and, seemingly satisfied, said that she was going to go and get lunch. Paulo waited for her to go and then shuffled across the room to the curtain that hid their bathroom. They didn't have the space for a shower, so Paulo filled a bucket with cold water. He reached his hands into the water and splashed it over his face. He looked down into his cupped palms and saw that the water was running red; he reached into the bucket again and splashed a double handful of fresh water over his scalp.

He needed money, now more than ever. Palito would keep coming for him until he had been paid, but, more important than that, he still had to find the money for Eloá's treatment. He had lost his car; how could he possibly find all the money that he needed without it? Racing had been his best hope, and now that had been taken away from him.

He washed his face again and looked in the mirror. The blood was gone, revealing a patchwork of bruising: his forehead, his nose, both cheeks, all were stained with purples and blues and blacks. His right eye socket was swollen, puffed up above and below his eye, partially closing it. He looked dreadful.

He soaked a flannel and used it to wash his body. He remembered what Felipe had said to him in the bar after the race.

Speak to Garanhão.

The gangster ran the *favela* and had made it known that he was prepared to lend to *cariocas* who needed financial help. Everyone knew that his willingness to lend had nothing to do with generosity or a wish to improve his reputation on the Hill. Garanhão was a vain man, and the role of benefactor was one that appealed to him. More than that, perhaps, was a more practical motivation: lending money was a very good way of washing the proceeds of his many illicit businesses.

Paulo was fresh out of options. Garanhão was his only hope.

He took his phone from the table and called Felipe.

"What's up?"

He swallowed. "You know what you were saying the other night? About what I could do to find the money?"

"Garanhão?"

"Yes. I need to... I think..." He couldn't say it.

"You want to meet him?"

Paulo's mouth was dry. "Can you arrange it?"

"You're sure?"

Paulo could hear the equivocation in his voice, and it made him angry. "What? You thought it was a good idea."

"I've been thinking about it. I'm not so sure now."

"Can you lend me the money?"

"I don't have that much lying—"

"Then I don't have a choice," he cut in. "Please. You said you knew a man who knew him. Call him. Set it up."

There was a pause and, after a buzz of static, Felipe said, "I'll call you back."

Paulo went back to the bed and took out a clean T-shirt and a pair of jeans. He dressed, grabbed his phone and the keys to the front door from the small table in the middle of the room, and went to the vestibule to pull on his sneakers. He locked the door and made his way out of the apartment.

He had to walk along a long, narrow alley to reach the street; it was dank and it smelled unpleasant for days after it had rained. He emerged, blinking, into the fierce sunlight. His head throbbed again with the brightness. An old woman called Luna had a stall just down from the apartment, where you could get a strong cup of coffee and tapioca crepes. He gave her one of his last remaining notes, and she prepared his breakfast for him. He took the polystyrene cup and the paper bag with the crepes and sat on the pavement with his back to the wall. The road bent around sharply here, and he was able to look down over the rooftops to the gleaming skyscrapers of the districts below and, beyond them, the sparkling blue of the sea.

He had finished his coffee when his phone rang.

"He'll see you at midday," Felipe said.

"Thank you."

"Be careful."

"It's too late for that. I don't have any other choice."

"I'm just thinking of your father. If he knew I'd done this—"

It was a little late for regret, Paulo thought. "I won't tell a soul."

"He's not someone to fuck with, okay? Be respectful. Don't piss him off."

"I won't," Paulo said. "Thank you."

He ended the call and put the phone away. He tossed the crepes into one of the torn-open garbage sacks that had been lined up along the wall; he had lost his appetite. He paused for a moment, knowing that he was at a crossroads that was both literal and figurative. He could turn right and head down the Hill, go to the garage and set up for the day. He would have to deal with Palito, but perhaps he could negotiate with him. Perhaps Palito would lend him the money for new parts and he could repair the car and offer it in exchange for the money that he owed, or race it with Palito as his patron.

Who was he kidding?

The other choice, the only choice, was to turn left and climb. That was where Garanhão had his business. That business involved drugs and extortion, prostitution, black-mail and violence. Paulo's father had been caught up in that world, and he was still paying the price for his involvement. Paulo had promised himself that he would never follow in his father's footsteps. He had promised the same to his father, too, and to Rafaela. He had responsibilities to her and to his child. They would be lost if anything happened to him.

Yet there were no other paths that he could take. The notion that he had a choice was illusory.

He didn't.

He was down to this. There was nothing else that he could do.

He swallowed down the bubble of vomit that crept up his throat and, one foot after the other, began to climb the Hill.

20

Milton and Drake finished their breakfasts, said goodbye to Sophia, and made their way down to the garage. Drake drove Milton across town to an industrial park in Barra da Tijuca and, after waiting for the gates to open, he rolled the Boxster inside and parked next to a small warehouse. The building was anonymous and, unlike the other warehouses around it, there was no sign to denote the business that carried on inside.

"This yours?" Milton asked.

"Yes," Drake said. "We keep the cars and the kit here. Come on—we need to get you sorted out."

The gates rattled again as they slid back to admit a second car. Drake stopped and shielded his eyes with his cupped hand as the car rolled up next to the Porsche.

"They work with you?" Milton asked.

"Yes."

The new car was a top-of-the-line Lexus, almost as ostentatious as Drake's Porsche. Not for the first time, Milton was uncomfortable about the lack of discretion that Drake—and now his employees—exhibited in a sensitive and dangerous job where it was far better to melt into the crowd. Milton would never have chosen such a gaudy car.

The doors of the Lexus opened, and two people stepped out, a man and a woman. The man blipped the locks and led the way to where Milton and Drake were waiting.

"Here you go," Drake said. He shook hands with the two newcomers and then turned to indicate Milton. "This is John Smith," he said. "He's an old friend of mine from the Regiment. This is Jannike Berg, and this is Dean Hawkins. Jannike was in the Norwegian special forces. Dean was in Delta."

The woman was tall and blonde, an almost stereotypically statuesque Nordic specimen. She took off her shades to reveal blue eyes and put out a hand.

Milton took it. "Norwegian special forces?"

"The *Jegertroppen*," she said.

"You were in Afghanistan," Milton said. "The unit, I mean. I've heard of it."

"That's right," she said, maintaining a deliberately firm grip. "What about you?"

"John was SAS," Drake said for him.

Hawkins stepped forward and offered his hand. "Hello."

Milton took the man's hand. Hawkins squeezed hard, and Milton held it without betraying even a flicker of the discomfort that he sensed Hawkins would have liked to see. The American held on for a beat too long; Milton regarded him, allowing a small upturn at the side of his mouth.

"You sure this is a good idea, Shawn?" Hawkins said.

"John knows what he's doing."

"Really?"

"Careful," Milton said with an innocent smile. "Unless you want me to show you."

Hawkins's face darkened, but just for a moment. He

smiled, exposing two rows of shining bright teeth, and took
his hand away. "Maybe we'll see about that later."

Drake had been watching with veiled amusement. "He's
just rattling your chain."

Milton found Hawkins irritating. He was no fan of
yahoos, and he found the exaggerated bonhomie that was
often evident in military personnel to be grating and tire-
some. His instant assessment of Drake, Hawkins and Berg
was that they had been working together for some time, and
that their familiarity had bred a confidence that, as far as he
could tell, might be unwarranted. Milton knew from experience that that kind of familiarity could easily lead to a
reduction in a person's awareness and professionalism, and
in a city like Rio, with the family of a man who had made
powerful enemies under their guardianship, that was something that made him uneasy.

"Don't worry about Hawk," Berg said to Milton. "He's
full of shit."

"You're *both* full of shit," Drake corrected.

Milton kept his eyes on Hawkins. He could see that the
man was going to hammer him on the shoulder, another
juvenile attempt to establish a pecking order, and he flashed
his right hand up and caught Hawkins's arm at the wrist. He
yanked his wrist down and bent it around, pinning it against
Hawkins's back and pressing it all the way up until it was
between his shoulder blades. The American gasped in
sudden pain; Berg straightened up and took a step, but
Milton froze her with a smile and a wink as he released
his hold.

"Don't worry," he said. "I'm full of shit, too. Nice to meet
you, Hawkins."

"Jesus," Drake said with mock exasperation. "Can't you
at least try to get on?"

Hawkins rubbed his wrist, glaring at Milton. Drake took a key from his pocket, nudged his way between them, and opened the door.

The warehouse was dark, but, as Milton's eyes adjusted to the gloom, he could see two identical black Range Rover Sports parked inside. It was a fairly standard choice of vehicle for those in close protection: four-wheel drive, powerful, and rugged enough to take a decent amount of punishment.

Drake went into the warehouse, flicked on the lights, and walked between the two vehicles to the back of the space. Milton followed and saw two large gun lockers fixed to the rear wall. Drake took a second key from his pocket and opened one of the lockers. There was a selection of firearms inside: Milton saw a variety of pistols, a Bernelli combat shotgun and two HK416s, which, upon further inspection, he noted were military issue with single, three-round, and fully automatic modes. The bottom of the locker contained boxes of ammunition for the firearms.

Drake moved along to the next locker and opened that, too. There were black flak vests inside.

"Help yourself," he said to Milton.

Milton went to the jackets first and took one out. It was made from Kevlar with pouches intended to house ceramic plates. The plates made the jackets too bulky to be worn underneath normal clothes, and they had been removed; the Kevlar was supposedly strong enough to stop a 9mm round on its own. Milton put his arms into the jacket and pulled it on over his T-shirt.

Berg and Hawkins had gone straight for the firearms. They took out the AR-15s and started to check them over.

Milton cocked an eyebrow at Drake. "Seriously? You

show up with those and you're going to terrify the kid. She's going to a recital—it's not the Alamo."

"We keep them in the back of the cars," Drake said. "Backup, just in case."

Drake took out one of the handguns and handed it to Milton. It was a Browning Hi-Power, the sidearm used by the Regiment. It had a single-action-only trigger that was light and smooth and broke evenly. Milton ran his finger along the steel frame. It was strong while also being light, lending the weapon a thinner profile than others Milton had used. He wrapped his hand around it and remembered how comfortable it was to hold.

"You need a licence to carry here?" Milton asked Drake.

"You need a permit to carry outside of the home. We're all registered."

"But I'm not."

"Yes," he said, shaking his head. "That's a shame. You're going to have to go without. May I?"

He held out his hand, and Milton returned the Browning.

"The judge is a stickler," Drake explained. "If he found out one of my men was unregistered..."

"What about if he found out you only had three armed guards instead of four?"

"I'm hoping he doesn't find that out." Drake grinned.

Drake went back to the locker and took out a clip-on holster and two spare magazines. He pushed the weapon into the holster and attached it to his belt, then put the spare magazines into his pocket. Berg pulled on a flak jacket and clipped an identical Browning to her belt. Hawkins slung his own jacket over his shoulder and took out another pistol. He made a show of racking the slide, shoved it into a holster, and went back for spare ammunition.

Milton looked at his watch.

"Eleven thirty," he said. "How long will it take us to get to where we need to be?"

"Twenty minutes," Drake said. "We need to be on the road."

21

The *favela* became more dangerous the nearer Paulo climbed to the summit; there was a stratification, with each upward step bringing him closer to the man who ruled the slum. Paulo needed to ascend to Rua Um—Road One—and the building where Garanhão had his office. The area of the Hill above Rua Um was known as Laboriaux, and, with Garanhão decreeing that no one was to add to the shanty beyond his own buildings, it offered a peaceful sanctuary from which it was possible to look down on the rest of the *favela* and, beyond it, the rest of the city.

Paulo followed Estrada da Gávea as it climbed, passing through the districts of Cachopa and then Dionéia, tightly packed slums that clung determinedly to the flanks of the Hill. He kept going, crossing over Rua Dois—Road Two—and climbing again until he reached Rua Um. The sides of the road were piled high with trash that had gone uncollected for weeks. The buildings on either side of the narrow road were crumbling and almost on the verge of collapse; graffitied gang tags had been daubed over every inch of free space, with fresher tags painted atop them. Stores had been carved out of the buildings: there were bars, places that sold mobile phones and SIM cards, and establishments where proprietors slept beside trays of rotting fruit and vegetables that were good for nothing but the dump. Vehicles crawled up the Hill, and hundreds of men and women picked their way between them, everything rendered sluggish and torpid by the monstrous strength of the morning sun.

Paulo tried to remember everything he could about Garanhão. His full nickname was Pequeno Garanhão, meaning 'Little Stallion,' or, more commonly, 'Little Womanizer.' Local legend had it that his nickname had originally been Pequeno Antonio, a diminutive bestowed upon him as a child when he had been so much smaller than the other boys that he played football with on the beach. Most people thought that Antonio Rodrigues secretly liked that his nickname might be considered unflattering; he looked at his lack of stature as a permanent reminder of where he had come from. By sheer force of will and a terrifying propensity for violence, Pequeno Antonio had risen faster and farther than any of his contemporaries. His appetite for women had led to his first name being dropped from his moniker and replaced with a more apt description.

Paulo reached the marketplace where Estrada da Gávea swung around to the left. There was a narrow passage to the right that led between Bar da Lúcia and a store selling parts for the mopeds that were one of the favoured forms of transport for getting up and down the Hill. Paulo turned around and looked down the Hill. He was high up; from here he could see Gávea to the east and the lagoon at the foot of the Hill, the stretch of blue-green water that separated the valley of Botafogo from the gilded towers of the rich middle class who lived in Ipanema and Leblon. He thought about the banks that had their offices down there and how they would have happily lent the money that he needed to their customers, men and women who would just fritter it away on a new car or a holiday. But the banks would not entertain the likes of him. The security guards on the doors would not let him cross the threshold, so, because he had nowhere else to go, he had to find another way.

He resumed walking. The alley was just wide enough for two people to pass, and, in those spots where barrels of cooking oil or pallets of rancid vegetables had been left against the wall, it was necessary to wait for a gap before continuing along the alley. He stepped over an open sewer and then a dead and rotting cat, and, at the next junction, he paused again. He could follow Rua Um to the southwest, where it would, eventually, deposit him at the foot of the mountain. Or he could turn left and continue into the heart of Garanhão's domain. He looked that way now and saw the seemingly idle women and children sitting with their backs against the walls or talking animatedly with one another. Paulo had never had reason to come up here before, but he had lived on the streets for long enough to know that they were lookouts and that the news of a newcomer's approach would, even now, be making its way to Garanhão's guards.

The drug trade was ferocious and vicious, with gangs always on the lookout for ways to expand into the territories of their rivals. Security was important, and this teeming district of alleys and passageways offered a natural advantage that a man like the don would be able to exploit. There was no prospect of making an armed incursion without his knowing of it, and, for anyone foolish enough to try, Paulo knew that there would be dozens, perhaps hundreds, of armed men in the buildings that fronted the passageway who would be able to flood it with crossfire and turn it into a killing zone.

He felt sick with fear and doubt, but then he closed his eyes and pictured his daughter's face once more.

He couldn't go back.

He swallowed on a dry throat, clenched fists that were damp with sweat, and walked on.

22

Milton took one of the Range Rovers with Drake, leaving Berg and Hawkins to take the second. Drake tried to deflect the abrasive introduction that Milton had received from the others, but Milton told him to forget it.

"They're good," Drake said, still defensive.

"I'm sure they are," Milton said.

"But?"

"I don't have to like them to be able to work with them."

"True," Drake conceded. "And it's not like we're going to have to do anything."

The traffic was heavy, and it took them thirty minutes to reach Ipanema. The Saverin family's accommodation was on Avenida Vieira Souto, a busy road that followed the coastline from east to west and linked the middle-class districts of São Conrado, Ipanema and Copacabana. Milton looked to his right and saw the ribbon of beach and, beyond the golden fringe, the waves that rolled in and out, the sun sparkling on the water. He turned to his left and saw the buildings, a collection of glass and steel high-rises that he had no doubt were extremely expensive. As they rolled slowly onward, Milton caught the occasional glimpse between the upthrusting skyscrapers of the multicoloured habitations that had seemingly been dropped onto the flanks of the hills that characterised this part of the city.

Drake noticed that he was staring. "The *favelas*," he noted. "That's Rocinha. And over there is Vidigal. I wouldn't go into either of them."

Milton gazed at the view: a shifting parallax with the vivid backdrop of the lush green rainforest, the crazy patchwork of the *favelas* and, standing against both, the sleek apartment blocks and businesses of the middle-class zone. Rich and poor; luxury and penury; all of it cheek by jowl. Milton thought it an apt juxtaposition.

Drake flicked the indicator and pulled over to the side of the road. Milton looked up at a tall building that was, judging by the sign above the door, reserved for apartments.

"We're here," Drake said.

BERG AND HAWKINS stayed down on the road in the second Range Rover while Milton followed Drake inside the building. The lobby area might have been smart, once, but now it was faded. The windows were dusty, and the posters and sheets of information that had been stuck to a corkboard on the wall were several years out of date. The space felt neglected and unloved.

Drake led the way to the two elevators and pressed the button.

"He can be quite aggressive," Drake said as they waited for the car to arrive.

A bell chimed and one set of doors slid apart. Drake

went inside and pressed the button for the sixth floor. Milton settled next to him as the doors closed and the lift took them up.

"He'll want to be satisfied that you're up to the job," Drake went on. "He says he has to meet everyone I put on the detail. There was one guy—another American, Prince, friend of Hawkins—he didn't like him. No idea why, but he said no, and I had to take him off the crew."

"So be on my best behaviour?"

"Exactly."

"Take it easy. I won't show you up."

The elevator stopped and the doors slid open. Milton waited, letting Drake exit first, and then followed close behind.

The sixth floor comprised a corridor that ran to the left and right, with the elevator lobby in the middle. Drake went left and stopped outside the door for flat sixty. There was a bell, and Drake held his finger against it. Milton heard the buzzer inside and then the sound of a raised voice. Drake straightened up and put his shoulders back. He was keen to make a good impression. This was his business, Milton supposed, and the Saverins were Drake's best clients. He was being professional. Milton had never really considered going into business for himself, and seeing his old friend making such an effort to impress someone else confirmed to him that he was not suited to it. Milton knew that he was prone to dark moods, and, knowing that, he couldn't think of too many things that would be worse than his livelihood depending upon what someone else thought of him. That didn't mean that he thought less of Drake—to the contrary, it was impressive what he was trying to build—but rather that a life like this was not for him. He knew what he preferred: an itinerant existence, a month or two in one place and then moving on, happy in his own company, no one to annoy, and no one to annoy him.

They heard a key turn in the lock and then two bolts as they were pushed back. The door was opened by a woman. Milton guessed that she was in her early forties, with creamy dark skin, black hair and dark eyes that flashed with suspicion until she recognised Drake.

"Hello, Shawn," she said, in excellent English.

"Hello, *senhora* Saverin."

The woman took a step back to admit Drake, and Milton saw that there was a young girl sheltering behind her legs. Milton had little experience with children, but he guessed that she was five or six. She was slender, tall for her age, and had the same brown skin and dark eyes as the woman, who must have been her mother.

Drake knelt down so that he was at the girl's height. "Hello, Alícia," he said. "How are you?"

"I'm very well, thank you, Shawn."

"Ready for this afternoon?"

The girl didn't answer, shuffling nervously from foot to foot.

"She's been practising all week," her mother said, reaching around to tousle her daughter's hair. "She's very excited."

"I'm sure she'll be excellent," Drake said, standing.

Milton stayed outside the doorway and observed the conversation: it was evident that Drake had formed relationships with the two people whom he had been paid to protect. Valentina Saverin had an easy, relaxed attitude around him; Milton was impressed, especially so given that Drake was carrying a weapon and that the holstered Browning was visible on his belt. Alícia Saverin might not have realised the significance of the pistol, but, despite her shyness, it was evident that she was comfortable with Drake, too.

Milton was still outside when a fourth person stepped into the hallway. He was tall, with thick black hair and a neatly clipped beard. He was wearing a suit, a pastel blue shirt and a dark blue tie with a subtle pattern of white dots. His eyes were as dark as the woman's, but his stare was given weight by heavy brows.

"Shawn," the man said.

"Good morning, Judge Saverin."

Felipe Saverin looked beyond his wife and daughter, beyond Drake, until his gaze fixed on Milton.

"*Senhor* Smith?"

"That's right," Milton said.

"Come in, please. I'd like to talk to you."

23

Paulo reached Laboriaux and the top of the Hill. It was quieter here, almost peaceful, the atmosphere more serene than the clamour of the rest of Rocinha. The elevated position offered a panoramic view of the city. Gávea was to the right, with its mansions and villas sliced into the rainforest, oblongs of crystal blue marking out the pools from which the fortunate residents could look back at the Hill. The lagoon was behind those residences, with the affluent districts of Lagoa, Copacabana, Ipanema and Leblon encircling it. The thought struck Paulo that this was the best spot to observe the comings and goings in Rocinha. Its position, apart from providing the perfect place for a lookout, also made it easy to defend. In the unlikely event that a rival gang or the police made it all the way up here without being spotted, the maze of streets and alleys would make it easy to mount ambushes or, if the situation demanded it, effect an escape.

There were men, women and children on the street, some seemingly going about their business while others relaxed or played. The buildings here were often built with *lajes*: flat concrete platforms that usually housed large water butts, strong enough to withstand additional storeys when the funds of the owners allowed. Paulo saw lookouts —*olheiros*—lounging on the *lajes*, able to monitor the comings and goings on the streets below. He felt the eyes of the *olheiros* on him, the itchy sensation between his shoulder blades as he set off. He followed the road around to the warehouses that he had been able to see once he was three-quarters of the way up. Everyone knew that Garanhão was based here, and that some of the warehouses were used to facilitate the drug business that had made him a very rich man.

Felipe had sent a text with instructions on where he should go, and he followed them to a two-storey building set back from the road, opposite the row of warehouses. He approached it slowly, still entertaining the thought that he could turn around and scurry back down the Hill. Two young men—perhaps still in their late teens—idled out of the building and paused as they saw him. The man at the front of the pair was holding an AK-47 as if it was the most natural thing in the world.

"Who are you?"

"Paulo de Almeida."

"What do you want?"

"I'm here to see Don Rodrigues."

"Yeah?"

"My uncle spoke to him." He started to panic, and the words tripped out haphazardly. "He said I should be here for midday."

"Wait," the man said, turning to his partner and saying something that Paulo couldn't hear.

The second man took out a phone and turned away as he made a call. He put the phone away, turned back, and cocked his finger.

"Come with me."

24

Milton and Drake followed Judge Saverin deeper into the apartment. Milton got the very clear impression that the Saverins, while comfortably off, were not rich. They had passed more opulent buildings as they had travelled east from Drake's storage facility. This building, by contrast, was a little old and tired. The fatigue continued into the apartment. It was clean and tidy—almost scrupulously so—but the furniture was of only middling quality, and the apartment itself was small. Milton had no idea how much a judge in Brazil would be paid, but he doubted that it would be a fortune. He wondered how much it would cost to hire a four-man security detail and decided it would have to be in the order of several hundred dollars a day. Would the government pay it? If not, how hard must the Saverins have had to push the family budget in order to find the money? Milton imagined that the judge could have turned down the case that Drake had described, remained in Curitiba, and prosecuted crimes that did not have the allure—and the danger—of this particular scandal. He would have saved himself and his family a lot of money and stress. That he had not taken the easier path immediately endeared him to Milton. It suggested that he was a man of principle.

Saverin led the way into a compact sitting room. There was space for a settee and an armchair, and, on a low stand, a large television was tuned to a news bulletin on *Globo*. Saverin took a remote control from the chair and, with a stab in the direction of the TV, he switched it off.

"Please," he said, gesturing at the settee. "Sit."

Milton did as he was told.

Saverin sat down in the armchair and crossed one long leg over the other. Milton gazed at him and then at the view outside the window. The apartment might not have been the most stunning inside—it paled next to Drake's stunning rental, for example—but the view from the window was stupendous. There was nothing between the apartment and the ocean, and, by turning left and right, Milton was able to see all the landmarks of the city: the statue of Christ, Sugarloaf Mountain, and the stick-like figures of the thousands of men and women and children who had gathered on the golden crescent of beach below.

"Rio is beautiful, isn't it?"

Milton drew his focus back. "Yes," he said. "It certainly is."

"Yet, if one were to walk five minutes behind this building, you would be in the heart of one of the most dangerous places in Brazil. In all of South America. It is a city of contradictions."

Drake had not given Milton much of an idea of what he might expect from the judge; he hadn't warned him that he was likely to begin a conversation with someone he had never met with a philosophical flight of fancy. His English, though, was excellent; it carried a slight accent, but not an especially obvious one. Milton suspected that the judge had received his education abroad.

Saverin let the silence persist for a moment and then gestured first to Drake and then to Milton. "*Senhor* Drake says that he will vouch for you. That is good of him, but you will be looking after my wife and daughter. I will need more than that."

"What would you like to know?"

"How do you know *senhor* Drake?"

"He's an old colleague."

"From the army?"

"That's right. We were in the Special Air Service together."

"We served together for several years," Drake interposed with just a little too much eagerness.

Milton knew from what Drake had told him that Saverin had already been given all of this information; it appeared that the judge was cross-examining him for himself.

"And when did you leave the army?"

"A while ago," Milton said, unsure of how he would answer if Saverin probed too deeply. He certainly couldn't tell the truth, and Milton got the impression that the judge would not easily swallow a lie.

"And since then?"

Drake stiffened next to Milton; he didn't want Milton to reveal to a client that he was proposing to put a cook on the team that would protect his family.

"This and that," Milton said. "I've done some private work here and there. I've kept my hand in."

Saverin pursed his lips and regarded Milton coolly. The man had an air of studiousness to him, but, beneath that, it was obvious that his character was underpinned with steel.

Milton held his gaze, finding that he had the urge to straighten his back and square off his shoulders. He wondered whether Saverin was going to tell him that his services wouldn't be necessary, but, just as the pause was beginning to become uncomfortable, the judge gave a single short nod of his head.

He turned to Drake. "You will vouch for him?"

"Absolutely," Drake replied.

"Then it is good," Saverin said, and Milton could almost feel the tension drain away from Drake. "The other man on your team. The man that *senhor* Smith is replacing. What happened?"

"He's indisposed," Drake explained. "I asked John if he would stand in, and he said that he would. There'll be no difference in the service. John has experience of close-quarters protection. Diplomats, government officials... the same as me."

Saverin looked at Milton. "You know who you'd be looking after?"

"Your wife and daughter," Milton said. "I understand the responsibility."

"Rio is a dangerous city. It is particularly dangerous for my family and me."

"With respect," Milton said, "I've guarded diplomats outside the Green Zone in Baghdad. I'll be very careful, but Rio doesn't present anything I haven't seen before."

"Fine," Saverin said. He turned to Drake. "But you'll still be in charge?"

"Yes," Drake said. "It'll be just the same as it's always been."

Saverin shook his head and chuckled. "It's not as if I have a choice," he said. "How do you say—you have me over a barrel. It's my daughter's recital. She's already mad at me that I can't go. If I told her the whole thing was off, I doubt she'd ever talk to me again."

"I have all the details," Drake said. "We'll drive them to the school, guard them while they're there, and then drive them back."

"There's a small change of plan afterwards," Saverin said. "You'll bring them back here to collect their things and then take them to the airport. They're coming back to Curitiba with me."

"Why? The case isn't finished, surely?"

Saverin paused, as if contemplating whether he should say what he had in mind. "No," he said. "It's not, but we've had a breakthrough. We've arrested a man who can open it up for us. A very senior man. We arrested him yesterday—you probably saw it on the news. I've been with him all night. It will mean there is more attention on me. I would like them somewhere a little safer until it dies down again."

Milton wondered what that meant for Drake's contract but kept his face straight.

Drake remained professional. "What time do you need them at the airport, sir?"

"The flight is at six, so if you could have them there for four thirty? Five at the latest."

"Of course."

Saverin turned back to Milton. "It was good to meet you, *senhor* Smith."

"You too, sir."

"Take care of my girls. They are very precious."

"We will. You don't need to worry."

"I'm afraid that I do. I have a lot of enemies, and they would like to hurt me very much. I don't take them lightly. Neither should you."

25

The young man took Paulo into the building and up to the first floor. There was a corridor that led away from the stairs with a series of doors that opened onto it.

"Hands against the wall," the man said.

Paulo did as he was told, and the man frisked him, expertly running his hands down his body. Once he was satisfied that Paulo was unarmed, he opened one of the doors.

"Inside," he said. "You wait."

The room was simple: wooden floors, a decent sofa, a table with a decanter and two glasses, a television. There was a window on the other side of the room, and Paulo walked over to it. The window's shutters were ajar, and the thin muslin drape blew inside between the panels, ruffled by the gentle breeze outside.

Paulo took a deep breath to try to bring his racing pulse under control. When he held up his hands, he saw that his fingers were trembling.

He was left alone for ten minutes before the door

opened and Antonio Rodrigues came inside. Paulo knew plenty about Garanhão and had seen pictures of him, but he was different in person than he had expected. He was slender and short, a good three inches shorter than Paulo, and surprisingly feminine. His hair was bouffant, coiffed so that it fell down beyond the collar of his shirt. He was brown skinned, and his eyes were perfectly black. The don was accompanied by two guards toting AKs, and, compared to those soldiers, he looked almost insignificant.

"Don Rodrigues," Paulo said, bowing his head.

"You are Paulo?"

"Yes."

"I understand that you want to talk to me."

Paulo started to reply, but his throat was too dry to speak.

Garanhão saw his discomfort and smiled warmly at him. "There's no reason for you to be fearful."

Paulo swallowed again and found the moisture to say, "I appreciate your time, Don Rodrigues."

"Sit down, please."

Paulo looked around, decided that the sofa was his best choice, and sat. Garanhão turned to the two guards and dismissed them with a cursory wave of his hand. The two men glared at Paulo, whose attention was fixed on their weapons, and left the room.

Garanhão went to the table. Paulo could smell his fragrance as he drew near. The don took the glass decanter and held it aloft. "Would you share a drink with me?"

"Thank you," Paulo said.

Garanhão poured liquid into two glasses and handed one to Paulo. It was chilled, and the cold wetness of it refreshed his dusty mouth.

"It is *chá de abacaxi com capim-santo*," he said. "Do you like it?"

Paulo knew what it was: you infused the water with lemongrass and pineapple peelings and then chilled it down. "I've never had it."

"Really? I don't drink alcohol or do drugs. Bad habits. Iced tea and cigarettes are my vices. I prefer to keep my wits about me."

Paulo shifted uncomfortably. Garanhão noticed, smiled again, and came around to sit next to him. He folded one leg over the other, revealing a half inch of his tanned ankle and an expensive loafer. They were flat shoes; Paulo had wondered whether Garanhão might have worn shoes with lifts to compensate for his lack of height, but it appeared that the legend was true: he really didn't care that he was short.

"Do you know that I know your father?"

"Yes," Paulo said.

"How much has he told you about me?"

Paulo couldn't say what he knew: that his father hated Garanhão, that he described him as a cancer, and that he longed for the day when someone—the police or a rival—finally did away with him. He couldn't say that, so he said, instead, "Not a great deal."

"We worked together—years ago. Your father is a dear friend of mine. He is a loyal man. The police offered him a deal—he could walk free if he implicated me in the work that we were doing together. Did you know that? He went to Bangu rather than betray me. That tells me a lot about him as a man. And it makes me wonder—is it a characteristic that is shared by his son?"

Garanhão stopped talking. Paulo had been concentrating on keeping his fear at bay and didn't realise that he had been asked a question until he saw the don looking expectantly at him.

"I'm sorry, Don Rodrigues. Could you say that again?"

"I was talking about loyalty," Garanhão said, the smile still twisting the edge of his lip. "Are you as loyal as your father?"

"I don't know," Paulo said before he could consider what he should say. If he said yes, what would that mean? He was wrong-footed, and Garanhão's ambiguous motives were confusing him.

"Can I be honest with you?" Garanhão didn't wait for an answer. "I've always been interested in your well-being—yours and your mother's. Your father's silence has been a blessing to me, and, when I speak of loyalty, you must know that it flows both ways. I am grateful for what he has done, so I have always made sure that your mother had enough money to raise you. I have been paying her every month for the last ten years—ever since your father went to jail. Did you know that?"

Paulo's mother had never been explicit about the packages that were delivered on the last Friday of every month. She had always been secretive about them, opening them when she thought Paulo wasn't looking, but there had been occasions when Paulo had been able to peep through the crack in the door. Paulo had watched her open one of them, tearing away the brown paper wrapped in duct tape to take out a small bundle of banknotes. He doubted now that the payments had amounted to very much, especially not to a man as rich as Garanhão, but they had allowed them to keep their apartment and to ensure that they never went hungry. There had also been enough to pay for his mother's regular trips to the prison. Paulo had guessed that the money was dirty and that it was being paid in order to win his father's silence. He gave a single nod now to acknowledge this.

"It was the least I could do. I prefer not to talk about it." The don got up from the sofa and collected the iced tea from the desk. He refilled Paulo's glass and then his own. "Now—you have walked up the Hill to see me. What can I do to help you?"

Paulo took another sip of the tea as he composed himself; here it was, the moment he would rather have avoided, the opportunity that he had no other choice but to pursue.

"My daughter is unwell," he said. "She has cancer. The doctors say that she can be saved, but the treatment that they have recommended is expensive."

"And you don't have the money to afford it."

"No," Paulo said.

"What is your daughter's name?"

"Eloá."

"Do you have a photograph?"

Paulo found himself wrong-footed once again by the don's request but said that he did and took out his phone. He had hundreds of pictures of his daughter, and he selected one of his favourites and handed the phone over. Garanhão looked at it and smiled.

"She is very beautiful," he said. "How old is she?"

"Six."

The don handed the phone back to him. "How much money do you need for her treatment?"

"Thirty thousand *reais*."

"And how much do you have?"

"Nothing," he admitted.

"Nothing?"

Paulo had not intended to tell Garanhão about what had

happened two nights ago, but he found the man's charm disarming and was unable to stop himself. He explained that he had been gambling on his racing to put the money he needed together, and that he had lost it all thanks to the sabotage of his car.

"And who did this to your face?" Garanhão pointed to Paulo's bruising.

"I owe money to a moneylender."

"Who?"

"Palito."

"Really?"

"Do you know him?"

"Of course I know him. I told him he wasn't welcome in Rocinha." As Garanhão spoke, a flicker of menace passed across his face. "Leave him to me, please, Paulo. I'll take care of it."

Paulo was confused by the direction that the conversation was taking and, in his bewilderment, he found he was fixated on the amount of money that he had just asked for and the person to whom he would be in debt. Now that the don had suggested that he might say yes, Paulo found that the consequences of his request were coming into focus. "I know it's a lot," he said. "Perhaps I should ask for less."

"And how will that help Eloá? It's all or nothing, Paulo. She needs to be treated. Please—wait here."

Garanhão got up, crossed the room, and called out to the men waiting outside. Paulo couldn't see through the door, and the noise of the street outside meant that he couldn't hear what Garanhão was saying. The don closed the door and came back to sit down on the sofa again.

"The money will be waiting for you when you are ready to leave," Garanhão said. "Thirty thousand. All of it."

"Thank you," Paulo said, trying hard to ignore the fresh

fear that had started to worm around in his gut. "You're very generous, Don Rodrigues. I can't tell you how much that means to me—to my family. You've saved my daughter's life."

Garanhão smiled and, instead of acknowledging Paulo's gratitude, he stood and collected the decanter again. He refilled Paulo's glass and then his own. "There is the question of repayment, of course," he said blandly. "What do you propose? Do you have a job?"

"Yes," he replied. "I'm a mechanic."

"But it doesn't pay very well?"

"I make four hundred *reais* a week."

Garanhão smiled gently. "I charge interest on the loan, of course. I doubt you would be able to service it with a wage as small as that. Something else, then."

"Yes," Paulo said. "Of course. What do you suggest?"

"You said you raced cars."

"Yes."

"So you are a mechanic and a good driver?"

"I am."

"Excellent. Then you will work for me."

"I'm sorry?" Paulo said, confused.

"It's the best way. The job I have for you is safe, it pays very well, and it will give you more than money. The demands on your time will be light, so you would be able to spend more time with Eloá and Rafaela."

Garanhão dropped Paulo's wife's name into the conversation with flippant ease. Paulo had no idea how he knew it, but it was not difficult to see it for what it was: a demonstration of his command of the *favela* and a thinly veiled threat.

Paulo's throat was dry once more. "What would I have to do?"

"You would drive," he said. "Sometimes for me, sometimes for others. There are many people in Rio who would like to see me harmed. I am well protected, and my name is warning enough for most to respect me, but there are some who are less sensible than others."

"So I'd be your chauffeur?"

"Yes," he said. "I suppose so. I would pay you generously: I was thinking fifteen hundred *reais* a week with a week in advance as a bonus for saying yes. How does that sound?"

Paulo felt dizzy and was grateful that he was still sitting down. Six thousand a month? That was nearly two thousand dollars. He would be able to pay the debt back in less than a year.

"And you would be able to maintain my cars, check that they haven't been tampered with, that they are safe."

"Of course, Don Rodrigues."

"There will be other times when I need things delivered or people picked up. You can be responsible for that, too. Yes?"

"Yes—I can do that. Thank you."

Garanhão stood. "Tell your employer that you quit. Use my name if you have to."

"When?"

"You will start now," he said. "Today. Two of my men have business to attend to in Ipanema. You will drive them there and bring them back again."

Paulo knew that there was no way that he could say no. Any choice that he might have once enjoyed was gone. He had sold himself to Garanhão in order to save Eloá's life. He had no option but to do what he was told. And although he knew it was foolish greed, he could not ignore the change to their lives that six thousand *reais* would make once the debt was repaid. They could find a bigger place, for a start, somewhere that didn't leak when it rained, somewhere without mould on the walls. He ignored the part of him that was yelling out that it couldn't be as simple as the don had suggested, that he wouldn't pay that much cash for a chauffeur and a mechanic, that he would want his pound of flesh.

"Where do I find them?" Paulo asked.

"In the warehouse," he said, gesturing toward the window in the direction of the industrial buildings. "The cars are kept inside the last one on the left. Go there now and ask for Alessandro. Tell him I sent you and that you will be driving them."

Garanhão stood, smiled warmly, and put out his hand. Paulo took it.

"Thank you."

Don Rodrigues withdrew his hand, put it on Paulo's shoulder, and guided him toward the door. Paulo thanked him again and allowed himself to be shepherded out of the door. The two young men with AKs were lounging around outside, their eyes and teeth shining in the gloom. Another of the don's men was waiting there; he had a white plastic bag in his hand and, as Paulo approached, he held it out so that Paulo could take it. He did.

"Thirty," the man said.

Paulo opened the mouth of the bag and looked inside; he could see bundles of banknotes, all of them stuffed haphazardly into the bag.

The man eyeballed him. "You want to count it?"

"No," Paulo said. "Of course not."

Paulo put his back to them all and descended the stairs. He heard the sound of their voices, and then Garanhão's, and then a peal of discordant laughter. He swallowed down on his dry throat and stepped out into the bright light and the heat of the early afternoon. He stopped. He felt dizzy, buffeted this way and that by a riot of emotions. He opened the mouth of the bag again and looked more closely at the contents. There was a rainbow of yellow twenties, brown fifties and blue hundreds. The money was Eloá's salvation, and he felt numbing relief that he had managed to find it.

He was jostled out of his daydream by the clatter of automatic gunfire somewhere below him in the streets of the *favela*.

The relief collapsed into the fear upon which it had been built.

He stared across the road in the direction of the warehouses.

What had he just done?

26

Milton rode in the back of the Range Rover with Valentina Saverin and her daughter. Milton was on the passenger side of the vehicle, and the girl was next to him, with her mother on the opposite side.

"I'm good at singing and dancing," the girl said.

Milton's attention was on the window, and he hardly heard her.

He felt a hand tapping against his leg. "*Senhor* Smith?"

He turned from the window; the girl was looking up at him.

"I'm sorry, Alícia," Milton said. "What was that?"

"I said I'm good at singing and dancing. It's my favourite thing."

"So you must be excited about today."

"I am," she said. "What about you?"

"Am I excited?"

"No," she said, her nose crinkling as she shook her head in childish exasperation. "Are you good at singing and dancing?"

"Oh," Milton said. "No. I'm afraid not. I'm terrible at both."

"You don't like music?"

"No," Milton said. "I love music. Very much. But no one would want to hear me sing."

Milton glanced up and saw that Alícia's mother was watching the exchange with an amused expression on her face.

Milton couldn't help but smile, too.

"I've heard *senhor* Smith's singing," Drake offered from the front of the car. "Trust me, Alícia. He's right. I don't think there's anything that could be done for him."

"*Everyone* can sing," Alícia protested. "I'll teach you."

"Well," Milton said, keen to change the subject before she could go any further, "I'd certainly like to hear *you* sing."

"You can hear me today," she said and, with that, she turned to the front and looked out of the windshield, a happy smile on her face.

Milton saw Drake's beaming face in the mirror and looked back out of the window, stifling his laugh before it could come. The child had a naïve innocence that was impossible not to love, and a way of expressing herself that was both charming and entirely guileless. Milton had never been paternal and had long since decided that to bring a child into his own life would be both the height of selfishness and entirely impractical, but he found that Alícia charmed him. He gazed back at her now: her hands were folded demurely in her lap, and she watched out of the window with an open, inquisitive face.

Valentina caught his eye and smiled at him.

Milton smiled back. He was enjoying the afternoon rather more than he had expected he would.

27

P aulo took the road around to the back of the last warehouse on the left, as the don had instructed. There was a slope that led down to a large opening that, in turn, led to the interior of the building. The room had a double-height ceiling with dirty skylights set high above. There was an old loading bay and a raised platform that was guarded by a metal rail. There were two beaten-up vans parked against the platform and a Jaguar XF next to the trucks.

Paulo made his way inside and walked across to a man in a blue-and-white-checked bandana.

"Excuse me," he said.

The man turned to him. "What?"

"I'm here to see Alessandro."

The man pointed to the corner of the loading bay. "In the office."

Paulo followed the man's directions, climbing a flight of stone steps to the raised loading dock and then continuing across it until he reached a wooden door. The door was closed, but there was a dusty panel of glass set into it and, as he looked through it, he saw an office space with a table and filing cabinets. He couldn't see all of the room, but he could see that there were at least two men inside. They were playing cards, both of them with their backs angled toward him.

He knocked on the door.

"What?"

Paulo opened the door and stood in the doorway.

One of the men turned around. He was bearded and was wearing a sleeveless vest that exposed the tattoos on both arms. "Yes?"

"I'm Paulo. Don Rodrigues sent me."

"You're the driver?"

"That's right."

"So don't just stand there—get in here."

"And close the door," the second man said without turning away from the table.

Paulo did as he was told, closing the door and stepping up to the table. The man with the beard laid his cards down and stood up. He hawked up a ball of phlegm, turned his head and spat it onto the floor. "I'm Alessandro," he said. He pointed to the man at the table, who still had not turned around. "That's Junior. You're driving us."

"Where are we going?"

"Ipanema," he said.

"What for?"

"You just worry about driving us down there and back here again. That's all you got to concern yourself about."

Paulo decided not to press it. He felt a little frisson of disquiet, but he told himself he was being paranoid. It was a simple enough job. Garanhão had told him: take them down the Hill and bring them back again.

Junior stood. "You okay with that?"

"Yeah," he said. "I'm okay with it. Where's the car?"

"Outside," Alessandro said. "The Jaguar. Go make sure it's ready. We need to be down in Ipanema by one thirty."

"Then we have to leave in five minutes—"

"Just as well you came when you did, then. Get on with it."

28

The Our Lady of Mercy School was found between Lagoa and Botafogo, a short drive from the Rodrigo de Freitas Lagoon. Traffic remained heavy, and it took them twenty minutes to make the short four-mile transit from Ipanema. The entrance to the school was on Rua Visconde de Caravelas, a side street that was too narrow for the line of cars as parents waited to drop off their children. Milton looked up and down the street anxiously; it would be impossible to make a quick exit here if they were put under attack. There was a drop-off zone to their left, marked by a dotted white line and a painted yellow box, but it was jammed with cars. The driver of one car—an expensive Lexus—was trying to slide his vehicle into a space that was much too small for it, bullying his way ahead in an attempt to persuade the driver of the big SUV ahead of him to get out of the way.

Drake was anxious, too, and he pressed on the horn as a Honda pulled out without warning and blocked his way ahead. The car had left a space, though, and, with the second Range Rover blocking the rest of the traffic behind them, Drake seized the opportunity. He reversed into the space and raised his hand in thanks as Berg and Hawkins went by in the second car.

"It's not normally as busy as this," Drake said. Milton knew that Drake would have been embarrassed to have driven them into a spot like this and, although Valentina might not have appreciated the risk, he knew that Milton most certainly would.

"The recital is always popular," Valentina offered. "It was like this last year. Everyone comes. All the parents."

Milton got out of the car first and checked up and down the street. Cars were parked on both sides, with others slowly trying to pass between them. He turned to the school itself: the doors that led inside were set into a modern-looking brick façade, with coils of barbed wire set atop tall walls composed of concrete slabs that were still scarred by the ghostly markings of graffiti that had been partially cleaned away. There were a lot of parents gathered around the entrance, and an enterprising young woman was hawking inflatable balloons as the children passed on their way inside.

Drake got out of the car.

"I don't like it," Milton said over the roof.

"I don't either," Drake said.

"It's a choke point."

"I wouldn't have brought them in this way if I'd known," Drake replied, a little defensively.

There was an old saying that Milton remembered from running protection operations: 'If you're not mobile, get mobile. If you are mobile, stay mobile.' Drake had dropped the ball. Milton was about to tell him that he should have known the lay of the land, that a little reconnaissance would have made the issue self-evident, but he bit his tongue. He didn't want to embarrass an old friend in front of his client.

The second Range Rover found a space ten metres ahead of them and pulled up next to the kerb.

"Berg will stay out here and watch the car," Drake said. "Hawkins will stay by the entrance and wait for us."

"All right," Milton said.

Drake went to the door and opened it. Valentina Saverin came out first, then reached back into the cabin to take her daughter's hand so that she could help her out.

Milton went around the car and joined them as they passed through a gap in the slow-moving line of cars. Valentina was on the left and Milton the right, with Alícia between them both.

The little girl looked up at him. "Are you coming in, *senhor* Smith?"

"I am," Milton said. "Is that all right?"

The girl gave a solemn, satisfied nod of her head. Milton looked back to the road and felt her small hand slip into his. He felt her fingers lying across his palm and looked down; her hand was small and dainty. She felt his eyes on her and smiled up at him. Milton found himself smiling again, too. The shadow of his unease faded in the brightness of her expression.

They went through the entrance and into the school beyond. It was squeezed into the cramped city block and did not have the space for grounds or any sort of outdoor facilities. Valentina led the way down the corridor and then out into an enclosed concrete yard that looked as if it was where the children went outside to play. They crossed the yard and entered another building; this one opened onto a performance space. It was designed as a rotunda, with the small stage surrounded on all sides by seating. Alícia was more confident now that she was in a place that she, rather than the grownups, recognised, and she led the way across the space to a man who turned to meet her with a smile.

"Alícia," the man said. He turned to her mother. "*Senhora* Saverin."

The man—Milton guessed that it was Alícia's teacher—spoke in Portuguese, and Milton was unable to translate. He and Drake took a step back, finding a discreet position where they could observe the room without standing out too much.

"Is this expensive?" Milton asked.

"Not cheap," Drake replied. "But there are more expensive schools."

"The Saverins aren't rich, then."

"No. Between us, I agreed to a reduced rate for the job. It's not really about the money for me. This is good for the CV. And for introductions to the other people Saverin knows."

Milton nodded, but, before he could respond, Valentina came over to them both. She had an awkward expression on her face.

"That was the headmaster," she said. "I'm very sorry—he says the hall will be full today. School policy is for parents only, but, given that my husband isn't here, he said it would be all right for one of you to stay." She turned to Drake apologetically. "I'm sorry, *senhor* Drake, but Alícia asked if *senhor* Smith could stay. I hope that's not a problem."

"Of course not," Drake said. "Let me just speak to *senhor* Smith, and then I'll wait outside."

She nodded her assent and went to take one of the few empty seats in the middle of the nearest bank.

"I'll go outside," Milton said. "You should stay here. The wife knows you."

"It's fine," Drake said, waving the suggestion away. "There's only one way into the hall, and the school has guards, too. I don't need to be here. I can wait in the yard."

"Are you sure?"

Drake grinned. "You've made a new friend."

"So it would seem."

Milton turned. Valentina was looking in his direction, and, as their eyes met, she raised her hand and then pointed down at the empty seat beside her. Milton ignored the feeling that a six-year-old girl was calling the shots and, raising his hand to acknowledge the girl's mother, he started toward her just as the doors to the yard were closed and the lights started to dim.

29

The recital was charming. The school catered to children from Alícia's age all the way up to sixteen years old, and a selection of musicians from across the age range entertained the audience for an hour. An older teen gave a dazzling performance of Beethoven's 'Waldstein' sonata, and others followed with an extract from Rachmaninov's third piano concerto, Haydn's Sonata No. 42 and Chopin's Polonaise-Fantaisie. Classical music wasn't Milton's favourite, but it was impossible not to be charmed.

At ten minutes to the hour, a fifteen-year-old who had just dazzled them all with Mozart took his applause and left the stage. There was a pause, and then Alícia appeared. The girl walked confidently to the front of the stage, faced the parents, and gave an exaggeratedly deep bow. The adults clapped enthusiastically. Milton turned his head a little so that he could look at Valentina; the girl's mother was absorbed in the moment, caught between clapping and raising her hand to catch her daughter's attention.

Alícia turned away from the crowd and took her seat before the big piano. She looked tiny, her legs barely long enough to reach down to the pedals. She took a moment to compose herself, and then, resting her hands on the keys, she started to play. Milton looked down at the program and saw that Alícia was going to play the first movement from Beethoven's 'Appassionata.' Milton didn't recognise the particular piece; the music was fiery and rebellious, with a hint of darkness beneath it that Milton found impossible to miss. The girl was extraordinarily talented. Her hands flew over the keys, her nimble fingers picking out the notes with a fluency that, if not perfect, was still remarkable for one so young. She finished the piece with a bravura flourish, and the audience rewarded her with an enthusiastic ovation.

Milton clapped, too, and, as he looked over at Valentina, he saw that her eyes were wet with tears. The girl's mother saw that Milton was looking at her and, for a moment, their eyes met. Valentina smiled at him with a sort of bashful pride, and Milton gave a single nod of his head, a gesture that he hoped she would interpret as a mark of how impressed he was with her daughter.

Alícia came to the front of the stage, gave a second bow, and, still tiny next to the big piano and on the wide stage, she gave a third bow before turning and heading back to the room from which she had emerged.

The applause petered out.

"That was outstanding," Milton said.

Valentina smiled her gratitude. "Thank you, *senhor* Smith."

"You should be very proud."

"I am. I just wish that her father could have seen her."

"Yes," Milton said. "But I imagine he can listen to her at home."

"He can," she conceded. "He does. But it's not the same as being here." She paused, biting her lip until the flesh whitened. "It's difficult. His work is very important. But sometimes..." She paused again and, this time, did not continue.

Milton felt uncomfortable. He doubted he had the empathy to finish the conversation in the right way, without appearing gauche or patronising, but he knew that he had to say something, so he offered, "I'm sure it won't be forever." Then, before she could respond, he told her he would meet her at the door and made his way down the stairs to the exit.

30

Valentina and Alícia met them in the yard, and Drake led the way back through the school to the entrance. He had called ahead, and Hawkins was waiting at the entrance, while Berg had brought the first Range Rover up to the kerb. She left the engine running as she got out and opened the rear door for first Valentina and then Alícia. Milton went around to the front and got into the passenger seat. Berg shut the rear door, conferred briefly with Drake, and then jogged down the road with Hawkins to get into the second car. Drake slid into the driver's seat and rolled away from the kerb. He slowed down and flashed his lights, and Berg and Hawkins pulled out in front of them. They headed west in formation and then turned to the south, following the road around the lushness of the Parque da Catacumba.

"*Senhor* Smith?"

Milton turned to look back. "Yes, Alícia?"

"Did you enjoy the recital?"

"I did," he said. "Very much. You're very talented."

The girl screwed up her face and turned to her mother,

who translated for her. She smiled when she looked back to Milton again. "Thank you."

"Thank *you*," Milton corrected her. "Thank you for asking me to come. I had a lovely afternoon."

Milton gazed past the girl and her mother and looked out at the vast Honda dealership on Rua Real Grandeza. The traffic was still heavy, and Drake had no choice but to keep their speed low. The second Range Rover was just ahead of them, the brake lights flashing on and off as Berg reacted to the intermittent flow ahead of them. Milton felt a knot of disquiet in his stomach. They were vulnerable. There was no easy way to get off the road. If he were planning a hit with the Saverins as his target, *this* would be precisely the kind of place that he would choose. A couple of attackers on motorbikes, a drive-by with MP5s or a magnetic mine slapped onto the chassis... He sucked his teeth.

"This isn't unusual," Drake said, gesturing to the traffic ahead of them. Had he sensed Milton's unease?

Milton wanted to tell him to keep his eyes open, but he didn't want to betray his anxiety in front of the girl and her mother. And, he reminded himself, it was probably just his paranoia. He had seen nothing to make him suspect that an attack was a possibility. It was his habitual wariness. He had spent so long working out how to get to difficult targets and, less often, how to defend potential targets from attack, that it had seeped into his bones.

"How long do you think it will take?" Valentina asked.

"Half an hour from here," Drake offered.

"We have to get to the airport," she added.

"Not a problem. Your husband said we've got plenty of time."

Milton concentrated on the view out of the window. The traffic moved sluggishly.

31

The Jaguar was the XF Sport in black, with tinted windows, and looked as if it was new. It was the 3.0-litre V6, with 376 horsepower and a six-speed manual transmission. Alessandro and Junior got into the back, and Paulo drove them out of Rocinha and then east along the coast until they reached Ipanema. Alessandro told him to go to Avenida Vieira Souto, the exclusive road that separated the high-end apartments, restaurants and hotels from the beach and the sea. Paulo had been here just two nights earlier, racing in the opposite direction. It seemed longer ago than that now. A lot had changed in the meantime. He had lost his car and the money that he had been saving, he had been beaten and threatened by Palito, but then—perhaps—his luck had changed. He had been given all of the money to pay for Eloá's treatment.

But it wasn't that simple, Paulo reminded himself: Garanhão had not offered him the money because of some altruistic motivation; he wanted something in return, and Paulo would have to start paying it back now.

Paulo glanced in the mirror at Alessandro and Junior.

The latter, now that Paulo had seen him properly, was fear-some-looking: he had a tattoo across his face, the design attesting to his membership in the Red Command gang, of which Garanhão was the local leader. The two men were silent, but Paulo had the impression that they were both keyed up by the prospect of whatever it was that they were here to do. He wondered what that was. Garanhão had said only that it was 'business,' that he was to drive the two men to and from Ipanema. He knew that anything to do with Garanhão was likely to be illegal, but he hoped that the scale of that illegality was minimal.

They approached a red and white building from which the owner rented beach equipment to those going down onto the sand.

"Turn around," Alessandro said. "You want to be over there."

The road had three lanes on either side of a central island. Alessandro pointed to the other side of the island, to a spot just outside an apartment block. Paulo drove east for another fifty metres until he reached a spot where he could turn left onto the road heading back to the west. He waited for the lights to turn red, stopping the onward traffic, and edged the car around.

"See the apartments?"

"Yes," he said.

"Park on the other side of them."

Paulo fed in a little gas, drove past the block, and then indicated that he was going to pull over at the side of the road.

"Leave the engine running," Alessandro said.

"What's going on?"

Alessandro ignored him.

"What is this?" he pressed. "We're picking someone up?"

"Be quiet," Junior snapped. "You do as you're told when you're told to do it. And keep your mouth shut or I'm gonna lose my temper."

Paulo looked at Alessandro; the other man held Paulo's eye coolly.

Paulo started to feel more concerned about what it was that he had signed up for. What was this? A robbery? Was he the getaway driver? He wondered whether he could go back and tell Garanhão that he didn't want his money, thanks but no thanks, he'd find another way to fund the treatment. But then he remembered how much he needed, how much he owed Palito, and the fact that he had nothing and no way to make anywhere near enough to meet all his obligations. Paulo felt sick. He couldn't leave. He was trapped. He had to see this through.

Junior's phone buzzed. He put it to his ear and listened to whatever it was the other person was saying. He delivered a curt, "Yes," and put the phone away.

Paulo waited for instruction, but it didn't come. He looked out of the window as a pair of good-looking girls in bikinis jogged across the road and hopped down to the beach. He tried to ignore the churning in his gut.

He wanted to be *anywhere* other than here.

He glanced up in the mirror as a truck pulled out of the traffic and slid up against the kerb outside the hotel. He recognised the livery: it was one of the dry-cleaning trucks that served the businesses down here.

Paulo was still looking in the rear-view mirror when Junior leaned forward so that he could speak directly into his ear. "You remember what I said?" he hissed. "No questions. You do exactly what we say when we say it. You don't do that, or you ask questions, then I'm going to put a bullet in your brain and drive this fucking car myself. You understand?"

Paulo swallowed.

"Say it."

"I understand," he said.

"Good boy. You want to know why we're here? We're here to pick up two passengers. They're not going to want to get into the car, but we're going to make them. And then, once they're inside, you're going to drive us away, all the way back to the top of the Hill. You got it?"

"I got it."

Junior leaned back in his seat once more.

"Good," he said.

32

They turned onto the road that ran along Ipanema beach and headed back to the apartment. Milton kept his eyes open all the way, scanning ahead and to the sides and then behind them to ensure that they weren't being followed. It was difficult to make an assessment; there was so much traffic that it was tricky to spot patterns, but, as far as he could see, Milton was satisfied that they were not being tailed.

They reached the apartment block.

"Here we go," Drake said as he flicked the indicator. "We'll leave the car down here while we get your luggage. Do you think you'll need long?"

"No," Valentina said. "We're already packed. We'll need ten minutes, that's all."

There was a van parked at the side of the road opposite the entrance to the block. It was marked with RIO FRESH and a logo of a pile of neatly folded sheets, and a man was lowering the loading ramp. The rear doors of the van were open, but, as Milton glimpsed the inside, he saw something that concerned him.

"Go around again," he said quietly.

"What is it?"

"See the man on the truck? He's not in company uniform."

"So—"

"And the truck's empty. Nothing inside. Keep going."

Drake turned the wheel and edged carefully back into the traffic again. Milton watched carefully as they went by the truck. The man on the back of the truck was watching them. Why would he be paying them attention?

Milton took the radio and opened the channel.

"It's Smith," he said.

Berg responded. "What is it?"

"Check out the van," Milton said.

"He's picking up laundry from the—"

Milton spoke over her. "Check it out," he said. "We're going around again."

"Copy that."

Milton glanced behind as the second Range Rover swung into the parking space that they had just avoided. First Berg and then Hawkins opened their doors and stepped down from the car.

Valentina leaned forward. "Excuse me?" she said. "What's happening?"

"We're just being careful," Drake said. "There's a van outside the apartment that wasn't there when we left."

"I saw it—it's the laundry van. There's a hotel next to us."

"It's probably nothing," Milton said. "But I'd like to be sure before we get out of the car."

Milton looked at the satnav unit in the car's dash. There was a right-hand turn just ahead that would allow them to get off the main road. The streets were arranged in a grid, and if they took it, they would be able to follow Prudente de Morais until they reached the rear of the apartment block.

"Is there a way into the building at the back?" Milton asked.

"I don't know," Drake admitted. "*Senhora* Saverin?"

"There's a goods entrance," she said.

"Thank you," Milton said, and then, to Drake, "Take the next right."

Milton reached down to where he would have holstered his weapon before remembering that he was unarmed.

"In the glovebox," Drake said quietly.

Milton reached forward and opened it. He saw a Glock 17 in a polymer clip-on holster. He took the gun, removed it from the holster, and automatically checked the chamber and the magazine. There were sixteen rounds in the mag and another in the spout: seventeen shots in total. He pressed the magazine home again.

He watched, looking through the front and side windows and into the rear-view mirror, switching his attention through a circle that encompassed the car and its surroundings. There was a median between the eastbound and westbound Vieira Souto; it accommodated trees for most of its length, but the stretch adjacent to the car was crowded with mopeds and motorbikes that had been left there by owners who had then made their way down to the beach. The road had three lanes, and each was full of traffic waiting for the lights to change. There was a black Chevrolet to their immediate left; Milton looked through the window and discounted it as a threat: the female driver was applying lipstick as she looked in the vanity mirror. They were at the front of the queue, but the lights were holding them as pedestrians in swimsuits and flip-flops crossed to get to the sand.

The lights changed.

"Here we go," Drake said.

Milton looked up into the mirror as the car edged forward and started to turn. The laundry van was blocking his view of the Range Rover, but he could see Berg standing between it and the line of stationary traffic. It looked as if she was in conversation, gesticulating animatedly as she spoke.

And then Milton saw a flash, a puff of red mist, and Berg toppled straight back to sprawl across the hood of the car that was next to her.

"Drive!"

Milton's shout had barely left his lips when he saw a large vehicle rushing out of the street that they were turning into. It happened too fast for him to be able to make out the details, save that it was a silver Chevrolet Suburban with tinted windows. The SUV raced across the pedestrian crossing and slammed into their Range Rover. The Suburban was moving quickly; the Range Rover's progress was abruptly arrested, and the rear end leapt up and then slid around to the left. All of the airbags detonated loudly; Milton bounced back against the seat and then whiplashed forward, his face and torso absorbed by the bag.

Their car continued to slide around, eventually stopping as the offside rear wheel caught against the kerb on the other side of the road that they had been trying to take.

Milton heard screams from behind him: Valentina Saverin's shriek and the distinctive, higher pitch of a panicking child.

The airbag was already deflating, and, as it shrank away, Milton looked through the cracked windshield. Two men were getting out of the Suburban. They were both dark-skinned, wearing jeans and T-shirts and dark glasses. The man getting out of the passenger side was holding a pistol in his right hand, and Milton glimpsed the driver reaching down to his belt, most likely going for a weapon of his own.

Milton raised the Glock, pointed it at the windshield, took aim at the passenger, and pulled the trigger. The bullet punched a hole through the safety glass. Milton's aim was true, and the passenger dropped to the road.

The driver had brought up his own pistol and, before Milton could switch his aim, the man pulled the trigger.

The bullet raced across the short distance between them and punched its own hole through the windshield. Milton flinched as it deflected downwards, whistling by his torso and thudding into the floor.

Drake's Browning roared, deafeningly close, his round drilling the man in the middle of the chest. He stumbled back against the wing of the Suburban and slowly slid down to the road.

"Drive," Milton urged again.

Drake put the car into reverse and stomped on the accelerator; the engine whined, but they barely inched back. Milton guessed that the cars had been jammed together by the crash. Drake cursed.

Milton turned to look out of his window. The line of traffic had stopped, and angry horns sounded from those drivers waiting down the road who hadn't seen the crash. Milton could see two men running toward them from the west. One of them was on the sidewalk, and the other was in the road. They were both armed. Milton assumed that they had taken out Berg and Hawkins.

"Come on," Milton said to Drake.

"We're stuck."

Milton caught a quick flash of Valentina and Alícia in the back. They looked terrified. Milton opened his door and stepped out.

"Get them away from here," he called back to Drake as he stood and turned. "I'll cover you."

33

M ilton quickly assessed the tactical situation. The two men who had come at them from the SUV had been shot, and, for now, were out of the picture. There were another two who he assumed had taken out Berg and Hawkins. They were approaching from the west and must have seen what had happened to the men in the Suburban. They had slowed their approach. Milton looked east. He couldn't see anything that gave him cause for concern.

The Range Rover had swung around enough so that Milton was able to duck down beneath the open door. It was average cover, at best, but it was better than being exposed in the open.

He felt the weight of the Glock in his hand. One shot fired, sixteen shots left.

"Go west," Milton called back. "I'll cover you."

"Affirmative. On your mark."

Milton took a breath, calming himself for action.

"Three. Two. One. *Go!*"

Milton waited and, as Drake threw his door open, he

popped up and raised his Glock. He aimed at the only one of the two men that he could see. The man was twenty feet away, a tough shot to make, but he didn't need to hit the target to buy Drake the time that he needed.

He squeezed the trigger—once, twice, a third time—and the man scurried back until he was out of sight.

Milton heard the boom of a big handgun and flinched as a round rushed by his cheek. It missed, crashing into the back of a car that was trying to bully its way through the jam and out of danger.

Milton saw the shooter crouched behind the row of parked motorbikes and returned fire, his three rounds cracking into the raised windshield of a Vespa.

He glanced back. Drake had placed himself between Valentina, Alícia and the two shooters, and now he was switching his attention from front to back as he ushered them down the street. Valentina had Alícia pressed close to her body, her hands on the girl's shoulders, and, at Drake's instigation, she shepherded her around the smoking Suburban and along Vieira Souto to the west.

Milton saw a flash of movement from the sidewalk. The shooter had popped out of cover and unloaded three rounds in Milton's direction. Milton ducked down behind the open door; two rounds thudded loudly into the panel. He rose up ready to return fire, but the man had fallen back into cover again, and he had no shot.

Milton had counted each shot as he fired and knew that he had ten rounds left. He was sweating badly. They were in trouble. He had to assume that both Berg and Hawkins were dead. Drake had his hands full getting the Saverins to safety; it was down to Milton to give him the time that he needed. He thought of the AR-15 in the trunk. The increased firepower and capacity would even the odds. It was a risk to go and get it, but maybe it was a bigger risk to stay.

He decided that he had no choice. The Glock squirmed in his sweaty palm as he took three deep breaths, readying himself to move.

Three.

Two.

One.

Go.

The man near the motorbikes made a run at the exact same time that Milton raised his Glock and came up from behind the door.

The man fired and missed.

Milton fired back at him.

The round was badly aimed, but Milton got lucky. The man skidded to a stop, and the bullet punched him in the leg. He collapsed and his leg kicked out from beneath him. He fell face first and ate the sidewalk. Milton sprinted to the rear of the Range Rover and pressed the button to pop the trunk. He grabbed the rifle and brought it up at the same time as the final attacker came out of cover. Milton aimed and pulled the trigger three times. The man was twenty feet away, and all three shots found their marks. The second man was on his belly, crawling for cover. Milton swivelled his hips, took fresh aim, and fired again. Two shots missed, blowing out chunks of asphalt, but the third drilled him in the ribs.

Milton's relief was short-lived. He heard the sound of automatic gunfire. It wasn't coming from the east, from the direction of the laundry truck; rather, it was coming from the west, the direction that Drake and the Saverins had taken.

Milton spun around. A Jaguar XF was parked on the

same side of the street. Two men were standing outside the vehicle, each aiming small submachine guns at Drake. He had put himself between the men and the Saverins; Drake had his arms raised, and, at a shouted command from one of the men, he dropped his Browning to the ground.

Milton knew what was about to happen. He aimed the AR, supporting the forestock with his left hand as he pressed the side of his head against the buffer tube so that he could look right down the iron sight.

One of the two men approached Alícia and grabbed her by the wrist. Valentina screamed and seized her daughter around the waist. She had put herself between Milton and the potential abductor, and Drake blocked his line of fire to the second man; Milton had no shot at either man.

Milton heard the rattle from one of the automatics and yelled out as Drake fell to the ground.

Valentina and Alícia screamed as one.

Drake was on the ground, but at least he was no longer in the way. A gap had opened up; Milton had an opportunity.

Valentina and the man who had grabbed Alícia were still wrestling with one another. Milton aimed at the man who had shot Drake. He took a breath, exhaled and, in the moment of calm that came between breaths, squeezed the trigger a single time. The man spun like a top as the bullet hit home; Milton was too far away to be sure, but he thought he had struck him in the shoulder.

The other man elbowed Valentina in the face, and she fell. Milton watched, horrified, as he scooped Alícia up and, clutching the girl to his chest with one arm, backed toward the Jaguar, then turned and shoved her into the car. The man Milton had tagged was on his feet again, too, struggling across the road to the open rear door and falling inside.

Milton aimed at the first man again, but he had moved quickly and was now in the car beside the child; he had no possible shot that would not also risk her being hit.

The man backed into the Jaguar and, even before the door was closed, the engine roared, the tyres squealed, and the car raced away.

Paulo watched what was happening outside with a quickening sense of dread. This wasn't a normal pickup. It was a kidnapping and, worse, it was a woman and a little kid. Junior was aiming his submachine gun at one of the men who had come out of the Range Rover. Alessandro and the woman were fighting over the girl, dragging her toward the car as the woman tried to pull her in the other direction. Paulo heard the clatter of automatic gunfire and saw, with horror, that Junior had fired on the man.

He wanted to be anywhere but here.

Fuck.

He couldn't take his eyes off the mirror.

Alessandro struck the woman with his elbow. She fell. Alessandro scooped up the girl and started to back toward the car.

Fuck.

Paulo saw the other man who had come out of the Range Rover. He had found a long gun from somewhere, and now he was aiming it in their direction. Even as Paulo fought the urge to lift his foot off the brake, he saw a puff of smoke and heard the crack of a single shot.

Junior cried out and fell to the ground.

Fuck, fuck.

The engine roared as Alessandro shoved the girl into the back of the Jaguar. Junior hauled himself into the back through the opposite door; Paulo caught a quick flash of red and saw that Junior's hand was pressed to his shoulder.

"*Filho da puta!*" Junior grunted.

Alessandro got in next to the girl.

"Go!" he yelled. "Move!"

Paulo released the brake and, tyres squealing as they laid rubber down on the asphalt, the car leapt ahead like a bolt of lightning. The back fishtailed at the sudden acceleration, but Paulo had anticipated it and was able to nudge them back straight without having to let go of the accelerator.

He knew the way back to the *favela* without having to look at the satnav. Vieira Souto followed the beach until it reached Leblon, and then he would be able to stay on the coast road through Vidigal or, if he needed an alternative, he could go north around the Ecological Park. There would be traffic, but he knew that he would be able to carve a way through it.

It was six miles from here to Rocinha.

Fifteen minutes to get them back there and off the street.

MILTON KNEW that there was nothing that he could do for Drake; he had been shot at close range, and he hadn't moved since he had fallen to the ground.

He had to assume that he was dead.

Drake, Berg and Hawkins. Four bad guys. Seven dead.

Valentina Saverin was on her hands and knees. "Alícia!" she wailed. "Help!"

"Call the police!" Milton yelled at her.

He ran across the road. The traffic had jammed up as panicked drivers had tried to escape the shoot-out; one car had crashed into the back of another, and a line had formed up behind them both. The nearest car to Milton was a red Honda Civic. He raised the AR-15 and aimed it at the driver, jerking the muzzle to the left in an order that the man should get out. The driver froze; Milton reached his door, opened it, and, as the driver finally managed to disengage the seat belt, Milton grabbed him and hauled him onto the street. He put the AR-15 on the passenger's seat, slid into the car, threw it into drive, and yanked the wheel around so that he could mount the median and cross over to the opposite lane. He straightened up and stomped on the accelerator, smoking the wheels as he left the Civic's driver behind.

The Civic was nimbler than the bigger Jaguar. Milton raced along the road, darting in and out of gaps in the traffic, slowly closing the distance to the lead car.

"*Puta que pariu*," Junior cursed.

Paulo glanced in the mirror. The gangster was slumped against the inside of the car door, his left hand pressed to his right shoulder. Paulo could see the blood that was seeping between his fingers, and, as Junior raised his hand, Paulo saw the red all over his palm and heard the squelch as he pressed it back down again.

"*Que merda!*"

"Is he all right?" Paulo called back.

"Just drive," Alessandro shouted back.

"*Foda-se*," Junior grunted. "Who the fuck was that?"

"I don't know," Alessandro said.

"Garanhão said it would be easy. He shot me. The *puta* shot me!"

"It's just your shoulder. You'll be fine."

"You ever been shot in the fucking shoulder?"

The two men bickered as Paulo hammered the accelerator, swerving the big car into a gap between a bus and a delivery truck. He looked back again: the little girl was in the middle, tiny and delicate between the gangsters. She was sitting up straight, her eyes wide, and tears rolling down her cheeks. She was petrified. Junior was still cursing, but Alessandro had ignored him to look out of the rear window.

"Someone's coming after us!" he yelled out.

Paulo checked his mirrors. There was a red Honda Civic ten car lengths behind. It was obvious that the driver was giving chase; the car had switched over to the wrong side of the road, accelerating along the quieter lane faster than the Jaguar was able to travel.

"Get rid of him," Alessandro ordered.

Paulo swerved left so that they were running down the middle of the road. There was just enough space for them to carve a path ahead: they overtook cars to their right and narrowly missed the cars that approached them on the left.

"Look out!"

Everything slowed down for Paulo, just as it always did: he saw how the road changed up ahead, with the median between east- and westbound traffic given over to a line of parking spaces that were occupied by cars that had delivered their occupants to the beach. He couldn't continue on the same line without slamming into the back of the queue. He yanked the wheel to the right, sliding into the opposite lane and then touching sixty as he slalomed around slower-moving cars.

"He's still coming," Alessandro yelled over the sound of the engine.

There was a gap in the long line of parked cars, and Paulo bent the Jaguar into it, finding the sweet spot where grip and momentum intersected so that it was almost as if the car were on rails. He looked back into the mirror and saw that the Honda had followed them through the gap.

They were on the wrong side of the road now, facing oncoming traffic. Paulo swerved in and out, tracing a route in the gaps between the cars, instinctively calculating angles and closing speeds and escape points, all of it done without thinking. He caught a quick glimpse of the frightened face of the girl in the back; his passengers were flung left and right as Paulo muscled the wheel.

Alessandro opened the window all the way down and turned himself around so that he was facing backwards.

"Let him get closer," he said, raising the submachine gun.

Paulo ignored him.

"Slow down! Let him get close!"

"I can lose him."

"Slow down *now*."

Paulo hit the brakes, and the Civic quickly closed the distance between them. Paulo was able to see the face of the driver: he was in his middle age, white, and had dark hair. His face was set in a grimace of determination.

Alessandro brought the submachine gun up and leaned out of the window with it.

36

Milton changed down, pumped the accelerator, and then changed back up again. He glanced down at the dial and saw that he was doing seventy; the engine was screaming, and he could feel the slip and slide of the rubber on the road.

The driver of the Jaguar hit the brakes, the taillights burning a sudden red. Milton closed quickly, then saw the man leaning out of the passenger window with the submachine gun. Milton jagged the Civic to the left, getting behind the Jaguar as the gun chattered. He had been fast, but not quite fast enough; rounds chimed against the bodywork of the Honda, a pattern that tracked up the hood and into the wing mirror, blowing it clean off its housing.

The Jaguar swerved away, heading into a side street. Milton hit the brakes a fraction of a moment later and spun the wheel around. He felt the inside wheels lift off the road as the car fought for balance, but Milton had bled off just enough speed to stay upright, and the car slammed back down as he straightened the wheel and planted his foot again.

The Jaguar swerved to the left, the rear end crashing against the wing of a car heading west. The driver of the struck car sounded his horn as the Jaguar fishtailed, slowing rapidly. Milton put his foot all the way down. This road was emptier than Vieira Souto, and Milton was able to take advantage. He closed in again until he saw a truck reversing into the road from a building site. A banksman was in the road behind it, beckoning the driver to reverse; it was a big eighteen-wheeler, and, as it kept backing out, it quickly blocked the road.

The Jaguar swerved into a junction, heading north. Milton stabbed the brakes and downshifted all the way to second. The car started to slide, and he cranked the wheel all the way across, then stomped down on the pedal. The Honda went sideways, sliding into the street. Milton pushed the speed back up to seventy and swerved hard onto Rua Visconde de Pirajá, close to the Jaguar again.

The two cars raced together, side by side, and Milton took a moment to chance a fast glimpse across at the other car. The driver looked young, perhaps in his late teens or very early twenties, with hair that he wore close to his scalp. He was looking dead ahead, his eyes fixed to the road. There were three people in the back: there was a man with the submachine gun and a second man with a tattoo across his face. The third person was Alícia, the girl's face a mask of the purest terror.

Milton fought a blast of fury. He looked back to the road, saw that it was clear, and turned the wheel to send the Civic into the flank of the bigger car. The Honda bounced off, too light to do much more than nudge the Jaguar away. But it forced the driver to brake, and Milton was able to draw ahead far enough that, when he swerved into them again, he was able to strike the front wing.

THE CIVIC CRASHED into the Jaguar, nudging them toward
the sidewalk before Paulo turned the wheel and corrected
their course.

"Who is this fucker?" Alessandro yelled out.

Paulo knew what was coming up: the sharp right-hand
hairpin where he had dumped Aldo during the race. The
turn passed through more than ninety degrees as Avenue
Niemeyer swung from west to northeast and started its
ascent toward Estrada da Gávea, the run into Rocinha and
home. He had to lose the other guy here or risk being
followed into the *favela*.

He did not want to disappoint Garanhão. He knew how
dangerous that would be.

He turned the wheel to hug the inside of the right-
hander. The rocky outcrop and the wire mesh fence that
guarded against rock falls were almost close enough to
reach out and touch. He hit the brake, losing speed until he
was down to fifty, and waited for the Civic to draw closer.
Paulo could see the ragged petals in the bodywork from
where Alessandro had shot at it, but the car's performance
was unaffected. The driver of the Civic brought the front of
his car alongside the rear of the Jaguar.

Paulo hammered the brake and twisted the wheel
sharply to the left.

The Jaguar crashed into the Honda hard, with enough
force to bump it off course. It was too late for the driver of
the Civic to slow down. He tried to stop, but he had too
much speed, and the manoeuvre unbalanced his car. Paulo
glanced across as the front end danced left and then right
before the front rubber caught too much traction and the
back end slid out. Paulo watched in the mirror as the Honda

rolled, tumbling side over side until he couldn't see it. He didn't see the crash, either, but he heard it.

He turned back to the road, managing the sharp turn and then punching all the way down on the accelerator as they took off again.

Paulo turned off the main road. They approached the warehouse, and Paulo turned into the road that led to the loading bay. He drove slowly, following the passage around as it gently turned to the left and ascended before it levelled out and widened a little in front of a roller door.

"Hit the horn."

Paulo did as he was told. They were left there for a moment, and Paulo had the distinct impression that they were being observed. Paulo knew that Garanhão would have spotters with automatic weapons posted here to defend the building; the narrowness of the passage meant that it would be impossible for a vehicle to approach quickly or, indeed, to retreat before it could be shredded in a crossfire.

Paulo slapped the horn again; the roller door lifted up and started to fold back. He drove forward, slowly sliding beneath the door into the loading bay. Alessandro opened the door and called out a name that Paulo did not recognise, adding that Junior had been shot.

"Help him get out," Alessandro called to Paulo.

Paulo stayed where he was. He had been tricked, and now he felt stupid and vulnerable. Alessandro reached back into the cabin and, as Paulo looked up into the mirror, he saw the pale face of the little girl as she was half-carried and half-dragged out of the car.

He thought of his father and what he had said about Garanhão all those years ago.

He had listened then.

This was what happened when he forgot.

"Are you deaf? *Help him!*"

Paulo switched off the engine, opened the door, and went around the car to the back. He opened the door and looked down. Junior was pale faced and sweating. His shirt was soaked with blood, and there were swipes of it against the upholstery and on the back of the seat in front of him. Paulo reached down and tried to slide his arm behind the man's back. He gasped in pain, swore loudly, and pushed Paulo away.

"What the fuck is going on?"

Paulo turned. Garanhão was there.

Alessandro suddenly looked very nervous.

"What?" Garanhão said. "Why is he shot? What happened?"

"It wasn't as easy as we thought," Alessandro said.

Junior struggled out, his hand still clasped to his shoulder.

"What happened?"

"The security, Don Rodrigues," Junior groaned.

"We knew they would be there. Four men. We had six. And they didn't know we were coming."

"There was one guy," Junior mumbled. "He shot me."

Garanhão swept around Junior, dismissing him, and looked into the car. "Where's the wife?"

Alessandro shook his head.

"What does that mean? You don't have her?"

"I mean they put up a fight. We didn't get her."

"And the other car? Pedro and Luiz? Fabrício? Gael? Where are they?"

Alessandro shook his head again. "Dead."

Garanhão raised his arms and pressed his hands against the sides of his head. "This was supposed to be easy," he muttered, and then, in an eruption of anger that was as sudden as it was frightening, he cursed and slammed both hands against the side of the car. "Where did this happen? Ipanema?"

"Outside the apartment."

Garanhão cursed again.

Alessandro held Alícia by the collar of her shirt, and he shook her now. "We got her, Don Rodrigues," Alessandro said, trying to placate him. "His girl. She's more important than the wife."

Garanhão tamped down his anger. "Put her in the basement."

"I need to speak to Barbantinho," Alessandro said. "I need to make sure the police don't know anything."

"For fuck's sake." Garanhão exhaled irritably. He turned to Paulo. "Fine—you do it."

Paulo turned to him. "What?"

He stabbed a finger into his chest. "You've got a daughter —you deal with her."

"*Deal* with her?"

"Are you stupid? You want to start paying off what you owe? Thirty thousand *reais,* you motherfucker—you can be the best-paid babysitter in all of Rio."

"Where? Where should I take her?"

"There's a room on the other side of the office,"

Alessandro said. "Down the stairs. Take her there."

"I want her quiet," Garanhão said. "She doesn't make trouble. Make her understand."

Another question came to his lips before he could stop it. "But what are we doing with her?"

Garanhão looked at him scornfully. "Are you fucking stupid? Just make sure she doesn't cause any trouble—can you do that, Paulo?"

Paulo could see that he needed to tread carefully; Garanhão's previous bonhomie toward him was a distant memory. Paulo knew that he had been fooling himself. The don's good-natured generosity was a mask; this—the malice and the callous disregard for the girl—*this* was Garanhão's true self. The stories that Paulo had heard of the man—the things that he had done to complete his ascent to the top of the Hill and then secure his position—they all came back to him now. Paulo was nothing: just a driver and dispensable. Garanhão was not his friend. He never was, and he never would be. Paulo needed to remember that.

"Of course, Don Rodrigues," he said. "I'll make sure she's no trouble."

Garanhão said nothing.

Paulo went to the girl. She had backed up against the side of the car, as if trying to hide. He crouched down in front of her. Her face was pale, and her eyelashes were plastered down from the tears that still glistened on her cheeks. He reached for her hand, but she flinched and drew it away.

"Come with me," he said gently. "I'm not going to hurt you."

She turned her face away from him. Paulo reached one arm behind her knees, put the other around her shoulders, and lifted her up. Her body was stiff with tension. He started toward the stairs.

38

Paulo carried the girl and the bag of money down the stairs into the basement of the warehouse. It was damp, with pools of stagnant water spread out across the cracked concrete. Mildew stained the floor; it was hot, and the air was thick with humidity. There was a single door in the bare brick wall. It was smaller than usual, and he could see that he would have to stoop if he wanted to go inside. There was a key in the lock. He put his fingers on the key and left them there for a moment. The metal was cold to the touch, and he focussed on it and tried not to think about how far he had already been dragged into the world that his father had always tried so hard to keep him away from. But who was he kidding? He was already implicated. And, worse, he had taken Garanhão's money and put himself into the don's debt. He was Garanhão's man now, bought and paid for, and there was no way out.

He felt sick as he put the money on the floor, turned the key in the lock, and opened the door.

The space inside was dark. A little light from the basement seeped into the room beyond the door and, as his eyes adjusted to the gloom, Paulo could see a light switch on the wall. He flicked it, and the space was illuminated with golden light. It was little more than a crawlspace, and it was not pleasant: it had a low roof and a rough concrete floor, with a plastic crate that he assumed was intended to be used as a seat. There was a plastic bucket for a toilet.

He put the girl down, rested his hands on her shoulders, and gently turned her around so that he could look at her.

"What's your name?" he said.

She didn't answer; she didn't even look up.

"What's your name?" he said again. Still the girl didn't look up. He dropped down to his haunches so that he was at the same height as her.

"I'm Paulo," he said before wondering whether it was sensible to give her his own name.

Still she didn't look up. She was tiny and seemingly even smaller now than when she had been in the back of the car. Her long hair fell forward, cascading over her face. Her bare limbs were thin and delicate and, as he looked, he saw a trace of Junior's blood on the side of her arm.

"I'm not going to hurt you," he said. "I'm going to look after you."

He heard the sound of a snuffle, but still she didn't look up. Paulo's eye was drawn down, and he saw that the fabric of her jeans was a deeper blue around her crotch. He realised, with a withering blast of shame, that she had wet herself.

"Listen," he said, pointing into the crawlspace. "You need to wait inside there. I know it's not nice, but you'll be safer there than you would be out here. I'm going to get you some new clothes. I have a little girl—just like you. Her clothes will fit. And I'll get you something more comfortable to sit on. And a blanket." The words tumbled out helplessly, as if a display of kindness might absolve him from what he had already done. "I'll get you food and drink, too, and then I'll be back."

Finally, she looked up at him. Her eyes welled up and a fat tear rolled down her cheek.

"You need to wait for me inside," he said, hating himself a little more as he took her by the shoulder and gently moved her toward the door. Unresisting, she shuffled into the crawlspace. "I'll be back as soon as I can."

Paulo fought down a bubble of fresh disgust and closed the door. He turned the key in the lock and stood there for a moment, his hand pressed against the knotted whorls of wood. He was sweating. *What had he done?*

He grabbed the money, turned and hurried up the stairs to the ground floor. He would be quick. He didn't want to leave her on her own for any longer than he had to.

39

There it was again: a *sound.*

Milton couldn't place it. It was muffled, as if he were hearing it from deep underwater. He listened for it and thought that he heard it again. But now he wasn't so sure; *had* he heard something? Whatever it was, he tried to ignore it. He was tired, and the darkness was wrapped around him in a warm, comforting embrace. The sound wanted him to wake up, but he didn't want to. He wanted to go back to sleep.

But there it was again.

This time he thought he felt something, too. He felt as if he was being gently shaken. A hand on his shoulder, perhaps?

"Senhor?"

He rose from the depths of his sleep just a little, enough to become aware of an ache that swept dull waves of pain around his body. He was definitely being shaken; he could feel someone gripping his left shoulder.

"Olá? Senhor?"

He tried to open his eyes. It was an effort—they seemed

to be weighted down—but he tried again and was rewarded with stabs of pain from light that banished the last of the darkness. He blinked, trying to clear the gumminess away. He saw dim shapes around him and, above, an artificial light burned through the blur.

He remembered: the crash.

He closed his eyes and concentrated on his body: he felt the ache of pain but couldn't pinpoint it. He felt numbed, and the pain pulsed with every beat of his heart.

"*Senhor?*"

He remembered more.

Drake shot and killed in the street.

Berg and Hawkins, likely dead. The four bad guys, all put down.

But the girl... Alícia... taken.

He opened his eyes, blinking into the light. He felt a blast of panic. The fuzz resolved into detail: there was a woman leaning over him, middle-aged, dark-haired and dressed in a white coat. He looked beyond her and saw that he was in a hospital ward. He looked left and right: there were beds packed into a medium-sized room, with barely enough space between them for someone to stand; there was a woman in the bed to Milton's right, and he would have been able to reach out and touch her shoulder if he chose to.

"*Olá?*"

Milton looked up at the woman. She was gazing down at him; her face was kindly, and her eyes shone with compassion.

"No Portuguese," Milton mumbled. His mouth felt as if it had been stuffed full with cotton wool.

"No Portuguese?" she repeated.

"I'm English."

The woman nodded and smiled. "I speak a little," she said. Her brow furrowed as she looked for the right words. "How do you feel?"

"Sore," Milton said.

"You were in a car crash," the nurse said.

Milton raised his head from the pillow, choking down the urge to vomit, and looked down at his body. His clothes and shoes had been removed, and, instead, he was wearing light blue hospital pyjama bottoms. He was topless, with bloody scratches across his chest and stomach and down both arms.

"I need to leave."

The woman frowned as she tried to decipher his words. "No," she said, lighting onto his meaning. She reached down her hand and gently rested her finger on his forehead. "*Concussão.*"

Milton could translate that easily enough: concussion.

Milton tried to sit; nausea swept over him. The nurse rested her hand on his chest and pushed him gently down again. She shook her head. "You must rest."

Milton took a breath. "How long have I been here?"

"I am sorry?"

Milton searched for the words and failed. He pointed up at a clock on the wall. It was four. He tried to remember the time when they had been ambushed, but he couldn't recall it. "When did I come here?"

"Today," she said. "This afternoon."

It was too vague to be useful, but Milton couldn't delay. He needed the nurse to leave. "Thank you," he said.

"What is your name?"

"Smith," he replied, so woozy that he almost gave her his real name. "John Smith."

"And you are... *Inglês?*"

"That's right."

"We look after you. You must wait here. Okay?"

"Yes," Milton said, smiling again. "Of course."

The nurse turned and walked away from the bed. Milton watched until she had turned the corner and was out of sight, and then slowly raised himself to a sitting position. The nausea came again, but he swallowed it down. He felt numbed, and he could taste something metallic in his mouth; he shuddered again at thought of the drugs they must have given him for the pain. He felt weak and vulnerable. He knew that the voice in his head—the voice that told him he was worthless and always would be, that he owed so much to so many, that he would never be able to make amends—he knew that the voice would start to drip its poison again, telling him that it didn't matter anymore, that he wasn't sober, that his long run of sober days was over, that he had been pumped full of drugs so what did it matter if he found a cheap bar and drank until he was out of his mind.

He clenched his right hand into a fist and cracked his knuckles against his forehead. He didn't have the luxury of self-pity.

Self-pity would kill him, in more ways than one.

He had to leave. Now.

He had been out for two hours. The men who had ambushed them were professionals. They wouldn't be in the business of leaving witnesses behind, especially those who had seen their faces. If Milton had been in their shoes, he would have checked to see if the driver of the car that had given chase had survived the crash. If he was still alive, Milton would have taken steps to ensure that he wasn't for much longer.

They would come for him. He was in danger.

And the police would have found the AR-15 and the Glock from the car. They would know that he was involved in the shoot-out. At least six people were dead; the nurse had probably gone to tell them that he had come around.

He had to leave

Right now.

40

Milton swung his legs out of bed and lowered his feet to the cool tile floor. He felt weaker than he expected; they must have given him something to ease his pain. He shuffled forward and, using his arm to brace himself, pushed himself to a standing position. A bout of dizziness forced him to put his arm down again in order to hold himself upright. The moment passed and, gritting his teeth in frustration at his debilitation, he took a step away from the bed.

The ward was busy. He scoped it out quickly, counted ten occupied beds, some of them with friends and relatives gathered anxiously around them, and a handful of nurses who were too busy to notice that he was on his feet. The ward was accessed by an open corridor to his right, where the nurses had a station. Milton could see the nurse who had come to wake him up; she was talking to a man in a police uniform. Both had their backs to him and hadn't noticed that he was up.

There was a paper sack on the chair next to the bed. Milton opened it and took out his clothes; they were stained with blood from his scrapes and scratches, the smudges still tacky in the humidity of the ward. He dressed and walked slowly toward the corridor. He felt awful, constantly on the verge of being sick, and was sweating by the time he reached the intersection with the corridor. There were windows on one side of the corridor and, as he glanced out, he saw that he was several storeys above the ground. He kept walking until he reached a vestibule, where there were doors for two elevators and a plain door that was marked as an emergency exit. He pressed the button for the lift and, to his relief, the door opened at once. He stepped into the elevator, pressed the button for the ground floor, and braced himself against the wall as the doors slid shut and the car descended.

The elevator arrived at the ground floor and the doors opened. Milton got out, stepped around a porter with a patient in a wheelchair, and walked through the lobby area to the exit. A sign on the wall of the building announced the Miguel Couto Municipal Hospital. There were three ambulances waiting to discharge their occupants and a police car behind them. Beyond that was a collection of taxis waiting to pick up passengers. Milton signalled to the driver at the front and waited for him to bring his car alongside.

Milton tried to remember the address that he needed. "Rua General..." He couldn't remember the rest.

"Rua General Glicério?" the driver offered. "Urquiza?"

"No," Milton said. He remembered the district. "It's... in... Laranjeiras."

"Rua General Mariante," the man suggested.

The address chimed with his recollection. "Yes."

The man grunted and indicated that Milton should get into the car.

"*Inglês?*"

"Yes," Milton replied. "No Portuguese."

Milton knew that making it plain that he didn't speak the language was the best way to shut down a conversation that he did not want to have. He felt dreadful: he was as weak as a baby and, even though the car was air-conditioned, he was still sweating profusely.

He looked up and saw that the driver was watching him with a worried expression. "You okay, *senhor*?"

Milton gave a feeble nod. "How long to Laranjeiras?"

The man held up three fingers. "Leblon to Laranjeiras —*trinta*."

Thirty minutes. Milton concentrated on trying to find a point of balance amid the buffeting dizziness that roiled around his head. He had to hold it together until he reached his destination. He tried to remember the house, but he had been drinking back then and all he got were vague fragments: the fragrance of a jasmine bush, a pretty walled garden, thin drapes that covered the windows. Milton didn't even know if the resident agent was still in Rio. The quartermaster had been old when Milton had last availed himself of his services, and that had been years ago. He might have been reassigned since then. He might have retired. He might have died.

But Milton had no choice.

Harry Marks was the only person in Rio to whom he could turn to for help.

41

Paulo climbed the stairs to the apartment. The rooms beyond were normally a riot of noise, but now they were quiet.

"Hello?"

There was no reply.

He went through into their room and saw that it was empty. A piece of paper had been left on the bed. He picked it up, unfolded it, and read the note.

He banged his palm against his forehead.

Oh shit.

He remembered: Eloá had an appointment at the hospital. He had attended every one so far, no matter how trivial, and now he had missed this one. He read through the note again. Rafaela didn't sound angry, just disappointed. That made him feel even worse.

He had lost his grip on his life in the space of half a day. Things were completely out of control. He tried to think of a way to fix it, but he could not. He was up to his neck in it now, and it was all his fault.

He looked down at the bag of money in his hand and

tried to think of a safe place to keep it. He didn't have a bank account and, even if he did, he wouldn't have wanted the inevitable attention that a cash deposit of thirty thousand would have attracted. He glanced around the room, remembered that the floorboard that he stood on when he got out of bed every morning was loose, and went over to it. He knelt down and used a pen to help pry it up. There was a small void beneath it, more than enough space for him to hide the bag. He took out two twenties, zipped the bag back up, and dropped it into the space. He pushed the bag down and replaced the floorboard. It wasn't perfect, but it would have to do.

He went over to the basket where they kept Eloá's clothes and picked out a T-shirt and a pair of jeans that he thought would fit the girl. He found a pair of fresh underwear and some socks and put them into a plastic bag. He stood and, about to turn for the door, his eye was caught by the shelf that held his daughter's toys. Money had always been tight for them, even before her diagnosis, and there was little spare to buy her things beyond the essentials. His mother had found some extra cash after their world had been brought crashing down with the discovery of Eloá's cancer, and she had bought three cuddly bears: one red, one green and the other blue. Paulo felt terrible at what he was considering, yet he knew he would feel worse if he left the little girl alone without anything to comfort her, so he grabbed the paw of the nearest bear, the red one, and put it, too, into the bag.

He wanted to stop, to put everything back as it was, and forget what he had done, but he could not. Things couldn't be changed now: the girl would still be locked in that room, and Garanhão would still expect Paulo to watch her, and he couldn't allow himself the indulgence of self-pity. He didn't deserve it.

He was to blame.

He stuffed the bag under his jacket, left the apartment, and hurried back up the Hill.

42

Paulo reached the confluence where the two main roads met. There were fast-food stalls set up around the perimeter of the square, and, after trying to guess what the girl would be most likely to enjoy, he walked over to one of the vendors and ordered chicken *coxinhas*. The young man who ran the stall scooped up half a dozen croquettes, bagged them up, and handed them to Paulo. He wondered whether the girl might be vegetarian and, in case she was, he ordered *empanadas*. The man bagged those up, too, and handed them over. Paulo gave him one of the twenties and took seventeen in change.

He reached the top of the Hill and walked to the warehouse. He made his way inside and went through into the office. There were two men he didn't recognise sitting at a plastic table with a bag of weed set out before them; one of the men was rolling a joint, putting it to his mouth and licking the paper to seal it. He handed the spliff to the other man and started to roll a second; the other man put the cigarette to his lips and lit it, staring balefully at Paulo through the blue-tinged smoke. Paulo turned his eyes away from him, passed through the room, and then climbed down the stairs to the basement.

He was worried that the light might have been switched off, but he could see the yellow glow beneath the bottom edge of the door. He turned the key and opened the door. The girl was sitting with her back to the wall, her legs drawn up to her chest as if she was trying to make herself as small as possible. She turned to look at him.

"Hello again," Paulo said.

She didn't speak; instead, she bit down on her bottom lip.

"I've got you some clothes," he said. He put the bag down on the floor and took out the jeans and the underwear. "Here," he said. "You'll feel much more comfortable." She didn't respond, so Paulo pushed the clothes inside the door and then stepped back. "I'll let you get changed."

He started to close the door. "No," she said, almost too quiet to hear. "Leave it open."

"I'll leave it like this. Tell me when you're ready."

He went to stand behind the door. He wondered whether she would ignore him again, but, as he waited there, he heard the sound of scrabbling movement and then a zip being worked down.

"My name is Paulo," he told her again as the sound of movement continued. "What's yours?"

The girl didn't answer.

"I know you're frightened. I understand that—I'd be frightened, too. But you're not on your own. I'd like to be your friend if I could. I have a little girl, too. Her name is Eloá Vitória. She's six—are you the same age as her?"

Still the girl did not reply.

"You don't have to say anything," he said. "You can be quiet if you want to—it's fine. But I bet you're hungry." He reached into the bag and took out the *coxinhas* and *empanadas*. The smell was pungent and quickly filled the room. "I've got you some food. Have you finished changing?"

She didn't speak, so he stepped around the half-open door and stooped down so that he could shuffle inside. She had changed into the new jeans, and, from the pile of clothes at her feet, he could see that she had taken the fresh underpants as well. She had not changed her top. Paulo collected the dirty clothes.

"I'm going to get these washed," he said. "I'll bring them back tomorrow, but you're welcome to have those ones. Is the food okay?"

The girl glanced down at the food, up at him, and then back down to the food again.

"I need to go again," he said. "I'll be back again later. I have to lock the door, but I'll leave the light on again for you. The best thing to do is to be quiet and patient. You won't be here for long. You'll be able to go home soon—I promise."

The girl looked up at him, and he wondered whether she was about to speak, but, instead, she turned away and bit her lip again. Paulo closed the door, turned the key, and took a moment to try to ignore the guilt. He thought of the two men in the room upstairs and, on impulse, he took the key out of the lock and held it in his fist.

He climbed up to the ground floor. The men were smoking their weed; the room was thick with the sweet odour.

Paulo was about to leave the room when one of them stretched out a leg and blocked the way. "She okay?" he asked.

Paulo clenched. "She's fine," he said. "I've given her some food. You just leave her to me."

The man looked to his mate and laughed. "What does that mean? You telling us to stay up here?"

"Garanhão told me to look after her," he said, struggling to stop his voice quivering from the fear and anger that he felt. He knew that invoking the name of the don like that was a threat—*If you do anything, I'll tell the boss*—and he knew that they were the type who would kill him as soon as look at him, but, for that moment, he found that he didn't care.

"What's your point?" the second man said.

"I'm going to get her something to sleep on," Paulo said. "I won't be long."

The man shrugged, pulled his leg back again, and turned his attention back to his spliff. Paulo clenched his fists tight, the edges of the key digging into his flesh. He didn't trust either of them, their judgement or their intentions, and he didn't want to leave the girl alone with them so close to her.

But he had to go home. He had to see Rafaela and Eloá.

He left the room before either of them could say anything else.

43

The taxi driver took Milton through Flamengo, passing the stadium where both Flamengo and Fluminense played, and then into the pleasant streets of the middle-class neighbourhood of Laranjeiras. They exchanged the asphalt of the highway for cobbles and followed the road up the hill until they reached a series of houses that were secured behind neat walls. The walls were covered with ivy and topped with spikes and wires to keep unwanted visitors outside. The driver asked which house Milton wanted; he wiped the sweat out of his eyes and looked out of the window. It had been years since he had been here; he wasn't sure that he would remember. They reached a property that Milton thought he recalled: the door was secured behind a metal grille, with the entirety of the wall around it clad in ivy and clematis. Milton looked at the top of the wall and saw the corrugated metal roof of the property behind it. He hadn't visited for ten years, but he was as sure as he could be that this was the place. He remembered the smell of the flowers.

Milton paid the driver and got out of the cab. He tried to

stand, but the wave of dizziness that washed over him was so intense that he had to hold onto the roof in order to stop himself from falling. He shuffled forward and rapped his knuckles against the window. The driver lowered it.

"Help me," Milton said.

The driver put his hazard lights on, got out of the car, and came around to where Milton was standing. "Where?" he said.

Milton gestured weakly to the gate.

The driver ducked down so that Milton could loop his right arm over his shoulders and then supported him as they crossed the cobbled street and climbed the shallow kerb. A small section of the wall to the right of the door had been kept clear of vegetation, and an intercom with a camera was set into it. Milton blinked the sweat out of his eyes and looked down at it: a strip of card was protected by a Perspex cover, and written on the card was a single name: MARKS. Milton felt a wave of relief and pressed the button.

There was a pause, and then the intercom crackled with static.

"Who is it?"

The voice was cracked with age and carried a grouchiness that Milton remembered very well.

"Hello, Harry," he said. He shuffled to the right so that his face was in front of the camera. "It's me."

The intercom clicked off and, for a moment, Milton wondered if he was going to leave him on the street. He needn't have worried; he heard a door open somewhere behind the wall, and then the door was unlocked.

Harry Marks stood in the doorway. Milton remembered him: his face was wrinkled, there were deep lines around his mouth, and bags bulged beneath his eyes. His hair was all white, although he had much less of it now than he'd had when Milton had last seen him. He had been in his late fifties then, and the erosion of the last decade was writ large. The lines were a little deeper, his eyes a little less bright, and he seemed to stoop a little as he stepped out onto the street.

"Jesus Christ," he said.

"I need... help. Can I..."

Harry came to Milton's side, and the driver stepped aside so that Harry could take his place. Milton draped his arm over the old man's shoulders and allowed him to take his weight. Milton could feel that there was still strength in the old man's back and shoulders.

The driver held out his hand. "Extra."

Harry frowned, said something in Portuguese, and then, when the driver stood his ground, he reached down with his left hand and fumbled his wallet out of his trouser pocket. He took out two notes and gave the first one to him. The man looked at the second expectantly. Harry said something to him, the man grunted his agreement, and Harry gave him the note.

"Told him to keep his mouth shut," the old man said as he turned Milton around and helped him to shuffle across the pavement.

The doorway in the wall was too narrow for them to pass through side by side, so Harry went through first and then helped Milton to follow. There was a pleasant court-yard beyond that contained a number of potted plants and small shrubs. Milton remembered the fragrant jasmine.

Marks went around and looped Milton's arm over his shoulder again. "What happened?"

"Car crash," Milton said weakly.

"And I take it you'd rather not go to a hospital?"

"Was in one," Milton said. "Discharged myself."

"Anything else I need to know?"

"Ambush," Milton said. "Ipanema. It was..." The words degraded into gibberish; Milton knew that he was mumbling, but he suddenly found it impossible to speak clearly.

"I'll look into it," Harry said. "I've got a spare room. You can go in there."

A pair of French doors opened off the courtyard, and Marks led the way inside. Marks took him through the room to a corridor that led deeper into the house. There were two doors at the end, and Marks opened the one on the right. They slid through it sideways and stepped into a small bedroom. There was a bed, a single wooden chair, and a small chest of drawers. Marks helped Milton over to the bed. Milton sat down. The window was closed and the room was stuffy. Marks opened it, and a gentle breeze started to ruffle the thin taffeta drapes.

Milton winced with pain as he managed to slip his shirt off his shoulders. All of his muscles ached. Marks put his hand on Milton's chest and gently pushed him back. Milton was too weak to resist. He sank down onto the mattress, feeling the coolness of the sheets against the clammy skin of his back. He felt fresh sweat on his brow and on his body, more of it gathering despite the breeze that blew over him from the open window. His eyes were heavy, and he allowed them to close. He was tired. He needed to sleep.

PART IV

THE FIFTH DAY

44

Milton became aware of the sound of birdsong. It was light and cheerful, a pleasant noise that was close at hand. He could see the glow of light from behind his half-closed eyes and, focussing on the chirping of the bird, he opened his eyes. He was lying on his back, and the first thing that he saw was a ceiling that he did not recognise. There was a fan above him, spinning slowly and sending a gentle breeze down onto his body. He turned his head a little until he could see an open window with taffeta drapes pulled aside and, beyond the window, a colourful jasmine. It was loaded with purple flowers and, when he inhaled, he could smell their fragrance. A small bird had taken up a position in the branches of the tree, and it chirped merrily, oblivious to its audience.

Milton turned his attention back to the room. It had whitewashed walls, bare save for a framed Mondrian print. He was lying on a bed, with linen sheets folded back down to his waist. There was a small table to his right with a glass of water standing on it.

He lay back on the bed, stared up at the ceiling, and remembered.

Drake.

Alícia Saverin.

He closed his eyes.

He took a moment to gather himself and then opened them again and tried to sit up.

The effort sparked an explosion of dizziness. He was weak and lethargic. He gave up, falling back down on the bed.

"Hello?" His mouth was dry. "Hello?"

He heard the sound of footsteps and then the squeak of old hinges.

"You're awake."

Milton turned his head toward the voice and saw Harry Marks standing there. The old man was wearing a linen suit and a pale lilac shirt. He was drying a glass with a tea towel.

"Hello, Harry," Milton said.

"How are you feeling?"

"Shitty. How long was I out?"

"Bit more than a day. You—"

"What?" Milton protested. He tried to sit again. "That long? I can't—" He felt a wave of weakness and lowered himself back onto the mattress. "Ouch."

Harry came closer. "Take it easy. You have a very bad concussion. My friend was concerned."

"Your friend?"

"Used to be a doctor. He's been very helpful."

Milton groaned. "What happened?"

"You don't remember?"

He closed his eyes and tried to recall what had happened. "Not all of it."

"You came here straight from the hospital. Remember that?"

"No."

"I went out to get my friend, and when I came back, you were on the floor in the other room, saying something about how she was just a little girl and how you couldn't stay here. He said you needed to sleep, and he put you under. You've been out the whole time."

"Thank you," Milton said. "And I'm sorry. It was unprofessional of me not to call ahead."

"You were in no fit state," Marks said. "Forget it. You thirsty?"

"Yes."

Marks helped Milton to sit, putting two pillows behind his back and then giving him the glass of water from the table next to the bed. Milton drank it with careful sips, wary of gulping it down and bringing it straight back up again.

Marks took the glass and replaced it on the table. "You want to go through what you *do* remember?"

Milton told Marks as much as he could recall. He told him about Shawn Drake and agreeing to stand in for the missing man while they took Valentina and Alícia Saverin to and from the girl's recital. He told him about the ambush outside the apartment in Ipanema.

"Hold on," Harry said.

Milton waited as Harry disappeared into the other room and returned with a copy of the previous day's *O Globo*. He opened the newspaper to the second and third pages and started to read.

"'Seven people have been killed in Ipanema after gunmen attacked a car containing the wife and daughter of Felipe Saverin, the anti-corruption judge. Police would not say how many suspects were involved, but Mrs Saverin and her daughter were targeted by at least four assailants at around 2 p.m. The attackers were confronted by private security guards, and a shoot-out followed. Mrs Saverin was able to escape, but her daughter was abducted and taken by three men, who fled the scene in a Jaguar. Witnesses said that one of the guards gave chase, but that the car that he was travelling in was subsequently involved in a crash at Avenue Niemeyer.'"

"I remember," Milton said. "He forced me off the road. I rolled the car."

"That adds up," Marks replied. He read on. "'The guard was taken to hospital but discharged himself before the police could speak to him.'" He laid the newspaper on the bed. "Is that true?"

Milton said that it was. "Do you know how I got here?"

"Taxi," Marks said. "And, yes, before you ask, the driver would definitely remember you. We're going to have to be a little bit circumspect until the fuss dies down."

"I can't hide away," Milton said. "They took the girl. She's six. I have to find her, Harry. Help me up."

"Take it easy," Marks said, but, at Milton's insistence, he reached down a hand and helped him to his feet. "You must be hungry."

"I am."

"So let me fix you some breakfast. Then we can work out what to do."

45

M arks had set up a table and two chairs in the courtyard next to the jasmine. An awning had been fitted to the wall, and it stretched out to provide a little shelter from the sun, which, despite the early hour, was already burning bright. Marks told Milton to take a seat and then went into the house to fix breakfast. Milton lowered himself into the canvas chair and breathed in the fragrant air. He closed his eyes and assessed how he felt. His muscles ached, he was bruised, and his neck was sore from whiplash, but, those ailments aside, he felt stronger than he had any right to feel. He knew that he had been lucky; he could very well have been killed in the crash or during the firefight that preceded it. He thought of Drake. He had been less fortunate. And then he thought of Alícia, and his anger boiled up again. He was going to find her, and then he was going to punish the men who had taken her.

Marks returned with a tray laden with two mugs, a jug, a basket of bread and a bowl of sliced papaya. "*Café da manhã*," he said, setting the tray down. "Morning coffee. Want one?"

Milton said that he did, and Marks poured strong black coffee into both mugs.

"Thanks, Harry," Milton said. "I owe you."

Marks waved his gratitude away. "Forget it."

Milton sipped the coffee. The natural bitterness had been ameliorated with a lot of sugar. "What else can you tell me?" he asked, setting the mug back down.

Marks sipped his coffee. "So," he began once he was finished, "I made a few calls while you were sleeping. I have a friend who used to work in the police, and he asked around for me. The newspaper is right—the police are looking for a man who walked out of Miguel Couto Municipal Hospital two days ago. He was admitted after being pulled unconscious out of the wreck of a car on Avenue Niemeyer. White, mid to late forties, believed to be English."

"He say anything else?"

"He did. An AR-15 and a Glock 17 were found in the wreck, and seven people are dead. This kind of thing happens in the *favelas*. They can forget about it up there, but not when it happens in a place like Ipanema. That's why the police are interested. And because of the girl who was taken. Saverin is a big deal. This is already a big story."

"Do you know anything about the dead?"

"Funny you should say that." Marks took a small leather-bound notebook from his pocket and flipped pages. "Shawn Drake, Jannike Berg and Dean Hawkins. All three working in private security, contracted to guard the Saverins."

"And the bad guys?"

He looked down. "Pedro Santos, Luiz Belle, Fabrício Moretti and Gael Alves. All reputed to be members of Red Command, and all with criminal records as long as your arm."

"Red Command?"

"It's one of the gangs—there are three: Comando Vermelho, Terceiro Comando Puro and Amigos dos Amigos. Red Command runs Rocinha, the biggest *favela*. You don't know any of this?"

"No. Nothing."

"So this isn't a Group job?"

"You didn't hear? I'm not in the Group anymore."

Marks shook his head. "I didn't. But that's not the kind of information they'd share with an old stringer like me. What happened?"

Milton exhaled wearily. "I told them I didn't want to do it anymore."

"And how did that go down?"

"About as well as a cup of cold sick."

Marks chuckled. "What was it Control used to say? 'The only people I owe my loyalty to are those who never made me question theirs.'"

"I forgot you knew him," Milton said.

"I've known him for years. We served in West Berlin together, but he was always a little more ambitious than I was. And a little more ruthless, too. I heard some unsavoury things about him. Were they true?"

"Probably. He was playing both sides. He betrayed one of his agents."

"And?"

"And that particular agent is not the kind of woman I would have betrayed."

"So he's out of the way?"

"He's dead."

Marks didn't look surprised. "We weren't close. He wasn't the kind of man I was ever completely comfortable about trusting. Brilliant, but he always had his own agenda. He would have sold his mother down the river if he thought it would be good for his career." He finished his coffee and refilled both mugs. "So this isn't work?"

"I came here for the festival and to see an old Regiment friend. Shawn Drake. He owned the security business. He said he was a man short for a job the next day, and I offered to step in."

Milton thought of the meal that he had enjoyed with Shawn and Sophia. When had that taken place again? He had lost track of the days. Three days ago? Two days? And then Drake, Berg and Hawkins had been shot, and Alícia had been taken. He would have to go and see Sophia, to tell her what had happened, but not yet. He had to work out exactly what *had* happened before he did anything else.

"Do you have a map?" Milton asked.

"Of course."

Marks went inside and returned with a folding map. He opened it and spread it over the table. Milton found Avenida Vieira Souto and the Saverin apartment. "This was where they hit us," Milton said, pressing his forefinger against the map. "They had men waiting and backup. It was well organised and well equipped."

Marks looked back at the map and drew his finger along it, following the coast road. "You crashed here," he said, laying his finger on a sharp right-hand bend. "It's the edge of cartel country. If it *was* Red Command, they would have headed for Rocinha."

Milton looked at the map. Rocinha was a mile square, a misshapen district between São Conrado, Vidigal, Leblon and Gávea, with a splash of green rainforest bordering it to the north. "What's it like?"

"Brutal. The police won't go in there. They shot a helicopter down with an RPG two years ago. They don't even fly over it now."

"I told the judge I'd bring his daughter back safe and sound."

"It's not your fault, Milton. You're not responsible. And it sounds like you did all you could to stop them."

"Doesn't matter. I promised. And she's six years old, Harry. I'm not abandoning her."

"Still stubborn?" Marks asked him with a wry upturn to his mouth.

"When I say something, I do it."

"Still stubborn, then." Marks looked down at the map again. "Rocinha's a big place."

"I know where to start looking," Milton said. "But I'm going to need a weapon—do you have anything?"

Marks smiled. "Oh yes."

46

Milton's shirt and jeans were covered with blood from the crash and, despite Marks's best efforts to wash them, the garments were stained; Milton binned them both. Marks had anticipated the issue and presented Milton with a plastic carrier bag that contained three plain black T-shirts, two pairs of jeans in different sizes, and underwear. Milton thanked him and went through into the bathroom to change. He looked in the mirror at his reflection. His skin had been scratched in several places, and there were two ugly bruises, one across his torso and the other on his forehead. The first had been caused as his seat belt snapped tight against his sternum; the second—a dark blue line with purples and reds radiating out from it—was from where he had cracked his head against the steering wheel. It was a vivid bruise that would be impossible to miss. Milton hated the thought of anything that might draw unnecessary attention to himself, but there was little that could be done about it now.

He filled the sink with cold water and dunked his head in it, leaving it submerged until his skin tingled. He took his head out of the water and stared at his reflection: droplets of water ran down his skin, falling back to the basin. He looked into his own cold, blue eyes, and made himself a promise: whoever had killed Drake and taken the girl was going to pay a steep price. He would find them and, when he did, he would make them wish that they had never been born.

He dried himself off, dressed in the new clothes, and then went to find Marks.

There was work to do.

~

MARKS HAD a beaten-up old BMW parked in a garage at the end of the street. He brought it up to the front door and, after confirming that the road was empty and that the property was unobserved, he tapped the horn. Milton stepped outside, closed the door behind him, and hurried across to the car.

Marks released the brake and set off.

"Where are we going?" Milton asked.

"Up near Bonsucesso," he said. "Half an hour if the traffic is kind."

Marks drove north through Santa Teresa. Milton wound down the window and let the warm air blow onto his face. He still had a dull throb in his head and the unsettling feeling that he might be sick without much warning. He'd been concussed before and knew the symptoms. The fresh air took his mind off it, at least a little.

"So how long ago has it been, Milton?"

He turned away from the window. Marks was looking over at him.

"Ten years?" Milton offered, although he wasn't completely sure.

"At least that. You were Number Eleven then."

"Might be longer, then. I lose track."

"You remember the job you were here for?"

"Of course."

The dates were fuzzy, but Milton remembered the operation very clearly. He remembered all of his victims: their faces, whether they had families, the things that they had said in an effort to ward off the inevitability of their ends. The memories were his curse, the revenge that the men and women that he had killed took from beyond the grave.

One particular man was a British businessman who was working for a defence contractor. He had been selling his company's secrets to the Russian government, and MI6 had collected enough evidence for his file to be passed across Whitehall desks to end up in the scruffy building near Vauxhall Cross that housed Group Fifteen. Control had summoned Milton and had sent him to Rio with orders to eliminate the man. Marks had been the Group's quartermaster for this part of South America, and he had provided Milton with the compound derived from the toxic gelsemium plant that had been chosen as the means of causing the target's demise. The man had dined at the exclusive Pérgula restaurant every night. It had been a simple enough matter for Milton to infiltrate the kitchen and lace the man's foie gras. The target had expired at the table as the dessert plates were being cleared away; Milton was on a plane out of the country while his body was still warm.

Milton closed his eyes in a vain effort to banish the memory.

"You been back since?" Marks asked him.

"No," Milton said. "Not until now. Did you ever leave?"

"The wife and I split up. She went back home, but I found it agrees with me here. The climate is reliable. I suffer with my joints—the thought of going back to England now..." He shook his head. "Well, it's not going to happen. When I leave, it'll be in a box."

"Are you still working for the Group?"

"Just as a stringer," Marks admitted. "Now and again, if they need me, I'm here."

"When was the last job?"

"You ever meet Number Nine? A woman. Young. Very intense."

"She would have been after my time."

"They sent her over last year. She needed a place to stay, and she needed to be equipped. They gave her my details. Don't know exactly what she was over here to do, but two days after she left, I read that the chief executive of an oil and gas exploration company that was tangled up with a British project in Barreirinhas went missing. They said he loved deep-sea fishing. He had a boat that he kept in Fortaleza. He took it out, but he never came back. They found the boat a week later. Empty. The police said there was nothing suspicious. They said he must've fallen over the side."

"It was her?"

Marks shrugged. "She asked me to find her some scuba gear. You tell me."

They reached a junction, and Milton paused for a moment until Marks had successfully negotiated it. "So," Marks said, "what are you going to do? About the girl?"

"Find her."

"Won't be easy. These aren't just gangsters, Milton. They own the *favelas*. The streets, the buildings, the people who live in them—they all belong to them. You don't look like they do. You don't speak the language. You can't just go into Rocinha and ask questions. You'll stand out like a sore thumb. Someone will come up behind you and put a bullet in your head."

"I'm going to be subtle, Harry."

Milton could tell that Marks was unpersuaded, but the older man held his tongue. "So where do we start?" he said instead.

"I think it was an inside job," Milton offered. "And there's someone who can help me prove that."

47

G roup Fifteen maintained arms caches all around the world. Most countries were covered, with the larger or more politically interesting ones being accorded multiple sites. Standard operating procedure was for the agents to infiltrate the country under the cover of the legends that had been prepared for them—businessmen or women, tourists, diplomats—and then to equip themselves with whatever the operation demanded once they were in country. Milton had used many of them during his time in the Group and had taken advantage of them after he had left, too. Some of them were unattended, like the crate that had been buried in the bayou outside New Orleans. Others were maintained by local quartermasters, just as Harry administered this dump in Rio.

They were in Parada de Lucas, to the north of the city. Avenida Brasil was a large eight-lane highway that passed through a district that was given over to industrial and office use. Everywhere looked rough and down-at-heel. They passed a series of empty municipal buses that had been left at the edge of the road, and then went by the depot where the buses were maintained. Trash was dumped outside buildings, and the walls had been marked with graffiti. The road itself was in dreadful condition, and the BMW bumped up and down as they drove along it, the antiquated suspension groaning and whining with every new pothole.

Marks approached a high concrete wall that was surmounted by billboards advertising local businesses. He indicated, slowed down and turned off. The new road was typical for the area: ancient warehouses, some barely standing, lined both sides of the street. Lines of cars had been parked outside the warehouses, and a tangle of telephone wires stretched between the poles overhead. The wall, painted white and blue, bent around and ended with a pair of heavy corrugated iron gates. A hand-painted sign that had been fixed to one of the gates advertised a mechanic, and a sign on its twin offered praise to God.

"Nice area," Milton said.

"I'm sure you've seen worse."

Marks sounded the horn and waited for two men to open the gates. He leaned out of the window and spoke with one of the men in fluent Portuguese, reaching into his pocket and taking out a banknote that he pressed into the man's hand. The man nodded his thanks, raised a hand to acknowledge Milton, and then opened the gates the rest of the way so that Marks could drive through. There was a yard, with a series of brick garages built against the flanks of the larger warehouses that formed its northern perimeter. The garages had not been expertly constructed, and some looked as if they were ready to collapse.

Marks parked the BMW in an empty space and stepped outside. Milton followed. It was already almost unbearably hot, and Milton's head throbbed as he followed Marks to the garage at the end of the row. Marks knelt down and undid the padlock with a key that he carried on a loop in his pocket. He held onto the grips and pulled up, the old roller door grumbling on unoiled tracks.

"*Et voila,*" Marks said, standing aside.

Light poured into the garage. It was of normal dimensions, big enough for a reasonably sized family car. But, despite that, it would have been impossible to store a vehicle here. The garage was full of trash: large black plastic bags had been stacked up along one side of the wall, falling over each other to fill almost half of the space. There were old domestic appliances—washing machines and tumble dryers—and along the left-hand wall a long line of junk televisions had been stacked in two precarious courses. The garage smelled musty, with an underlying note of rot. It was unpleasant, and Milton took a step back for a breath of fresh air.

"Here?"

Marks switched on a light and then went back to the door and rolled it down again.

"This way."

"It stinks," Milton said. "That's deliberate, I assume?"

Marks turned back with a smile. "Of course."

There was a narrow passage between the stacked televisions and the heaped black bags, and Marks led the way along it into the rear of the garage. Milton followed. The passage ended at the wall at the back of the garage; the televisions did not end flush with it, leaving a narrow space that Marks could stand in. Milton watched as Marks placed both hands on the wall and pressed. A narrow strip of wall, half the width of a doorway, sank back with a click. Marks kept his hands on the wall and slid it to the left, running it behind the remaining length of wall.

"Very nice," Milton said.

"Took me a while to get it right," the old man said proudly.

Marks squeezed through the secret door into the dark space beyond. He had erected a plasterboard wall and crafted a compartment beyond it. The junk in front of the wall served two purposes: the first was to make it appear that the garage was used as a dumping ground, a less likely subject of attention should anyone ever break in; the second purpose was to baffle the eye and make it more difficult to discern that the garage was smaller than might otherwise have been expected.

Milton heard the flicking of a switch, and the secret compartment was lit. He turned to the side and passed inside.

"*Very* nice," Milton said.

The space was around five feet deep and nine feet wide. The brickwork that comprised the real back wall had been equipped with a series of tactical wall panels. Hangers and brackets had been fitted onto them, and from those were suspended a large armoury of weapons. Milton saw pistols, automatic rifles, sniper rifles, submachine guns and shotguns. Drawers at the bottom of the wall were marked with various calibres of ammunition. There were grenades—smoke and fragmentation—and magnetic mines that could be fastened to the undersides of vehicles. There was a selection of bugs and other surveillance equipment, and ballistic vests in different sizes were hung from hooks on the narrow wall behind Marks. The smell was different from the room next door. It smelled of oil and gunpowder rather than decay.

"I think I've got everything you'll need," the old man said.

"Are you serious? You could equip an army with this."

"I remember not being able to get the load-out I wanted when I was in the Regiment. Used to annoy the hell out of me."

Milton didn't need an arsenal for what he had in mind. He ran his finger along the slide of a Beretta and decided he wanted something a little smaller, a little less conspicuous, something that he would be able to carry unobtrusively. He took a Walther PPK/S from the rack and let it rest in his hand. It was the version of the pistol with the extended beaver tail grip that protected the shooter from catching the flesh between the index finger and thumb in the slide. It was chambered in .32 ACP, with eight rounds in the magazine. Milton looked down at the drawers, took out two spare magazines, and put them in his pocket.

"Got a suppressor?" he asked.

Marks took one from a drawer and handed it to him.

"That enough for you?"

"I don't need a cannon," Milton said. "I'm going to be as quiet as I can."

"We're done, then?"

"We are."

Milton went back to the roller door, waited until Marks had moved the hidden door back into place, and reached down to unfasten the padlock. He heaved the door up, and light poured inside. Marks followed him out before reaching into his pocket and giving Milton a key.

"A spare," he said. "In case you need anything else."

"Thanks," Milton said, pocketing the key.

"What now?"

"Can I borrow your car?" he said. "There's someone I need to see."

48

Paulo knelt down on the floor next to his daughter's bed and stroked her hair. Eloá was tired and, as he sat there, her breathing deepened and she fell asleep. He looked at the clock on the wall: it was early, just a little after six. Eloá would normally have been awake for another hour or two, but there had been no chance of that tonight.

They had had an appointment with the specialist that afternoon and had left the hospital having sketched out a plan to treat her cancer. They had the money to take a taxi home, but Rafaela had insisted that they take the bus, just as they had always done. The money would last longer if they budgeted responsibly, she said, and that meant avoiding unnecessary luxuries. The trip had been long and the bus had been swelteringly hot, and by the time they returned home, Eloá had been so exhausted that Paulo had had to carry her inside.

Rafaela came up behind him and laid her hand on his shoulder. "What do you think?"

For the first time in an age, he didn't have to pretend to

be confident; he *was* confident. "The doctor said it'd work, didn't he? She's going to be fine."

"Look at her," Rafaela said. "She's so tiny."

She was right: their daughter did look small with her legs curled up to her chest. He thought of Alícia locked in the tiny room at the top of the Hill, and felt a shudder of shame.

"I've got to go," Paulo said.

"Tonight as well?"

"I'm late."

She hadn't asked him where the money had come from, and Paulo had no idea how he could even begin to tell her. She must have known that it was illegal, or at least questionable; they had exhausted all of the legitimate options that were available to them in the frantic days that had followed Eloá's diagnosis. Rafaela knew that he was a racer—she had met him at a race night, after all—and he had explained to her that he was going to find the money on the road. But he hadn't mentioned that he had been any more or less successful than usual, yet the cash had appeared. Rafaela was no fool. But, after her initial surprise, and after Paulo's unconvincing assertion that he had won the money, she had never asked him again. They had been desperate and, now that they had what they needed, they would be able to give Eloá a chance to fight her illness. If it meant that Rafaela needed to turn a blind eye to the money's provenance, then so be it.

He kissed his wife on the lips and left the apartment.

49

P aulo climbed the Hill and, as usual, he worried about what he was going to find when he reached the top. He had come up here three times the day before, and he had already visited Alícia this morning. She had cried as he had started to leave and told him that she was frightened. He had only been able to stop her tears by promising to return and, as he looked anxiously at his watch, he saw that he was already much later than he would have preferred to have been.

He went through the warehouse door, climbed the stairs, and made his way into the office. It was empty. He climbed down the stairs into the basement and closed the door behind him. He took out the key to the lock and opened the crawlspace.

Alícia was sitting with her back to the wall, reading one of the books that Paulo had brought her that morning. He left the light on all the time now and she was able to read in order to pass the time. She was an intelligent girl; he had started out with some of the books that Eloá liked to read, but it had quickly become apparent that she was able to read at a more advanced level. He had gone down to the second-hand bookshop at the bottom of the Hill and bought a selection of books, and he had been pleased to see the wide smile on her face when he had given them to her.

She was reading *O Pequeno Príncipe*, one of the books that Paulo remembered from his own childhood. She put the book down on the floor and crawled out of the space and into the basement. Paulo knew that Garanhão would not like the thought of her coming outside like this, but she was a six-year-old girl; what was she going to do? And, more important even than his fear of displeasing the don, Paulo couldn't stand the thought of her inside the damp and fetid crawlspace for a moment longer than was necessary.

"Did you bring them?" she asked him.

"I did." He took a deck of cards out of his pocket and held them up. "What shall we play?"

"Mau Mau," she said.

Paulo sat down with his back to the wall and took the cards out of their pack. Alícia sat opposite him and waited as he dealt five cards to them both, laying the rest face down between them.

Paulo had brought her dinner with him, too: a paper bag of chicken and cheese *coxinha* that he had bought from a street vendor on the way up the Hill and a bottle of chocolate milk. She ate the croquettes as they worked their way through the pack of cards. Paulo was pleased to see that she was unloading hers faster than he was; she laid down her last at the same time as she finished the final croquette.

"Well done," he said. "Too good for me."

She took a swig of the milk and then placed the bottle on the floor next to her. "Paulo?"

"Yes?"

"I want to see my mother."

"I know you do," he said.

He didn't know what he should say to the girl. He wanted to be honest—it was the least she deserved after what had happened—but, at the same time, he didn't want to upset her. They had a precarious relationship at best, and he didn't want to jeopardise it. That, at least, was what he told himself. He knew that he was being cowardly, just like always.

"When will I be able to go home?"

"Soon," Paulo said, hating himself for his lie.

Paulo had seen Garanhão in the warehouse yesterday and this morning, but the don had not acknowledged him, let alone shared his plans. Yesterday's *O Globo* had reported that Alícia had been kidnapped, but there had been nothing about a ransom. Perhaps, Paulo concluded, there was no ransom. He knew that the girl was the daughter of Judge Saverin, and he wondered if perhaps she was being held here to ensure that he did not prosecute the cases with the same vigour that had made him into a national hero. That seemed possible, at least. But, if that were true, what motivation was there for them to let Alícia go home? Paulo had told her it would be soon, but that was a lie. He hated himself anew. It could be weeks. It could be months. It might be never.

The girl looked as if she was going to say something, but she bit her lip and raised the bottle to her mouth again. She looked so small and helpless. Paulo wanted to put his arm around her and tell her that it would be all right, and to know, when he said it, that it was true. But he couldn't say that. The longer she stayed here, the more likely it was that something terrible would happen to her.

The thought started without him even being aware that he was thinking about it: if he *really* wanted to look after her, if he *really* wanted to ensure that nothing bad could happen, then he should take matters in hand. It was no good telling her that she would be able to go home soon, when he knew that was not true; he needed to make it happen.

He caught the thought before it had a chance to develop and stamped it down. What was he *thinking?* What was he going to do? Take her out of here, somehow get her away from the Hill, and deliver her to the police? He wouldn't get more than ten paces before they put a bullet in his back. And, even if he did get away, assuming that he could dodge the guards and the snitches and then find a cop who wasn't on Garanhão's payroll, what would happen to him then? The police would arrest him for his part in her abduction. His family would be punished. Garanhão would make an example of them, and then, when he was in Carandiru or Bangu or some other shithole prison, another inmate would visit him with a shiv and a message from Garanhão.

This is for crossing me.

Paulo blinked his eyes, trying to send the thought away.

"Paulo?"

He opened his eyes. The girl was looking at him. "Yes?" he said.

"What is it?"

"I was just thinking about something, that's all. It's fine."

"Why am I being kept here?"

She had asked that before, too. This time, Paulo tried to answer it in a different way. "Because your father is an important man," he said. "The men who took you want him to do something that he doesn't want to do. They know he loves you very much—they know that he will do what they ask if he knows he can have you back at home again."

"But what if he doesn't do what they want them to do? He is very stubborn."

"But he loves you more."

"Yes," she said.

"Then you don't have anything to be worried about."

Paulo wished that he could believe that.

50

M ilton stood on the corner of the street, close enough to the house to see the comings and goings yet not so close as to draw unnecessary attention to himself. He had bought a cheap ball cap and shades from a street vendor near where he had parked Marks's car, but, even with the disguise, he felt a little tremor of disquiet when a police car rolled down the road past his vantage point. He was not ready to talk to the police about what had happened in Ipanema. He knew enough about the police department in Rio to know that there would be plenty of officers who were not averse to supplementing their pay packets by passing interesting information to the *traficantes* and *vagabundos*. There would be others, more culpable, who would be directly employed by the gangs. Beyond that, Milton wanted to exhaust his own investigative options before he cooperated with the authorities. He had faith in himself and was confident that, if there was a lead to be followed, he would be more effective working alone. Following due process and the law would only impede his progress.

Milton checked his watch: twenty minutes to seven. He had been here for two hours. He was starting to wonder whether Sophia would ever show when he saw a car slow down and pull into the driveway. A woman stepped out. She was wearing a large pair of dark glasses, but Milton could see that it was Sophia. She wore a cream dress and she had a leather tote bag over her shoulder. Her long black hair was glossy in the bright sunlight. She left the car and walked to the door, pausing for a moment to find the key in her tote, and then opened the door.

Milton crossed the street. He walked up to the front door, waited for a moment to listen for anything that might suggest that there was someone else besides Sophia inside, and then tried the handle. It was unlocked. He opened the door and stepped inside.

He could hear the sound of movement in the kitchen and followed it. Sophia was at the refrigerator, her back turned to him.

"Hello, Sophia," he said.

Sophia gaped in shock until she realised it was Milton.

"John?"

"I'm sorry to surprise you like this."

She took off her glasses. Her deep, soulful eyes were different. The spark that he had found so attractive at dinner that night was gone. There was a deadness there now, a loss. It lent her a hardness that Milton found unsettling.

"I'm sorry about what happened to Shawn."

Her face clouded with pain.

"Have the police told you what happened?" he asked.

"They said he was shot, but they won't say anything else."

"Did you have to identify him?"

"They said they didn't need me to do that." She went to the kitchen table and sat down. "Fuck," she said, raising her hand to her brow. "I don't know what to think. Were you there?"

"I was. How much did the police tell you?"

"Almost nothing," she said. "Most of what I know is what I saw on the news."

"We'd just got back to Ipanema," Milton said. "They attacked us. There were six of them and a driver. They were heavily armed and it was well organised. Did you know the man and the woman who worked with Shawn? Berg and Hawkins?"

She nodded.

"They shot them first. Shawn and I were in the car with the family. We tried to get away, but they blocked us with another car. Shawn tried to get Mrs Saverin and her daughter to safety, but they shot him."

"But you're still here."

Milton wondered whether he could detect a little resentment in her observation. It was true: he *was* still here, yet Shawn was not. He wondered what to say and, as he paused, Sophia shook her head and apologised.

"I'm sorry," she said. "I didn't mean it like that."

"It's fine," Milton said. "They took Alícia Saverin."

"The little girl. I saw her picture on the news."

Milton nodded. "I chased them, but they got away from me. I crashed my car and woke up in the hospital."

"And then you left? That's what the police said—you were there and then you weren't."

"They spoke to you about me?"

She nodded. "They came to see me that evening. They want to speak to you."

"It wasn't safe for me to stay," he said. "I saw the men who attacked us—I'm a witness. They won't be the sort who like to leave loose ends."

The suggestion evidently frightened her, and she didn't respond.

"They have no reason to go after you," Milton said. "But they might be looking for me. That's why I'm being careful."

"So who did it?"

"I'm going to find that out," he said.

She bent her head and looked down at the table. Milton gave her a moment to compose herself and, taking advantage of the opportunity, glanced around the room. Nothing was out of place. Nothing was suspicious.

She drew in a deep breath and looked up at him again. "This was two days ago, John. Where have you been?"

"I had a concussion," he said. "I've been staying out of the way until I felt better."

"Where? You said you didn't know anyone in Rio."

"A hotel," Milton lied. "It really doesn't matter, Sophia. It's better that no one knows."

Sophia opened her tote and took out a packet of tissues. She pulled one out and dabbed at her wet eyes with it.

"I need to ask you some questions," Milton said. "Is that okay?"

She snuffled and wiped her eyes again. "If it helps you find them, then good. The police said they'd investigate, but they're useless. If they're not corrupt, they're incompetent. They won't get justice for what happened to Shawn. They don't care. But maybe you do."

"I do care," he said.

"I'll help if I can."

"I want to know about the man Shawn couldn't reach. One of the men who worked with him—the man I replaced. He never told me anything about him."

Her forehead wrinkled in concentration. "Jorge? No—Xavier. His name's Xavier. What do you want to know?"

"Anything that might be useful. What's his full name?"

She screwed up her face as she thought. "I can't remember," she said. "I'd have to look."

"Where is he from?"

"Rio," she said. "Shawn wanted to have at least one local on the books."

"Has he been in contact?"

"Not with me," she said. "But he wouldn't be—he doesn't know me. And if he's tried to speak to Shawn, I wouldn't know." She stopped, sniffed again, and then, looking directly at Milton, asked, "You think he might be involved?"

"I don't know. But the one day he doesn't show up for work..." Milton let the sentence drift. "I'd like to talk to him, if only to rule him out. Can you help me with that?"

"I'll have to look through Shawn's papers," she said. "They're in his study. He kept good records. It shouldn't be too hard to find."

"And anything else you can find out about him," Milton said. "A photograph, too, if you can find one."

"I'll look," she said.

52

S ophia left Milton alone, and he took the opportunity to look around the sitting room. There were magazines on the table; Milton flicked through them but found nothing of interest. He went over to the sideboard and opened the doors; there was an amplifier and a DVD player, together with an untidy stack of DVDs and CDs. He closed the door and shuffled through the loose correspondence that had been left on the top. There were utility bills for the gas and electricity, but, again, nothing of note.

He heard the sound of a printer and then, a minute later, approaching footsteps as Sophia returned. He confirmed that he had left everything as he had found it and sat down before she came into the room.

"Any luck?"

"I think so." She nodded. "His name's Xavier de Oliveira. He wasn't in the army—it was the police: BOPE."

Milton shook his head. "I know them by reputation."

"Batalhão de Operações Policiais Especiais. It's a special unit of the military police. Tough guys with a bad reputation. They're the ones who get sent into the *favelas*."

"How did Shawn know him?"

"I don't know. He never really spoke about him to me."

"Do you have a picture?"

"Yes," she said. "Here."

She handed him a printout. There was a photograph of a man on the paper: he was ugly and unshaven and had dark eyes and a flattened nose.

"He's a charmer," he said.

"I remember meeting him now. I always found him unnerving. He's really into guns—he said the gangs he used to go after would have given a lot to have him killed. He said it didn't bother him. He said he kept a shotgun in his bedroom closet and he'd use it if he ever felt threatened."

Milton folded the paper and put it in his pocket. "What about an address?"

"He's got a place in Barra da Tijuca. I've written it down for you."

She handed him a second piece of paper.

"Anything else?"

"That's all I could find. I could go through the files more thoroughly tonight if that would help."

Milton said that it would. He folded the address and put that in his pocket, too.

"You think he's involved, don't you?" she said.

"Not necessarily. But I'd like to speak to him."

"Will you let me know what he says?"

"I will," he said.

She hesitated. "What should I do now?"

"What do you mean?"

"Should I..." She paused. "Do I need to be careful?"

"No," Milton said, trying to reassure her. "You didn't have anything to do with what happened. Just keep your eyes open." He took a pen from the table and wrote on yesterday's edition of *O Globo*. "Here's my number. Call me if you're worried, but try not to overthink it."

"What about the police? They said I should contact them if you got in touch."

Milton had anticipated that. "Tell them I've been here— I don't want you to get into trouble. Tell them I said that I'll go in and see them myself in a day or two. I just want to look into a couple of things first. But it would help me if you didn't mention that we spoke about Xavier."

Milton gave Sophia what he hoped was a reassuring smile. She put her hand on his shoulder and kissed him on the cheek. Milton told her to keep in touch, turned his back, and left the house. He paused on the drive for a moment and turned back. Sophia was looking at him through the window, and their eyes held before he turned away and moved off.

Milton took out his phone and called Marks.

"Progress?" the old man asked.

"Maybe. I might need your help with something."

"What kind of something?"

"You still have access to GCHQ?"

"Of course."

"I need them to do some digging for me. There's a man called Xavier de Oliveira. Used to be in the military police. Ask them to run a background check: background, convictions, associates. Full spectrum."

"When?"

"As soon as possible. Tonight if they can."

"You think he's involved?"

"I think he might be."

PART V

THE SIXTH DAY

53

P aulo had trouble sleeping and woke early. He lay in bed, feeling the warmth of his wife's body next to him, and stared up at the ceiling. It was the guilt that had roused him. He had been sleeping lightly, and his fitful dreams had led him back up the Hill to the basement of Garanhão's warehouse and the crawlspace where he had left Alícia. She had been upset again last night and had asked him not to go. He had told her that he had to leave, that he had no choice, but that he would be back as soon as he could in the morning. He had hated himself as he had made his way down the Hill to his apartment, and he hated himself now.

It was fear, too. Marcos had called him last night with the news that a body had been found on the Hill. Two kids had walked up beyond Rua Um to the spot where the *favela* ended and the rainforest began. There was a spot there that they called Terreirão, or the Big Ground, where they played soccer and basketball. Terreirão was also a dumping ground for the dismembered body parts of those who crossed the gang. A head and a collection of butchered limbs had been found there last night.

It was Palito.

Paulo had forgotten Garanhão's promise that he would take care of the loan shark, but the don, self-evidently, had not. And this was how the don went about his business. Paulo had struggled to stop his imagination from picturing the scene.

He heard a buzzing noise. It took him a moment to realise what it was.

His phone was on silent, and it was vibrating with an incoming call.

"What time is it?" Rafaela mumbled next to him.

Paulo fumbled for the phone and squinted at it until his eyesight cleared. "Six," he said.

"Who's calling you at six in the morning?"

"I don't know."

"Answer it before it wakes Eloá."

He took the call and put the phone to his ear. "Yes?" he said quietly. "Who is it?"

"Alessandro."

"What do you want? It's—"

"I need you."

"It's six in the morning."

"I don't care what time it is. Get up here. You've got thirty minutes."

Paulo lay back on the bed and felt his heart race. Was it Alícia? Had something happened? Why else would they need him on short notice?

"What?" Rafaela asked him. "Who was that?"

"Work," he said, trying to regulate the racing of his heart. He had to lie. How could he possibly tell Rafaela the truth?

"Marcos? Why is he calling now?"

He closed his eyes and exhaled. "I have to go in. He's got a big job, and Jose has let him down."

He flinched, expecting her to press; his lies were so painfully obvious now that they were almost insulting, yet the moment passed and she said nothing. He was about to get out of bed when she reached across and laid her hand on his arm.

"Be careful," she said. "I know, whatever you've done, that you've done it for Eloá. For us. But the money means nothing if she doesn't have her father."

Paulo wanted to reply, but he found that his throat was suddenly clogged with emotion. Rafaela was upstanding and moral, and he hated that he had put her into a situation where she had persuaded herself to put her ethics to one side. He had co-opted her into his foolish scheme; what kind of soulless monster had he become?

"I'm always careful," he said, leaning over to kiss her on the forehead. "Everything's fine." He added, "We can talk about it later," even though that was the last thing that he wanted to do.

He got up before she could say anything else, washed his face with cold water, and dressed quickly, careful to be as quiet as he could so as not to wake Eloá. He opened the door, looked back into the flat and saw that Rafaela was leaning on one elbow and watching him. He would have given a lot to have ignored the summons and to have gone back to his wife and held her until their daughter awoke. He couldn't do that, though. Garanhão owned him, and he had no choice but to do whatever was asked of him.

He opened the door and stepped out into the dingy passageway beyond. It was already a quarter past six, and Alessandro had said that he was needed at half past.

He was running late.

54

Paulo was out of breath by the time he reached the top of the Hill. Alessandro and Junior were waiting for him in the empty warehouse: the former was sitting on a picnic chair, smoking a joint, his feet up on a matching white plastic table; the latter was pacing back and forth, his injured shoulder suspended in a sling. Paulo drew closer and saw that there were two pistols and a scattering of bullets on the table. Both men were agitated, and their eyes were bloodshot and lined with red. The smell of burnt plastic hung in the air; it was the smell of meth. It looked as if both men had been partying all night.

"I told you six thirty," Alessandro snapped as Paulo climbed the steps to the dock. "Not six forty."

"You only called me—"

"No excuses," Alessandro said, cutting him off. "You come when I tell you to come. What do you think Garanhão would say if I said you weren't taking your obligations seriously?"

"I am taking them seriously," Paulo protested, very aware that it sounded like he was whining.

Alessandro snorted. A muscle twitched in his cheek, and his fingers clasped and unclasped seemingly without him noticing; he looked very, very wired. Alessandro was usually more measured than Junior, and, until now, Paulo had relied on him to moderate Junior's more intemperate requests. The fact that he was unhinged now changed the dynamic, and that frightened him.

"What do you need?" he asked them. "Is it the girl? Is she okay?"

"Who cares?" Alessandro said. "Nothing to do with her."

Paulo felt a moment of relief. "So what are we doing?"

"You're driving us into the city," he said.

"What for?"

"Enough questions," Junior snapped. "Just do as you're fucking told."

Paulo was about to rise to that, but both of them were wound tight, and he didn't want a confrontation.

He stepped around them and started for the basement. Alessandro grabbed his arm. "What are you doing?"

"Going to see her," he said.

"Are you listening to me? We're going to the city."

"It'll just take a moment."

"You're a dumb fuck," Alessandro said. "What, you got a soft spot for her?"

"She's six years old," Paulo said. "She's scared."

"You think she's going to see seven?" Junior said with a smirk.

Paulo felt a knot of fear in his gut. He said, "What does that mean?" although he knew very well exactly what it meant.

"It means she's seen all of us," Junior slurred. "You think Garanhão is just going to send her back down the Hill to Mummy and Daddy?"

"She wouldn't be able to say who we were," Paulo protested.

Alessandro picked up one of the pistols and racked the slide. "You don't get where he is if you take chances. She stays up here for as long as it keeps her old man in line."

"And once it doesn't matter..." Junior didn't finish the sentence, but another smirk made his meaning obvious.

Alessandro got up out of the chair, lifted his shirt to reveal his skinny chest, and shoved the pistol into the waistband of his jeans. "You keep your eye on her, like the don said, but that's it. You got your own kid to worry about, right?"

"It's Eloá, isn't it?" Junior said, his smirk still fixed to his face. Paulo hated the sound of her name on Junior's lips, and he knew that the man was making a clumsy threat. The don was subtler when he did it, but the effect was the same.

Alessandro put his hand on Paulo's shoulder and gave it a firm squeeze. "You want a bit of advice?" He didn't wait for Paulo to answer. "Don't get too attached to the girl."

55

Milton took Marks's BMW and drove west. The address that Sophia had given him was located between Rio Comprido and Cosme Velho, a fifteen-minute drive from the safe house in Laranjeiras. It was nine in the morning, and this part of the city was still sleepy. Milton was pleased about that.

Marks had put in a flash request to GCHQ for as much information as they could find on Xavier de Oliveira: a full-spectrum sweep, including his history in the police, his family, anything that might suggest he was vulnerable to blackmail or extortion. Cheltenham had responded at three in the morning with a dossier of information. Most of it was irrelevant, but his bank account was heavily overdrawn, and there were debits to a local casino that suggested that the man had a gambling problem. It was beginning to look very much as if Drake's man had been compromised by his weaknesses and had compromised his employer as a result.

Milton followed the satnav's directions to Rua Professor Olinto de Oliveira. It was evidently a reasonably well-heeled neighbourhood. The road was cobbled, with walled properties on either side. The whole area looked as if it had been scrubbed clean: the roads were well maintained; the sidewalks were neat and tidy, lined with palm trees and verges that were watered by automatic sprinklers. A quick check with a realtor's website had suggested that the properties here would start at half a million dollars, with plenty going for two or three times that. Milton had doubted that a policeman in Rio would be able to afford a house up here without help, and now, after seeing the BMWs and Audis lined up with their wheels on the kerbs, his suspicions deepened.

The road bent around to the left. Milton parked the car, took the rucksack that Marks had given him from the passenger seat, and got out. The address was just ahead. The sun was beating down, and he was perspiring by the time he reached the house. He observed it as he approached: it was set back from the road, separated from the sidewalk by a well-kept garden. There was a gate and, behind that, a flight of stone stairs leading up to a veranda. Milton couldn't see any more from the street, but it appeared that the entrance would be found up there.

Milton walked on, looking for any sign that he had been noticed, but there was nothing that stood out to him. The street was quiet: he could hear the sound of children splashing in a pool around the back of a house on the other side of the street, and a maid was carrying dry-cleaning from her car into the house next door, but, save that, there was nothing else of note.

He turned at the end of the street and walked back toward the house again, but, instead of continuing, this time he opened the gate and climbed the steps. The veranda was enclosed by a fence; the space led back beneath the main bulk of the property, which was suspended on stilts. There was a pool with crystal-clear water, and dancing shards of light reflected against the walls of the property. There was a barbecue and, next to the pool, a sun lounger. Milton walked around the pool to the lounger. A novel had been left there, splayed open, its pages warped from being soaked by rain and then allowed to cook in the sun. There was a glass on the table next to the lounger; it had filled to the brim with rainwater.

Milton started to get a bad feeling.

The few windows that he could see were closed, but the curtains were not drawn, and he was able to see inside a little. There was no sign of anyone at home.

Milton reached around and took the suppressed Walther from his waistband.

There was a sliding door that offered access to the interior of the house. There was a blind behind the door, and it had been pulled all the way across. Milton put his face to the glass and looked to see if there was a gap in any of the slats, but there was not. He couldn't see beyond it. He examined the door. There were two glass panels: one was fixed and the other was designed to slide on tracks at the top and bottom of the frame. The sliding panel was on the outside of the fixed panel; that would make it easier to open. Although he couldn't see it, Milton knew that the catch on the frame would be nothing more than a hole or brace. The L-shaped latch on the door connected with the bracket, pivoting up from the bottom to lock the door. Milton took off his rucksack, opened it and took out the things that he would need. He pulled on a pair of latex gloves and stepped into similar latex overshoes. Marks had provided him with a small pry bar and, working quickly and carefully, he inserted the bar between the bottom of the door frame and the door about six inches from the corner, diagonal from the latch. He pried upward and tilted the door. The latch lowered, releasing it from the bracket, and Milton was able to slide the panel back. It took him less than twenty seconds.

He put the pry bar back into his bag, collected the pistol once more, and moved the blind aside so that he could step into the house.

Milton smelled it right away.

Death.

He gripped the pistol and crept into the gloom, treading carefully and listening intently.

Nothing.

Everything was quiet, but the smell was unmistakeable.

He reached back and moved the blind aside, leaving enough of a gap for the sun to shine a shaft into the room. Milton looked around: it was a kitchen-diner, longer than it was wide, with a cream sofa against the wall to his right and a breakfast bar to his left. There were kitchen counters on the left wall, a large oven, and an American-style fridge. The room had been designed to be clean and contemporary, but the effect was ruined by the detritus that had been scattered across the white-tiled floor. A bookshelf had been upended, and the books tossed here and there; the vases that might once have been placed on the breakfast bar lay in fragments on the floor. Milton stepped deeper into the room and glanced down to the sofa; two ring-binders had been left open on the cushions, papers ripped out and left to twitch in the gentle breeze that blew in through the open door.

Milton made his way carefully through the room. He led with his pistol, pivoting left and right as he took each fresh step, making sure that the room was clear.

He reached the door at the other end. It opened into a hallway. The light from the kitchen-diner was meagre, and Milton reached into his bag for the pencil flashlight that

Marks had provided. He switched it on, held it against the pistol, and swept the room. It was empty; coats and jackets that had once hung from a row of hooks in the wall had been pulled down and left on the floor. There was nothing else of note save two more doors. One of them was a bathroom; it was small, and Milton was able to clear it quickly.

He went back to the hall and approached the other door. The door looked thin and cheap, and it was ajar; he pushed it with the fingertips of his left hand, the pistol ready in his right.

It was a bedroom.

He saw it at once: there was a body on the bed. It was a man. He was on his back, lying at ninety degrees to the headboard. His arms were spread, and his head had fallen to the side so that he was looking straight at Milton. He recognised him from the photo that Sophia had shown him. It was Xavier de Oliveira.

Milton froze.

Had he heard something?

He closed his eyes, held his breath and concentrated.

He heard a car passing outside, the voices of the kids still playing in the pool on the other side of the street, a dog barking in a nearby garden.

And then he heard it again.

The crunch of footsteps across glass.

Someone else was inside the house.

ilton thought quickly: the door from the kitchen-diner to the hall was open, and he would be seen if he tried to retrace his steps.

He looked around the bedroom for somewhere to hide. It was a small room with a fitted cupboard to the left of the bed, a bedside table to the right, and a desk with a chair beneath the window on the opposite side of the room to the door. The bed was on a platform that brought it up to the same height as his thighs; the platform was solid, with no space for him to slide beneath it. There was no space for him to hide behind the door. He went to the cupboard, opened it, pushed the clothes aside so that he had a little space, and pressed himself all the way to the back. Some of the clothes were wrapped in plastic dry-cleaning sheaths, and they rustled as they rubbed up against each other. Other clothes had not been cleaned, and Milton could smell the odour of stale cigarette smoke coming off them.

He pulled the door almost all the way closed, leaving a crack so that he could see back into the bedroom.

He held his breath. He could still hear the footsteps.

Whoever it was, he or she was trying very hard to make as little noise as possible. The footsteps were barely audible, but now that he knew they were there, he could hear them. The steps padded through the kitchen toward the door to the hall.

The door to the bedroom was slowly pushed open.

Milton gripped the Walther firmly.

A man stepped into the doorway. There was almost no light, and Milton could make out very little save that the man was of average height and that there was a pistol in his left hand.

The man stood still; Milton couldn't see his face, but he could tell that the man was listening.

Milton could still hear movement.

There was at least one more of them.

Milton waited, his finger on the trigger of the pistol.

The man came fully inside the bedroom and turned a little. Milton saw that his right arm was in a sling and that he held his pistol in his left hand in an awkward, uncomfortable grip. He walked with slow, careful steps, his feet silent now that he was on the deeply piled carpet. He went over to the bed. He didn't register any sign of surprise at the dead body that was sprawled out on it. Milton assumed that the man had known the body was there; perhaps he was responsible for it himself.

Milton had surprise on his side, but that wouldn't last for much longer. He needed to know how many other people were in the house. A two-man team seemed most likely. He tried to work out what they might know: they would have seen the forced door to the veranda, so they would have been certain that someone had been in the house before them, and that the person might still be inside now. Milton didn't think that he had been seen as he had arrived, but it was unlikely that they were coincidentally here at the same time as he was. Milton gritted his teeth in annoyance. *Had* he been seen? Someone must have been watching, and he had missed them.

The man walked around the bed. Milton had only dared open the door a crack, and the angle became too acute now for him to see the man. He held the pistol and maintained his breathing, nice and easy, slow and even, keeping his pulse steady. He controlled the urge to kick the door open and shoot, waiting for just the right moment.

The man came back into view and, for a moment, Milton thought that he was going to continue all the way out of the bedroom. But he did not; he stopped, turned to the side, and took a pace toward the wardrobe.

Now.

The man passed through a faint sliver of light, and Milton saw his face: he had a tattoo across it. Milton recognised him: it was the man he had shot in the shoulder during the ambush.

Milton pushed the door open. The man's eyes bulged wide as he saw Milton and the gun pointed at his chest.

Milton pulled the trigger.

The gun barked, loud despite the suppressor.

Milton fired again.

Milton aimed both shots into the man's torso, and both found their mark. The first struck him in the right breast, shoving him back a quarter turn, narrowing his profile enough that the second round punched him in the left shoulder. The man stumbled back, tripped over a pair of shoes, and fell onto his backside. He tried feebly to raise his own weapon, but Milton made his attempt moot; he came out of the wardrobe, aimed down, and fired a third shot into the man's eye.

Milton stepped back and aimed at the door. "I know you're there," he called out. "Your friend is dead."

There was no response, but Milton could hear the sound of quiet footsteps in the hall. He couldn't work out whether they were advancing or retreating. The door was ajar, but it blocked Milton's view outside. At least it would restrict the view inside, too.

Milton stepped forward. There was a full-length mirror on the wall of the bedroom, opposite the door. He kept his pistol aimed at the door and slid his gaze sideways to the mirror. The reflection showed him a view of the hallway. It was empty.

"Get out now," he called, unsure whether whoever it was out there would be able to understand his English. "If you stay, I'll shoot you, too."

"Don't think so, John."

Milton froze.

It was Shawn Drake.

57

"You're outnumbered, John."

The voice was unmistakeable.

Milton struggled to put the pieces together: Drake was still alive.

How was that possible?

"Put the gun on the floor and kick it away."

Milton scrambled for answers.

Drake must have been involved in the abduction of Alícia Saverin, and now he was cleaning up. Had he been watching Sophia, seen them meet, and then followed Milton? No. He dismissed the suggestion as impossible; he would have had to have Milton under surveillance, and Milton was always alert to the possibility of his being followed. Did that mean that Sophia was in on whatever Drake had planned, then? Had she tricked him?

"What are you doing, Drake?"

"You're outnumbered," he repeated, "and you've got nowhere to go."

Milton would have to work out the angles later. For now,

he glanced quickly around the room. There was a window, but the curtains were drawn, and there was no way for him to see how easy it would be to open. And, to get to it, he would have to cede his shelter and step into the line of fire of anyone waiting in the hallway. He dismissed the thought; he would have to find another way.

Milton brought up his left hand and held the pistol in a two-handed grip to steady his aim. "This is a really bad idea, Drake."

"I'd rather it didn't have to come to this. You've been unlucky—wrong place, wrong time. That's just how it is. You got dealt a bad hand."

"So you set this up? You sold the Saverins out? Hawkins and Berg get murdered and a girl is kidnapped? For what?"

"Money," he said. "What do you think? I told you—I'm in the shit. I was going to lose the business. I tried doing it the right way, but you can make more playing both sides. A lot more."

Milton saw a shadow dart across the mirror. He listened hard, filtering out Drake's voice. How many were there? Drake on his own? He didn't think so. There was at least one more man besides him.

"Does Sophia know about what you've done?"

Drake didn't respond, but Milton could hear the sound of movement.

The thought of Sophia reminded him of something she had said to him about Xavier de Oliveira. He needed to keep Drake talking. "Let me guess what happened," he said. "De Oliveira here found out what you were up to?"

"Something like that," Drake said. He sounded close. He was in the other room, near to the door. Milton thought he heard the sound of someone whispering.

He backed up to the closet. "So what, then? He was going to go to the police?"

"He was, but not because he wanted to do the right thing. He wanted half of my take—greedy fucker. Couldn't have that."

Milton switched the gun to his right hand while he reached behind him with his left. He opened the closet door all the way and then crouched down, his eyes still on the bedroom door as he stretched out his arm and probed the closet.

"So you got rid of him," Milton said. His fingers touched cold metal.

"No," Drake said. "They did. He called to threaten me when we were at the concert. That was the last straw."

"But without him, the team was light."

"That's right. And then you said you'd stand in. Perfect timing for me, not so great for you."

Milton's hand closed around a long tube. Sophia had said that de Oliveira was paranoid and kept a shotgun in his closet; here it was. De Oliveira hadn't had the chance to use it to prevent his own death, but perhaps it would help Milton even the odds.

"I was perfect?" he called out. "How'd you figure that?"

"You're an old drunk, John. You said it yourself."

"And I wouldn't be a threat? Not looking like that now, is it? Want to reconsider?"

Drake laughed. "Maybe I underestimated you. Won't happen again. Come on, John. Come out. Time's up."

"I'm alright here, Drake."

"You don't come out, maybe I burn the place down."

Milton examined the shotgun: it was a Mossberg 590A1 with the twenty-inch barrel and bayonet lug. Pump-action, chambered in 12 gauge with a shoulder stock for more accurate shooting. He was lucky: the 590A1 was military issue and a solid defensive weapon. Milton turned the shotgun over, pushed back the cartridge stop lever, and let a shot-shell fall into his fingers. He checked the load—double ought buckshot—and then reinserted the shell into the magazine tube.

He pressed the stock against his shoulder, slid his right index finger through the guard and aimed at the door. "It's not too late, Drake," he called out. "Where'd they take the girl? Help me get her back."

"And you pretend nothing happened? No, thanks."

The shadow in the mirror returned. It was a man. He was hidden in the darkness, but Milton didn't think that it was Drake. The man was edging into the room, hiding on the other side of the open door, most likely assuming that he was hidden from view. He was standing side on, a pistol held in his left hand held up at head height. Milton knew that if *he* could see the man in the mirror, then the man would be able to see him, too. So far, though, it didn't seem as if the man had even noticed that the mirror was there.

Milton didn't wait. He squeezed the trigger. The buck-shot punched easily through the flimsy wood. The man screamed and fell back, crashing against the wall and then toppling forward into the room.

Milton had used the recoil to help him pump the weapon faster, the inertia pushing his shoulder back, allowing him to rack the gun at the same time. He moved quickly now, checked in the mirror that the hallway was clear, and then pressed himself against the wall. He heard a muttered, "Fuck," and then the sound of running feet. Drake was no fool. He probably had a pistol, just like the man Milton had just blown up, and he would know that the pump gun had completely changed the dynamic.

Milton sank low, took a breath, and then swivelled out into the sitting room with the Mossberg up. He saw a quick flash of movement in the yard outside and then nothing.

Drake was making a break for it.

Milton went after him.

58

Paulo waited in the Benz. Alessandro had told him that they wouldn't be long, and that he should be ready to move at short notice. Paulo had turned the car around and slotted it against the kerb next to the building.

He was nervous. Neither Alessandro nor Junior had told him what they were here to do, but it couldn't be good. They had waited nearby for two hours on Rua Alice until Junior's phone had rung. There had been a quick, clipped conversation, and then Junior had told him to drive to Rua Professor Olinto de Oliveira. A young teenage boy had sauntered up to the car, and Junior had given him a handful of notes before sending him on his way; the boy must have been a lookout, alerting Junior to the arrival of the person who was now inside one of the houses. Two minutes later a second car had arrived, and a man whom Paulo had never seen before had stepped outside and started a terse conversation with Alessandro. All three men had then gone into the house.

Paulo fidgeted; his fingers drummed the wheel, and he

couldn't stop the anxious tapping that animated his right foot. He thought how easy it would be to put the car into drive, press down on the accelerator, and be away from here. But what would he do then? He would have to tell Rafaela what he had done, and somehow persuade her that they would all have to leave Rocinha—leave Rio—and find somewhere they could hide. But he had already paid over a good chunk of the money that Garanhão had given him. If they ran, they would have to start over again: find more money and find another doctor who was able to treat Eloá. It was *impossible*. There was nowhere that they could go where the don would not find them, and when he did, Paulo knew that his revenge would not be limited to him alone. He would make examples out of all of them—Rafaela, Eloá, Uncle Felipe, maybe even his father in jail—a reminder to anyone else who might be thinking of betraying him that the price would always be too high.

He looked at his watch. The three men had been inside the house for five minutes.

He was wondering what was happening when he heard two gunshots, close together, and then, after a pause of a few seconds, a third. The noises were muffled from being inside, but Paulo had heard plenty of gunshots before.

Paulo gripped the wheel until his knuckles were white. It was Junior and Alessandro and the new man, obviously, but who had they come here to kill?

There was a longer pause, perhaps thirty seconds, and then a loud boom.

He squeezed his eyes shut and, when that didn't stop the panic, he rested his head on the wheel between his hands and started to pray.

He had his eyes closed when he heard the sound of footsteps. He looked up and saw the third man, the one who had been speaking to Alessandro, hurrying down the steps. He turned onto the street, sprinted to his car, and started the engine. Paulo watched, dumbstruck, as the car raced away, leaving rubber on the asphalt.

He leaned forward, craning his neck in an attempt to better see up the steps, but the angle made it impossible. He reached for the ignition with trembling fingers. There was no sign of Alessandro or Junior. Maybe the gunshots he had heard had not been fired by them; maybe they had been shot. Why was the third guy running? What had happened inside the house?

His heart hammering, he turned the key, bringing the engine to life and reaching for the handbrake.

His attention was fixed straight ahead. He didn't notice the man approaching from behind, not until one of the doors behind him was pulled open.

He raised his head and looked in the rear-view mirror at the same time as he felt something small and hard press up against his head.

"*Inglês?*"

Paulo flicked his eyes to the mirror. There was a man in the seat behind him, his face partially hidden by the head-rest of Paulo's seat. Paulo couldn't see him, but he could see what the man was holding against his head: it was a pistol.

"*Inglês?*" the man said again, his voice as hard and cold as iron.

"Yes," Paulo forced out. "A little."

"Good," the man replied. He gave a little push with the gun, jerking Paulo's head to the side. "Drive."

59

Milton called Marks from the back of the car and explained what had happened. The old man listened intently without interrupting, and, when Milton was finished, asked a series of questions that Milton was able to answer quickly and succinctly. Milton's main concern was where he could take his prisoner. He certainly couldn't go back to Marks's house; the road outside was far from quiet, and there was a good chance that someone would see Milton transferring his prisoner from the car to the inside. And, perhaps more important, he did not want his prisoner to be able to find the house again. Milton had not decided what he was going to do with the driver, but if he took him back to the house, then he would have little choice other than to execute him. That course of action was still a possibility, but Milton was not a butcher and he preferred an alternative, if one were available. The driver's prospects were better the less that he knew. Marks told him to head west, and he would text him in five minutes with the precise location.

Milton kept the gun trained on the driver and assessed

him. He was young and frightened. The blood had drained from his face, and his hands trembled on the wheel.

"What's your name?" Milton asked him.

"Paulo."

"Paulo?"

"Paulo de Almeida."

Milton lowered the gun to his lap but kept it trained on the driver. He had passed several police cars on his drive to the house earlier that morning, and the last thing he wanted was for some eagle-eyed cop to see his firearm and pull the car over. Paulo knew that he was armed, and Milton doubted that he would be foolish enough to try to escape. Milton would certainly shoot him if he tried to do that.

"I don't know who you are," Paulo said. "I can't do anything to you. I'm no one."

Milton didn't reply.

"I'm just the driver. They tell me where to go; I take them. I don't work for the gang. This is all a mistake. I shouldn't be here."

"We'll see," Milton said. "There'll be plenty of time for you to tell me all about it."

His phone buzzed as a text arrived. He opened it:

Joy Motel, Estr. dos Bandeirantes, Jacarepaguá. Room eight.

"How far to Jacarepaguá?" Milton asked.

"An hour. Maybe a little more."

"That's where we're going."

"Please, sir," Paulo said. Milton could see his eyes in the mirror: they were wide with fear. "Just let me stop the car."

Milton watched him as he spoke; there was something about him that was very familiar. He stared at Paulo's reflection and remembered: he had been there when Alícia was taken.

He had been driving the getaway car.

"Let me pull over," he pleaded. "I'll go—you'll never see me again, I swear."

"I don't think so."

"I have a daughter. A family. Please, sir. *Please.*"

Milton very nearly snapped that de Almeida should have thought of that before, but he held his tongue. There would be a time to ratchet up the fear, but that would come later; he needed him calm for now. "We need to have a talk," he said. "If you're honest with me, if you tell me what I want to know, you can go once we're done."

60

Paulo had never been to Jacarepaguá before, and, at the insistence of the man with the gun, he followed the satnav to Estrada dos Bandeirantes, a busy road on the very outskirts of Rio.

"There," the man said, pointing. "The motel on the right."

The place had a sign outside that announced it as the Joy Motel. It did not look aptly named. It was a collection of one-storey buildings set behind a white-painted concrete wall and eight sickly-looking trees. A neon sign proclaimed that rooms were available for sixty-two *reais* a night, or a minimum of three hours. A thick tangle of electricity and telephone cables passed almost directly overhead. Paulo turned off the road and rolled through a gate and into a parking lot beyond. There were two long single-storey buildings that stood on either side of the lot. Each building had a covered veranda and had been divided into a series of identically sized rooms. The rooms on the left were evenly numbered, and the rooms on the right were odd.

"Number eight," the man said. "Park outside it."

It was the room at the far end of the building. Paulo drove slowly ahead, then turned the car in and parked in the space directly opposite the door. He left the engine running, as if that might increase the chance that the man with the gun would change his mind and let him back out and drive back to Rocinha again.

"Switch it off," the man said.

Paulo's hand was shaking as he reached forward and killed the ignition.

"This is what we're going to do," the man told him. "We're going to get out and go into that room. The door's unlocked. You're going to go first, and I'm going to follow right behind. I'll have the gun in my hand the whole time. I'd rather not use it, but I will if you make me. Do you understand?"

"Yes," Paulo said.

"That's good. Okay, then. Nice and easy. Open the door and get out."

Paulo did as he was told. He stepped out into the baking hot morning and started to walk to the veranda. He could hear the fizzing and popping from the electricity cables and the nearby blare of a car alarm. The car door opened and closed behind him, but he dared not look back. He stepped up onto the veranda, crossed it, and put his hand on the doorknob for number eight. He turned the knob; it was unlocked. He pushed the door open and went inside.

The room was basic. It was bigger than the room that he shared with Rafaela and Eloá in the *favela*, and furnished with cheap pieces of furniture. Paulo stepped through the doorway, and the man came up close behind him, shoving him between the shoulder blades. He stumbled ahead as the man closed the door and drew down the blinds.

"Sit on the bed," the man ordered.

Paulo did. The man stepped closer and frisked him; his hands moved skilfully, and he quickly located and removed Paulo's phone and keys.

"How much English do you speak?"

"I speak it okay."

"Good." The man took a wooden chair, moved it so that it was in front of the bed, and sat down. He had the gun in his hand, holding it with the easy confidence of someone who had used it before. "Are you scared?"

Paulo nodded.

"You're right to be," the man said. "I would be if I were you."

The words came quickly now. "I didn't want anything to do with this," Paulo said.

"You're bound to say that now," the man said. "Do you think that'll persuade me to let you go?"

"You said if I helped…" He didn't know what to say; the fear felt like ice in his brain.

"I know what I said," the man said. "It's up to you what happens next. I have a few questions. You're going to answer them. You're going to be truthful and helpful. If you think you have information that might help me, even if I don't ask for it, you're going to volunteer it. And then, if I think you've been truthful and helpful, maybe I'll give some thought to you walking out of here in one piece. If I don't think that? Think about what I just did to your friends." The man let the sentence hang, leaving Paulo to join the dots. "Do we have an understanding?"

"Yes," Paulo said.

"Let's start with your friends," he said.

"They're not my friends," he insisted.

"What, then? Just two men you worked with?"

"It's not like that."

"Really? What *is* it like?"

"I'm in a lot of trouble," Paulo said.

The man raised the gun a little so that Paulo could see it and tapped his index finger against the barrel. "We can agree on that." The man paused. "Look at me."

Paulo looked from the gun to the man's face. He had the palest blue eyes that he had ever seen; they were almost limpid.

"You don't remember me, do you?"

Paulo found that he couldn't look away; the man's gaze was magnetic, and chilling. He thought of the calmness with which he held the pistol, and the shots that he had heard from inside the house. The man had killed Junior and Alessandro just an hour ago, and it seemingly had had no effect on him at all.

"I asked you a question, Paulo. Do you remember me?"

"I don't remember you."

"I was there when Alícia Saverin was taken. I was one of the men who was supposed to make sure she was safe. And then, when I tried to get her back, you ran me off the road. You nearly killed me." The man stared at him, his eyes even colder than before. "Do you remember now?"

"I'm sorry," Paulo said, because he didn't know what else to say. "I didn't know that was going to happen. He tricked me."

"Who did?"

"Garanhão," he replied, struggling to avoid being over-whelmed by the panic that he felt. "I owe him a lot of money. If I told him that I didn't want to work for him anymore, he'd take it out on my family. There's nothing I can do. I've been stupid, I know I have, but I'm trapped."

Paulo watched the man's reaction; his face was stern, and his expression didn't change.

"Who's Garanhão?"

"You don't know?" The question spurted out before he could tamp down his incredulity, and it was rewarded by another cold stare. "He runs the Hill. Antonio Rodrigues. He's the don."

"And how did he trick you?"

"He said I would just be driving for him. But he sent me with Alessandro and Junior—"

"Who?" the man cut in.

"The men—from today."

"The men who came into the house? One of them had a tattoo across his face."

"Yes," he said. "That's Junior. The other is Alessandro. Garanhão said I just had to take them to Ipanema. It was simple: we were just down there to pick someone up. And then they start shooting and they take the girl. I had no idea. I would never have done it if I had known. But I *didn't* know, I swear."

The man kept his eyes on Paulo as he spoke. "Where is the girl?"

"At the top of the Hill."

"Have you seen her?"

"Yes," he said. "Garanhão told me that I had to look after her. She is little. I have a girl the same age as her. I've made sure she has what she needs. I try to keep her safe. She shouldn't be there. She should be with her family. If I could get her away, I would. But it is *Garanhão*. What can I do?"

The man listened quietly and then reached onto the desk and picked Paulo's phone up and handed it to him. "Unlock it."

Paulo tapped in the passcode and handed it back. The man was silent for a moment, his finger swiping across the screen as he flicked through Paulo's photos. He turned the phone around and held it up so that he could see the photo-graph that he had stopped on. It was one of his favourites: Rafaela and Eloá on the beach at Ipanema, their happy smiles a reminder of how perfect their life had been before the diagnosis.

"Your family?" the man said.

Paulo nodded. "My wife and my daughter. Eloá is six. She is sick. She has cancer. We needed money for her treat-ment—I raced cars to try to get what we needed, but then that went wrong, and the only choice I had was to go to Garanhão. He gave me the money and said I had to work for him. And now, if I say no to him..." He stopped and then said, "You don't say no to Garanhão."

"You said the Hill," the man said. "You mean Rocinha?"

Paulo nodded. "Garanhão runs it. He lives at the top—everyone there works for him. He has warehouses there for his drugs business. They have Alícia in the basement."

The man stared at him again. "How much do you want to make this good?"

"Very much," Paulo said. "But how can I—"

"Can you show me where she is?"

"Yes," Paulo said. "But why? The police won't be able to help. Garanhão owns the police. They wouldn't even dare to go up there."

"The police aren't going up there," the man said. "I am."

Paulo wasn't immediately sure that he had heard him correctly. "You want to go to the top of the Hill?"

"Yes," the man said.

"But why?"

"Because I'm going to go and get her, and then I'm going to bring her down."

61

M ilton interrogated Paulo for another twenty minutes. The young man was terrified, with good reason, and once Milton got him started with a series of simple questions, the words flowed out of him. It would have been an exaggeration to suggest that Milton started to warm to him—Milton warmed to practically no one—but, as the story poured out, he did, at least, come to understand why Paulo had done what he had done. Milton was not prepared to absolve him, but he understood what it was like to be caught in a situation from which it appeared dangerous, if not impossible, to extract oneself. After all, Milton had once been in a similar situation himself.

More important than that, Milton started to believe that de Almeida meant what he said about wanting to help Alícia Saverin. He evidently felt guilty about his role in the affair, and, even though he said he was doing what he could to make the girl comfortable, he did not mistake his role for other than what it was: he was her jailor.

Milton had started to formulate the rough lines of a plan

when he heard the sound of a car pulling up outside. He went to the window and pulled the edge of the curtain back so that he could look out. It was Harry Marks's old BMW.

Milton opened the door so that Marks could come inside.

"Who's this?" the old man said.

"This is Paulo de Almeida," Milton said. "He's the man I told you about."

Marks looked at de Almeida with undisguised disdain.

"He's going to help me," Milton said. "Isn't that right, Paulo?"

De Almeida nodded, caught somewhere between the need to display enthusiasm for Milton's benefit and his wariness at Marks.

Milton gestured to Paulo. "Go and wait in the bathroom. I need to speak to my friend in private."

Paulo did as he was told. Milton had already checked that there was no way that he could get out from back there. He followed the young man as he went inside and pulled the door shut after him. He went back to Marks and quickly summarised the information that Paulo had given him. Marks listened intently, punctuating each new piece of intelligence with a nod of his head.

"What's next?" he asked when Milton was finished.

He gestured to the bathroom door. "He wants to make up for what he's done, and I'm going to give him a chance. He's going to go back to Rocinha, go to where Alícia is being held, and get me the information I need to plan an extraction. Do you have a camera he could use? Something very discreet."

"I have something," Marks said. "But it's been a while since it was updated."

"Does it transmit?"

"No. Just records."

"It'll have to do."

Marks took out a notebook and scribbled into it. "What else?"

"You need to go back to our friends in Cheltenham. I want a full workup on Antonio Rodrigues. His nom de guerre is Garanhão. I want to know who he is, where he lives, his known associates, criminal history."

"I'll get them on it today."

Milton thanked him.

Marks scratched his head with the end of the pencil. "Are you sure about this? Going up there?"

"What else am I going to do? You think I can trust the police?"

"No," he said with a grim shake of his head.

"So?"

"There must be another way. You were in bed with a severe concussion two days ago. You—"

"It's personal now, Harry," Milton said, cutting him off. "I came to stay here with a friend."

"You said."

"His name's Shawn Drake. It turns out he's not what I thought he was. He's been working for Garanhão. He sold the girl and her mother out—I'm guessing Garanhão, or someone who's paying him, wants to lean on Alícia's father. A man and a woman who worked for Drake were killed when they took her. And then he tried to kill me—he was there this morning."

"At the house?"

Milton nodded. "Three of them. I took his friends out, but he got away. But not before we had a nice cosy chat."

"You have a poor choice in friends," Marks observed.

Milton allowed himself a grim smile. "We made a lot of

noise this morning—the police are going to find the bodies of Garanhão's men and the man who was working for Drake. Tell GCHQ to monitor their investigation. I want to know if they start looking in the right direction."

Marks noted that down. "Understood."

Milton had taken quick snaps of the two dead men. He took out his phone, navigated to the pictures, and handed it to Marks. The old man looked at the photograph of the man with the tattooed face. "Not a looker, was he?"

"That's Junior."

Marks swiped left.

"His friend is Alessandro," Milton said. He took the phone back again. "I'll email these to you. I want Cheltenham to do full workups on both these men, too, and on Drake. Shawn Drake, spelled S-H-A-W-N. He was in the SAS at the same time as me, and then he came over here to work." Milton paused, wondering how thorough he needed to be; he decided, as usual, that more was much better than less. He swiped through the pictures until he found a selfie that he had taken at the festival. "This is him," he said, pointing. "And this is Sophia Lopes. She's involved with Drake. She told me that she's training to be a lawyer, but I'm not sure how much of that I believe now. I want a full workup on her, too. If there's anything interesting, I want to know it."

Marks scribbled in his book. "And what about you?"

"This *traficante*—Garanhão—he's going to find out what happened this morning pretty soon. He might know already." He nodded to the bathroom door. "It'll look better for the kid if he goes back up there now. The longer he's not up there, the better the chances Garanhão thinks he's involved or compromised."

"It's already been hours. He's going to need an excuse."

"Can you think of something?"

"Should be able to." Marks stood up. "So he just needs a camera? I can take him to get fixed up now. The kit's back at the cache."

Milton went to the door and opened it. "Get in here."

Paulo did as he was asked.

"You're going to go with my friend. He's going to fit you with a camera—a very small one that no one will notice. I want you to go back to Garanhão. You need to tell him that you heard shooting, you panicked, and then you drove. Nothing else."

The young man was pale with fear and didn't say anything.

Milton continued. "And then I want you to go to the warehouse and walk around. I want you to show me the guards, where they're posted, how many of them there are, the weapons they use. And then I want you to show me the building: how I get in, and then the way I'd need to go to find Alícia and get her out again."

"They'll see me," Paulo blurted. "The camera—they'll see it."

"It's very small," Marks said. "It looks just like a button. They won't even know it's there."

"No. No way. You don't know what—"

"This isn't a negotiation," Milton said sternly, cutting him off. "You said you wanted to help Alícia."

"I do."

"So this is how you do it."

"But you don't know what he's like."

"This is your chance to make good on what you've done. You decided to work for him—you didn't have to. Getting involved with men like him is dangerous. But crossing men like me is dangerous, too. Understand?"

"Yes," Paulo said quietly.

"Go with my friend. He'll fit you with the camera and tell you what to do. Get what I asked for and bring it to me this afternoon. And don't make me come and find you."

Milton opened the door and led Paulo to the Mercedes Benz that he had been driving. Marks joined them outside as the young man opened the door and slid into the driver's seat.

Marks shut the door to the room. "I've rented it for a week," he said as he came down from the veranda. "Thought it might be useful."

Milton closed the car door. "What do you think?" he asked Marks.

"You trust him?"

"No. But he's scared."

"He's definitely scared."

"And I think he wants to do the right thing."

"And if he doesn't?"

"All we lose is surprise. His boss finds out that someone who killed two of his men is coming for the girl. He doesn't know my name or where he can find me. If that happens, I'll find another way. But I don't think it will. And the intel could be valuable. I think it's worth the risk to get it."

Marks nodded. "I can get him sorted from here," he said. "I'll call when it's done."

"Thanks, Harry. There's one other thing I need you to get for me."

"What?"

"You got any bugs at the cache?"

"Some," he said. "Nothing fancy. Old stuff."

"It'll do. Can I have them?"

"Now?"

Milton nodded.

"I'll give you a ride. What are you going to do with them?"

"A little digging," Milton said.

62

P aulo drove east, following the old man in his beaten-up BMW. He was terrified. He had promised to do something that filled him with horror. The idea of spying on Garanhão was so frightening that the only way he could drive was to put it right at the back of his mind. He focussed on Alícia instead and told himself that he was going to do right by her, just as he ought to have done right at the start.

The old man indicated that he was turning off. Paulo did the same and turned into the forecourt of a Shell gas station next to a large derelict warehouse. The old man parked the BMW and got out. The man with the blue eyes waited in the passenger seat. The old man came over to Paulo. He opened the door and told him to step out.

"You need to wait here," the man said to him.

"Where are you going?"

"Wait," the man repeated, not bothering to hide his impatience. "There's a diner around the back of the station. Go and get a cup of coffee and wait for me. I'll be half an hour."

The old man got back into his BMW, started the engine, and rejoined the traffic.

Paulo walked across to the diner, ordered a coffee, and took it to an empty table by the window. He sat down to wait.

IT WAS NEARER to an hour by the time the old man returned to the gas station. Paulo was on his third coffee; he finished it, left a note on the table to settle the bill, and went back outside. The old man parked the BMW next to the warehouse and got out; he was alone, with no sign of the man with the blue eyes. He was holding a polo shirt in one hand and a small leather satchel in the other. There was a toilet block behind the gas station, and the old man started toward it, beckoning that Paulo should follow him.

The toilets were unpleasant and hadn't been cleaned for some time. There was a line of three stalls, three sinks on the wall—one of them had been smashed—and a cracked mirror above them. The old man checked that the stalls were empty and then tossed the shirt to Paulo.

"Put it on."

Paulo took the shirt and held it up. It was pale blue, with a collar, a three-button placket and an Yves Saint Laurent logo over the right breast.

"You need me to help dress you?" the old man said sharply. "Put it on."

Paulo took off his own shirt, put his arms through the new one, and tugged it over his head.

The man opened the leather satchel and took out a black plastic oblong, a length of wire and a roll of tape. He reached inside the placket and twisted the bottom upwards, revealing a thin square of plastic beneath one of the buttons that Paulo hadn't noticed. The square was on the inside of the shirt with the button on the other side of the fabric; it looked as if the two were connected. Paulo looked down as the man took one end of the wire and plugged it into the bottom of the plastic square.

The man held up the larger black oblong. "Turn around."

Paulo did so self-consciously. He looked in the cracked mirror and saw the man take the oblong and press it against the middle of his back. The man peeled off the end of the tape and cut a length off with a pair of scissors; the tape secured the oblong in place. Then, the man unrolled more, going from his back to beneath his arms to his chest and then back again, enough tape to go around Paulo's body three times. He cut it with the scissors and put the roll to one side. He took the other end of the wire and pulled it around to where he had secured the object against his back; Paulo heard a small click as the man pressed the wire into the oblong.

"This is a camera and recorder," the man said.

"Come on," Paulo pleaded. "They'll see it. It's obvious."

"No, it isn't." The man pointed to the mirror. "Look. Turn around."

Paulo did.

"The DVR is on your back. It's slender—if you leave your shirt loose, no one will be able to see it. You see it?"

Paulo couldn't see it. The shirt fell over the recorder.

He shook his head. "But they'll still—"

The man spoke over him. "The lens is hidden in the button. It's very sensitive—it'll work in low light, if you need it to. You've got nearly eighty degrees' field of view, so you don't need to be right in front of something. The recorder will last ninety minutes on a charge. You shouldn't need any longer than that for what you need to do. There's a single button on the back—press it to switch it on. Can you feel it?"

Paulo reached around and felt the depression against the otherwise smooth surface of the recorder. "This?"

"That's right. Make sure no one sees you pressing it. Understand?"

"Yes," he said weakly.

The man nodded his approval. "This is what you're going to do: you go outside, get into your car, and go back to where they've got the girl. Record everything that my friend asked you to record."

"And if I see anyone?"

"Act natural."

"How do I do that?"

"You prepare before you go up there. You get your story straight. You'd just taken the two men to the house. You heard gunshots. You saw someone come out of the house and leave in the opposite direction. You waited, but they didn't come back out—okay?"

"He'll ask why I didn't go back to the Hill straight away. I've been with you all morning. He'll know I'm lying."

"That's easy. You tell him you waited in the car for the men to come back. You waited twenty minutes. You realised something was wrong, and you went inside to check. You found three dead bodies and you panicked. But before you could get back into your car, the police showed up. They were cruising up the street. You panicked. You didn't think it was safe to get back to the car. So you walked. How long would it take to walk from Santa Teresa to Rocinha? Three hours?"

Paulo nodded.

"So that's how you explain where you've been."

"I don't know," Paulo said.

"You're scared already, right?"

Paulo swallowed and nodded.

"Then don't hide it. Use it. Be natural—he'll expect you to be scared."

The old man opened the door to the block, and the warm breeze blew inside, disturbing the layers of torpid heat and the underlying smell of excrement. "It's one o'clock now. I'm going to be here again at five. So are you. Don't be late."

The man stepped outside and disappeared from view. Paulo waited where he was, despite the unpleasantness, and turned to look at himself in the mirror. He faced it, then turned in profile, then turned around and looked back over his shoulder. Surely the recorder must be obvious? He looked for it, feeling it against his spine yet unable to see it beneath the fabric of the shirt. He turned back to the front and looked at his face; even if he couldn't see the recorder or the camera, then surely his guilt would be writ large on his face. He had heard the stories about Garanhão, about how it was said that he could sniff out a lie, an instinct for deceit that he backed with violence every time. And Paulo had always been a bad liar—it was a standing joke between him and Rafaela—and the audacity of this particular lie was several orders above lying about staying out for a drink with his friends when he had promised to return home. He was taking a camera into Garanhão's operation and then delivering the footage to a man who appeared crazy enough to consider attacking the don.

Paulo heard the slap of approaching footsteps and stepped outside before a man wearing flip-flops, shorts and a Fluminense shirt could go in. They blocked each other;

Paulo took a step to the left and the man mirrored him, then repeated the movement as Paulo went right. The man grunted irritably; Paulo apologised and stepped aside. He was sweating, yet his throat was bone dry.

He wanted to go home more than anything, but he shook his head, reminded himself that he still hadn't seen Alícia today and, with fresh stabs of guilt mixing with his anxiety, he hurried to the Benz.

63

M ilton took a taxi from the cache to a local car rental firm and hired a Fiat for the week. He drove east to Santa Teresa, parked at the foot of the Hill, and slung the rucksack that Marks had given him over his shoulders. He climbed the Hill on foot, paying careful attention to the cars and pedestrians that he passed as he made his ascent. He took the narrow flights of stairs that linked the snaking main road, cutting across the route he had followed for his morning run on the day after the festival. That all seemed like a long, long time ago now; he had been made to look a fool by a man that he had believed he knew. Milton was determined that there would be an accounting for that; the only question that he had to answer was whether Sophia was to be included in that accounting, too.

He reached Ladeira do Meireles, the narrow road that ended with Drake's rented villa, and made his way quickly along it. There was a wall to his left, with the same stunning view of the city that he remembered from before; to his right was a long stretch of wall, decorated by colourful

bougainvillea, with flights of steps leading up to the properties beyond. Milton checked that he was unobserved and
opened the gate to the property adjacent to Drake's villa. He
climbed the steps and looked through the open window: the
rooms beyond were empty, without furniture or anything
else that might have suggested that the place was occupied.
Milton watched Drake's villa. There was no sign that anyone
was at home there, either: the lights were off, and the white
Boxster was missing from the driveway.

Milton made his way across the lawned garden and
vaulted the low wall that marked the boundary between the
two properties. He approached a brick shed that accommodated the trash cans and ducked down behind it. He took
the rucksack off his shoulders, opened it, and pulled out a
pair of latex gloves and latex overshoes. He put them on,
then reached back into the rucksack for the suppressed
Walther. He waited where he was, straining his eyes and
ears for any sign that someone might be in the house. There
was nothing.

He jogged across the garden to the rear door. He remembered the layout of the house and approached the French
doors that opened out onto the patio at the back. The door
was much more secure than the one he had forced to get
into Xavier de Oliveira's home, and he needed to be subtler
than he had before. He opened the rucksack again and withdrew the lock pick set that Marks had given him. He took
out the instruments that he needed, knelt before the lock,
and quickly and expertly picked it. He didn't remember
seeing any sensors inside the property, so he was reasonably
confident as he pushed down on the handle and opened the
door that there would be no alarm to tackle. He heard
nothing and so started the stopwatch on his phone, drew
the Walther, and crept inside.

He cleared the property, moving quickly from room to room until he was sure that it was unoccupied. Then, finally satisfied, he took the rucksack into the sitting room and withdrew the surveillance kit. It was a small aluminium case; he popped the clasps and opened the lid, revealing a variety of bugs, keyloggers and tracking devices nestled inside a foam inset. He unplugged a standard lamp, took a small leather tool roll from the rucksack and opened it, selected a screwdriver and used it to unscrew the double wall socket that had powered the lamp. He found the breaker in a closet, killed the power to the house, then removed the socket and took out an almost identical one from the case. The replacement contained a mains-powered GSM bug that would allow real-time audio monitoring. Milton wired it in, screwed it in place, and plugged in the lamp once more. He flipped the breaker and checked that the lamp still worked; it did.

Milton checked his phone: he had been inside the villa for three minutes.

He went into the bedroom. Everything looked normal, with no sign that anyone had left in a hurry. The doors to the wardrobe were closed, and, when he opened them, he saw that the shoes and clothes were still neatly stored inside. He pulled the bed back and located another wall socket behind it. He replaced this one, too, wiring the bug into the mains and pushing the bed back into place so that his work was hidden.

He checked his stopwatch once more: nine minutes had passed. He wanted to be outside, but there was one final place to check. He went into the study. Drake had an old Dell desktop PC connected to a generic keyboard with a standard USB cable. Milton dropped down to his knees and turned the tower around so that he could get to the connections at the rear. He took out a small forensic keylogger that looked just like a normal USB memory key; he unplugged the keyboard, shoved the keylogger into the jack, and connected the keyboard to it. The logger would record every piece of data transmitted to it from the keyboard and then covertly text it to Milton's phone. He checked his work, and, content that it would be impossible to see unless Drake or Sophia were looking for it, he pushed the tower back into place and left the room.

Twelve minutes. There was no reason to wait any longer. He left through the French doors, closed and re-locked them, and stepped out into the warmth of the afternoon. He walked briskly back along the garden, vaulted the wall into the adjacent property, and started back to his Fiat at the bottom of the Hill.

64

P aulo parked the Mercedes in a quiet spot where it wouldn't be found and walked to the top of the Hill. He paused in a darkened alley, closed his eyes, and tried to compose himself. He was terrified. He looked down at the button on his shirt and tried to see the camera; he couldn't, but that didn't help. Maybe he just didn't know what to look for. Surely it would be obvious to someone else, and that wasn't even taking into account the recorder that was taped to his back. He arched his back and felt it there, the sharp edges digging into his spine. They would see the camera or the recorder, or his panic would give him away. He tried not to imagine what Garanhão would do when he found out that Paulo was spying on him.

But he had no choice. He couldn't run. The man with the pale eyes had killed Alessandro and Junior as if it was of absolutely no consequence to him. The man had warned Paulo that he would find him if he ran, and he frightened Paulo almost as much as Garanhão did.

He thought of Alícia locked in the basement not far

from here, and he knew that he had to do what he had promised he would do.

He squeezed his eyes shut until he could see little starbursts of coloured light against the lids and, taking a deep breath, he reached around his body until he could feel the depression in the body of the recorder. He pressed it, feeling the soft click as the button went down.

He stepped out of the alley and, blinking in the sunlight, walked the short distance to Garanhão's building.

PAULO SAID that he needed to see Garanhão, but he was told to wait in the antechamber outside the room. He sat down and clasped his hands in his lap. His palms were slick with sweat, and his damp fingers slithered against one another. He could feel the recorder against the small of his back; it felt enormous, surely too large for someone not to see it.

The door opened and Garanhão stood there. "Get in here," he snapped.

There was another man inside the room. He was sitting on the sofa, one leg crossed over the other. Paulo recognised him at once: it was the third man from this morning, the man whom Alessandro and Junior had met outside the house before all of them had gone inside.

"This is *senhor* Drake," he said. "He was there this morning."

"Yes," Paulo said. "I saw him."

"He has told me what happened. But I would like to hear it from you, too."

Paulo looked at Drake; the man shuffled uncomfortably, as if what Paulo might say would have consequences for him, too.

"Alessandro called me this morning. He told me to get up here, so I did. I drove him and Junior to Rio Comprido. We waited there until he got a phone call, and then I drove them to a house. They met *senhor* Drake"—he looked at the third man, who glared back at him—"and then they all went inside."

"Go on."

"I heard gunshots. Alessandro and Junior and *senhor* Drake had just gone in. I thought it was them."

"But?"

He looked back to Drake, swallowed down on a dry throat, and went on. "*Senhor* Drake came out of the house. He got into a car and drove away. I didn't know what to do. Alessandro and Junior didn't come out. I thought something must have happened to them."

"And then?" Garanhão asked. "Did you see anyone else?"

He nodded. "Someone else came out of the house."

"Describe him."

"Medium height. White, middle-aged. I was too far back to see much more than that, and he turned away from me."

"Did he see you?"

"I don't think so."

"What did he do?"

"Drove away."

"And then?" Garanhão said. "What did you do after that?"

Paulo recited the story that the old man had suggested. He said that he had gone inside the house, that he had seen three dead bodies, but that he had seen police outside before he could get back to his car. He said that he'd been scared that they would see him if he went back to the car, so he had walked back to the Hill.

"Why didn't you call?"

"My phone," he said. "It's in the car."

Garanhão eyed him. "Really? You couldn't get a taxi?"

"My wallet was there, too. I didn't have any money."

Garanhão stared at Paulo, unblinking, and, for that moment, Paulo was sure that he had seen straight through him.

And then the moment passed. Garanhão changed the subject. "This man you saw," he said. "Do you think you would recognise him?"

"I don't know, Don Rodrigues. I was down the road from him and—"

"But you will look at a picture?"

"Of course."

Garanhão nodded, and Drake took out his phone, woke the screen, and held it up. Paulo looked at a photograph. A man was looking straight into the camera. It was the same man with the same pale blue eyes who had taken him to the motel in Jacarepaguá.

"What do you think?"

"I don't know, Don Rodrigues. As I said—"

"Could it be him?" he cut in.

"Yes," Paulo said. "Maybe. It could be. Who is he?"

"*Senhor* Drake knows him," Garanhão said without attempting to hide his derision.

Paulo glanced across and saw Drake flinch. It was obvious that the man had irritated the don and that he was worried about what that might mean for him. Paulo found that he was relieved; there was someone else to absorb Garanhão's anger.

"His name is John Milton," Drake said.

Paulo didn't know what to say to that, or whether Garanhão wanted anything else from him. There was tension in the room, and it was obvious that Drake was as nervous as he was.

Paulo shuffled. "Is there anything else, Don Rodrigues?"

"No. You can go."

Paulo stood. Drake stood, too, but Garanhão froze him with an upheld hand. "Not you," he said. "You stay. We have things to discuss."

Paulo didn't need to be told twice. He made his way across the room, opened the door, and stepped out into the cool darkness of the antechamber beyond. One of the young bodyguards was lounging there, his AK propped against the wall, and it took all of Paulo's strength to put one foot in front of the other and make for the stairs down to the street. He was buffeted by a sudden light-headedness and an urge to vomit that was almost impossible to suppress. He heard Garanhão's angry voice as he stumbled down the stairs, pushed open the door, and stepped out onto the dusty street beyond.

65

Paulo went straight to the warehouse. He told himself that he should move slowly so that the camera could record everything that the man he now knew as Milton would need, but he was too scared to take his time. He went in through the open door, climbed the steps to the dock and hurried through the empty office. He descended the stairs to the basement and opened the door to the crawlspace. Alícia was sitting with her back to the wall. Paulo looked into her face and, in that moment, the doubts and fears were obliterated by a fresh surge of shame at what he had helped to make possible. Tears were running down her cheeks, which were already glistening. She lifted her head and looked at him.

"Where have you been?" she said, wiping her nose with the back of her hand.

"I'm sorry," he said.

"You've been gone so long," she said, her voice shaking.

"I had something that I had to do. Come here."

He knelt down and encouraged her to crawl over to him.

She sobbed, but came forward and allowed him to sweep her into a tight embrace.

"Are you all right?" he asked her.

"I want my mama."

He turned to make sure that they were alone and then, speaking quietly, he said, "You're going to see her soon."

"When?"

"Soon," Paulo repeated. "I'm going to get you out of here."

"Please," the girl said, clinging even more tightly to him. "Please. *Please*. I don't want to be here anymore."

"It won't be long, I promise. You just need to keep being patient, just like you have been."

"How long?"

"Very soon. Can you be brave?"

She sniffled.

"Can you?"

"Yes," she said quietly. "I'll try."

He put his hands on the girl's shoulders and moved her back so that he could look into her face. "You need to go back inside again," he said. "It won't be for much longer."

"You're not staying with me?"

"I have to see someone. It's important. It's about getting you out. Is that all right?"

She looked as if she was going to cry again; instead, she swallowed hard and nodded.

"Good girl," Paulo said.

He rested his hand on her cheek, gave what he hoped was his most reassuring smile, and then gently impelled her to go back into the crawlspace. She did, taking up the same position with her back against the wall. Paulo closed the door, locked it, and put the key back into his pocket. He reminded himself that he would have to give the key to

Milton when he delivered the recorder with the video footage.

He didn't want to leave her alone again, but he told himself that it would be the last time and, fighting back a mixture of contrition and fear, he climbed the stairs to the office once more.

Antonio Rodrigues looked out of the window at the vista laid out beneath him. *Rio*. That was one of the things about living at the top of the Hill that he liked so much: he could see everything, from the thousands of makeshift buildings that made up the *favela* to the spires of Leblon and Ipanema. The pleasure he felt was derived not from the impressive nature of the view, but by the knowledge that his influence extended as far as he could see.

He turned away from the window and the irritation returned. Shawn Drake was pacing the room. The man had annoyed him before, but that was nothing compared to the exasperation that he felt now. It had all been so promising before. Garanhão had approached him after his brother had asked him whether there was a way that he could exert influence on Felipe Saverin and the investigation that was systematically bringing down the pillars of Brazilian society. Garanhão was not interested in maintaining the status quo and had even enjoyed vicarious thrills as pompous politicians and businessmen had found their habitual immunities no longer protected them. He had smiled as they were paraded across the evening news and the morning papers, given the same inglorious treatment that was usually reserved for *traficantes*. But Garanhão had made many millions of *reais* from the corrupt men and women who were now in full-blown retreat, and it was in his best interests to keep the money flowing. He had told his brother that he would do what he could, and he had been true to his word.

Garanhão had paid a police officer he employed to investigate Saverin and to see whether there were weaknesses in his security that could be exploited. The officer had identified Shawn Drake as a particular weakness. Drake was greedy and vain and had overreached himself with expensive loans to finance his extravagant lifestyle. There was a woman involved, and Drake was pushing himself beyond his limit in order to impress her. He had been refused credit by the banks after defaulting on previous loans, and now his only recourse was the predatory lenders who preyed on the vulnerable. Garanhão had bought the loans and that meant, to all intents and purposes, that he had bought Drake, too.

He had then given him an opportunity to wipe the slate clean: deliver Saverin's wife and daughter and he would liquidate the debt. Drake had said yes with an alacrity that had both disgusted and amused Garanhão, and had assembled a plan that Garanhão had been happy to back. Drake would deliver the Saverins in return for his debt and an extra quarter of a million dollars to start a new life. Alessandro had shot him during the abduction, the flak jacket that he wore beneath his shirt preventing any serious injury, and Drake had been whisked away in the confusion that followed the shoot-out. Garanhão had plenty of other officers in his employ, and a few additional *reais* in their monthly stipends meant that there was no investigation into his involvement.

Everything had gone so well until this morning.

"This man," Garanhão said. "Milton. Tell me about him."

Drake stopped pacing and replied in Portuguese. "He used to be a soldier. We served in the same regiment. A long time ago."

"You told me that he was nothing to be concerned about. 'Nothing special,' you said. 'A pathetic drunk.' Did you underestimate him?"

Drake shifted uncomfortably. "Perhaps."

"And now he has caused me a very serious inconvenience. Six of my men are dead because of your mistake. Four when we took the girl, and now Alessandro and Junior."

"With respect, Don Rodrigues, we wouldn't be having this conversation if they had finished the job when they took the girl."

Garanhão felt his temper flare; he had never been very good at hiding it, and Drake saw at once that he had chosen his words poorly.

"This was *your* plan," Garanhão spat over Drake's half-finished apology. "This is *your* mistake. I hold *you* responsible. And don't ever talk to me like that again."

"Don Rodrigues," Drake said, his hands raised in an attempt to placate him, "I'm sorry. I didn't mean to insult you."

Garanhão dismissed the apology. "You want to make this right? Then find this man and kill him."

"That won't be easy. He—"

Garanhão clapped his hands together. "Stop making excuses!" he snapped. "Do I have to do everything myself?"

He swore under his breath and went over to the table where he had left one of his burner phones. He opened Telegram, the encrypted messenger service that he relied upon to communicate with the other members of the gang, selected the picture of a beaten-up BMW that had been sent to him an hour ago, and tossed the phone across the room to Drake.

"See the photograph? My lookout saw that car near de Oliveira's house this morning. He said a white man got out of it. He is sure that the white man is your friend. I have passed the details to one of the policemen who helps me. He will try to find the car. If we find the car, perhaps we can find your Mr. Milton. And, if we do, you can go and do what you should have done this morning. Kill the *filho da puta*. Make him wish he had never come to Rio."

67

Milton drove the Fiat back to the motel. He passed through the arch onto the lot and saw Marks's BMW parked in the same spot. He climbed the step to the veranda and knocked on the door.

Marks opened the door.

"Afternoon," he said.

"Is he here?"

"In the bathroom. He's just thrown up."

"And?"

"Come in. I'll show you."

Milton stepped into the room and closed the door behind him. The cheap television on the bureau was switched on, and a cable had been run from a port on the side to a small black DVR recorder.

The bathroom door opened and Paulo came into the bedroom. He looked pale and there was a film of sweat on his forehead.

"Just in time," Marks said. "I was just going to play it again."

"You okay?" Milton asked him.

"I feel like shit," Paulo said.

"You look like shit," Milton replied. "But you're nearly done now. Was it okay?"

"I felt like they all knew."

"Yet you're still here," Marks observed. "I'd say you got away with it. Sit down."

Paulo sat on the edge of the bed. Milton stayed where he was and waited as Marks fiddled with the playback functions. The TV screen flickered with static before a shot of the interior of a car replaced it.

Milton watched as the picture flared, the camera struggling for a moment with overexposure as Paulo came out of the car, walked out of a darkened space, and emerged onto a bright and busy street. The camera did not come with a microphone, and the street—full of traffic and men and women going about their business—was silent.

"Where is this?" Milton asked.

"The top of the Hill. That building over there is where Garanhão has his meetings. The building I've just come out of is the warehouse—that's where they're keeping Alícia. I go back there later."

Milton gestured, and Marks fast-forwarded the footage. They watched in silence as the POV shot accelerated along the street, turned to the first building, and halted by a closed door.

Marks ran the footage at normal speed.

"Tell us what's happening here," Milton said.

"They have guards on the door," Paulo said. "I told them I was there to see the don."

Milton watched as the footage rolled on. Paulo waited outside the door and then was led up to a room on what looked to be the top floor. He was met by a man who Milton, although he had not seen him before, knew at once was the don. He was young, slender, and had an air of nonchalant authority that was evident even without the sound to hear what he was saying.

"That's him," Paulo said. "That's Garanhão."

Paulo moved into the room, and Milton saw the second man sitting on the sofa with one leg crossed over the other. He bit his lip to stop himself from cursing.

Marks must have noticed him tensing up. "Your friend?"

"That's him," Milton said.

"His name is Drake," Paulo offered.

"Did he speak to you?"

"Not really. He was there to see the don. Garanhão was not happy with him."

"He's going to be thrilled with him when I'm done," Milton muttered.

The footage continued as Paulo moved across the room and Garanhão started talking.

"What did you tell them?" Marks asked.

"What you said I should: that I was outside the house and I heard gunshots. I said I panicked and left."

Milton only half heard Paulo's answer. His attention was fixed on Garanhão. He noticed the way he held the thumb and forefinger of his right hand together when he emphasised what he was saying; he saw the glint of a gold cap in his mouth when he yawned; he saw dead eyes, without life, and recognised a quality that he shared. A lack of empathy. The absence of compassion. The eyes of a killer. He was trying to do better, but he knew that they were cut from the same cloth.

"Did they ask about me?" Milton said.

"Yes," Paulo replied. "*Senhor* Drake showed me a picture. I said I couldn't be sure that it was you."

Milton was fine about that. Drake knew that Milton was

out there. He wouldn't know whether Milton would run or come after him. The uncertainty would keep him off balance; uncertainty often led to mistakes, and Milton would be ready to take advantage of even the smallest error.

"Garanhão knows your name," Paulo said. "John Milton."

Drake would have given the don everything he knew. It made no difference; Drake's information was incomplete.

"Did you go to where they are keeping Alícia?" he asked.

"Afterwards," Paulo said.

"Move it on," Milton said.

Marks forwarded the footage. They watched as the conversation with Garanhão and Drake ended and Paulo made his way back outside. He crossed the road to the warehouses. Marks slowed the footage and, at Milton's suggestion, Paulo provided a running commentary. Milton watched as Paulo went around to a loading bay at the rear of the building.

"The door is open during the day and closed at night," he said.

"Could you open it?"

"Probably."

They watched as Paulo went into the warehouse and climbed a flight of steps to a dock. Milton concentrated hard, committing as much of the building to memory as he could. He paid attention to the doors and corridors that led away from the bay, noted the vehicles that were parked, saw a walkway that ran around the wall fifteen feet up from the ground, noted the positions of the lights fixed to the wall and those suspended overhead.

"Keep going?" Marks asked.

Milton nodded. The footage continued as Paulo passed through an empty office and then descended a set of steps to a basement. There was a door in the wall with a light shining beneath it. They saw Paulo's hand reach forward to insert a key into a lock; the key turned and the door opened. The camera flared again as it adapted to the bright artificial light behind the door and then snapped back into focus: there was a girl sitting on the floor of a narrow crawlspace, her knees drawn up to her chest and her head down. She looked up, right at Paulo, and Milton felt a kick in his gut.

Alícia Saverin.

68

I t was ten in the evening when Marks drove Milton to the cache. He parked the BMW in front of the garage, and both men got out. The drive had been quiet. Milton didn't much feel like talking, and Marks, perhaps aware of that, let him sit and think about what he was going to do. Milton knew that he was taking a big risk. He knew that he did not have the element of surprise, but trusted, instead, that the audacity—perhaps even the stupidity—of an attack in the heart of the gang's territory would mean that Garanhão and his men would discount it. He had decent intelligence thanks to the footage that Paulo had provided, and, in the young *carioca*, he had an inside man who would be able to warn him of anything that he needed to know before he went too far to turn back.

Milton would have preferred to have had time to scout the target area himself, but Paulo had made it plain that time was not a luxury that they had. Beyond that, Milton did not want to leave the girl there for a moment longer than was necessary. He did not like to cut corners—his careful preparation was one of the reasons that he had lasted as long as he had in a profession where longevity was the exception rather than the rule—but he couldn't see how that could be avoided now.

"Get it unlocked," Milton told Marks. "I need to make a phone call."

Marks nodded. He unlocked the roller door and heaved it up and out of the way. He switched on the light, went into the garage, and lowered the door again so that it was almost closed.

There was no point in pretending otherwise: Milton was nervous. What he was proposing was dangerous. It was dangerous, but that was no reason to put it off. This would be his best opportunity to get the girl back again. Perhaps his only chance. The longer he waited, the longer the odds would be.

He took one of the burner phones that Marks had provided, switched it on, and dialled the number that GCHQ had found.

The call took a moment to connect.

"Hello?"

"Judge Saverin?"

"Who *is* this?" The reply was indignant; this was a personal number that would not have been made readily available to anyone outside the family.

"It's John Smith."

Saverin's reply replaced irritation with confusion. "Smith?"

"I was there when—"

"Where is my daughter?" he cut in.

"I'm sorry to call unannounced," Milton said.

"Where is she?" he said with sudden urgency. "Alícia— where is she?"

"I need you to listen very carefully, Judge. Shawn Drake

was working for Antonio Rodrigues. You know who he is? Garanhão?"

"Of course I know who he is," Saverin snapped.

"Garanhão has her. I expect he took her to order—if you asked me to guess, I would say that one of the men you're prosecuting hired him to do it."

Milton heard the sound of footsteps on the line and then a muffled, whispered conversation in Portuguese. He guessed that Valentina Saverin must have heard her husband mention their daughter's name.

"Please pay attention. It's very important."

"Jesus," Saverin swore. "*Jesus*. Do you know where she is?"

"I do. And I'm going to go and get her. I'll bring her to you."

"Where is she? In Rocinha? Please—just tell me."

"It won't be helpful for you to know that now."

"Of course it would," he snapped again. "I'll tell the police—they'll go and get her. They'll send a battalion."

"I think we both know that wouldn't work." Milton spoke calmly. "Even if we assume that Rodrigues doesn't have officers on the payroll—and we both know that he almost certainly does—his men will see the police coming as soon as they start up the Hill. If Alícia is lucky, they'll just move her somewhere else. If she's unlucky..." Milton let that end without elaboration. "If they do move her, I might not be able to find her again. I have an advantage—they don't know that I know where she is—but that's temporary. Involving the police would mean that we have no advantage at all."

"I'm sorry—I'm... I'm..."

"I know this is a surprise."

He heard the same female voice in the background and

then a more muffled conversation as, he guessed, Saverin cupped his hand over his phone.

"Judge," Milton said, "I don't have long. I just wanted to let you know that I'm going to go and get her."

"With who?"

"I have a little help, but I work better alone."

"It's the fucking Hill," Saverin said desperately. "You're going to go *alone*? You won't make it halfway up."

"You're going to have to trust me."

"You already lost her once."

The jibe was automatic and stinging, but Milton understood it. It was understandable; he might have felt the same way if the shoe had been on the other foot.

"I have some experience in this kind of work—it isn't the first time that I've done something like this."

"But..." His protest died out, and there was just the buzz of static on the line.

"I'll call when I have her," Milton said.

"Please be careful."

"I will," Milton said. "There's one other thing: if anything happens to me, you'll be contacted by a friend of mine. His name is Harry. He'll tell you everything that I know. Who is involved, where they are keeping her—everything. I hope that won't be necessary, but, in the event that it is, I want you to know that you can trust him."

Milton paused.

"*Senhor* Smith?" the judge said. "Hello? Are you still there?"

"You'll have her tonight," Milton said. "Goodbye."

He ended the call.

69

Milton lifted the roller door, ducked inside, and lowered it behind him. He followed the path between the trash and other detritus until he reached the false wall. Marks had already slid the door out of the way and was inside the hidden cupboard at the back.

He turned at the sound of Milton's approach. "All okay?"

"Fine," Milton said. "If anything happens to me, call Saverin. Tell him everything."

"I will," Marks said. He might have said that he hoped that wouldn't be necessary, but he did not; he knew, just as Milton did, that the night was going to be difficult, and there was no point in wasting time on platitudes that might suggest otherwise. "Let's get you equipped," he said instead. "Are you going in big?"

"Reasonably big," Milton replied.

Milton took off his jacket, took down one of the ballistic vests that hung from a peg, and slid his arms through the sleeves. His muscles ached; it was a reminder that he was far from one hundred percent. He would not have been allowed to go into the field after having been involved in a crash so recently, but, once more, caution was not something that Alícia Saverin could afford.

The vest was made of Nomex and had pockets on the front and rear for armour plates. It had an upside-down scabbard on the left side of the chest with an RAF Aircrew emergency knife fixed inside it. The scabbard was spring-loaded to keep the knife in place, and the weapon was released by pressing the two levers on each side of the handle. The blade was rustproof and had been kept in decent condition with regular sprays of lubricant.

Marks found an eight-inch-by-ten-inch plate in a cupboard and slid it into the front pouch. It was heavier and much bulkier now, but the addition would lend him significantly more protection. There was a very good chance that he would need it. The Nomex was dark and reasonably discreet against the black T-shirt that he was wearing. Milton put his regular jacket on over it.

Next, he took a plain leather sports bag from a cupboard on the floor and unzipped it. He couldn't take anything too bulky, so he ruled out all of the long guns. Instead, he selected a Heckler & Koch G36 for his main weapon. It was the K model with the shorter barrel, designed specifically for the German KSK special forces. Milton had had experience with the weapon at the training facility in Wiltshire before he'd left the Group. It was made from polymer fibre plastics and was light and durable. It was a 5.56mm weapon, and Milton stocked up with six full magazines. He put them and the gun into the bag.

Discretion was less important now, and he wanted a bigger pistol to exchange for the Walther that he had been using. Marks offered him a SIG Sauer P320. It held seventeen rounds in each magazine; he took three, shoved one into the magwell, and put the pistol and the two spares into the bag.

He was nearly done, but not quite.

"Grenades?"

"What do you want?"

"Flashbangs."

One of the cupboards contained a box that held a selection of grenades. Marks took out six G60 grenades and dropped them into the bag. Milton zipped it up and hefted it; it was already heavy.

"Anything else?" Marks asked.

"Night vision."

Marks opened another box. He took out an NVG monocle with a head mount composed of lightweight straps that ran around the crown, a forehead pad and a chin cup. Milton slipped it on and adjusted the straps until he was sure that it was secure and comfortable. The monocle sat over his left eye. He removed the monocle and put it into the bag with the rest of the equipment, grabbed the stick of camo paint that Marks offered and dropped that inside, too. They went back into the garage, closed up the cache, and made their way outside again. Marks gave the roller door a downward shove, sending it clattering down the rails to crash against the ground, and secured it with the padlock.

"Ready?" Marks asked him.

Milton slung the bag of gear across his shoulder. "Let's get started."

70

The traffic was heavy despite the hour as they drove to the Hill that accommodated the sprawling *favela*. A road branched off the main route, and Marks headed up it, but they were only able to drive for five minutes before the road narrowed until it was little more than an alleyway, with a series of other passages and alleys feeding off it like the tributaries of a river.

"This is as far as we can go," Marks said.

Milton had studied the map and had discussed the local geography with Paulo. This wasn't a surprise.

"We'll do it like we agreed. I'll take the rest on foot."

Marks eyed the passers-by suspiciously. "I won't be able to stay here," he said. "Too much attention—I'll stick out a mile. There was an opening back there." He angled his head toward the bottom of the Hill. "On the right. Did you see it?"

Milton said that he did.

"I'll put the car in there and wait. If it gets too hot, I'll move somewhere else, but I'll be close. Call me when you're on the way down again."

"You've got your weapon?"

Marks reached down beneath his seat and took out the Walther that Milton had exchanged for the SIG.

"When was the last time you fired it?" Milton asked him.

"I think I've got this, John."

"Just be careful."

Milton reached for the door handle.

"You know where you're headed?" Marks asked.

"Up," Milton replied, nodding to the confluence of alleys and passages, all of them tracking their way up the Hill. "And I can track Paulo. I can see where he is."

"Good luck, Milton."

Marks put out his hand and Milton shook it. "Thanks, Harry. For everything. I'll see you later."

He got out of the car, took the bag from the back seat, and followed the quietest alley around a bend until he found somewhere that he wouldn't be observed. He checked the holstered SIG that he wore at his waist, tightened the straps of the ballistic vest, and then arranged his jacket so that it covered both the vest and the gun. He put a cap on his head and pulled it down to cover his face, slung the bag over his shoulder, and set off again.

71

Milton heard the distant thump of bass. He followed the sound of the music until he reached Rua Um, the road that snaked up the Hill and around which the *favela* had coalesced. There was a late-night chemist on the other side of the road, and the posters in the window advertised shampoo and headache pills. The road ahead was blocked by a makeshift barrier: fuel barrels, shopping carts, and old vehicles had been put together to prevent anyone from continuing up the Hill. The blockade wasn't guarded, but, as Milton looked through the flickering flames of a bonfire that had been set just behind it, he could see men with automatic rifles. He doubted that was the extent of the defences. He knew that the *favela* had not yet been subdued by the military police, and he doubted that they would choose a night like this to try to begin an operation. No, Milton thought, these defences were against the other gangs who might regard what was going on tonight with jealous eyes and seek a slice of the action for themselves.

Milton watched the men from the other side of the

barrier and determined that they were not particularly vigilant. He waited for the next large group to squeeze around the barrier and followed close behind them. The guards were smoking cigarettes—Milton recognised the sweet smell of dope—and, perhaps since the rest of the group was comprised of kids who were obviously here for the party, they paid him little attention as he slipped through the line.

Paulo had explained what was happening tonight: this was a *baile funk*, a street party organised by Red Command, the cartel that controlled the *favela*. The *traficantes* had cordoned off the Hill partway up, transforming the area into what was effectively an enormous open-air nightclub. The street was thronged with people. Local entrepreneurs had set up counters made from breeze blocks and planks of wood; they sold bottles of beer and scooped ladles of something alcoholic from giant bowls and poured them into paper cups. Dealers were selling cocaine out of large plastic bags. Shirtless teenage boys paraded up and down the street, their sweat-slicked torsos decorated with tattoos that extolled the gangs and denigrated the police. Others held aloft AK-47s, and Milton heard the sporadic rattle of automatic gunfire as the rifles were fired into the sky. Apart from the AKs, Milton saw men and women with M16s and rocket launchers. No one cared.

There was no sign of the police, and Milton could see that it would have been impossible for them to intervene, or even to try to prevent the multiple breaches of the law that were being committed with impunity.

He followed the road to a section where it switched back on itself to continue its climb up the contours of the Hill. A square had formed around the turn, with businesses on all sides. The square looked as if it was the epicentre of the party. One end of it had been given over to a wall of loudspeakers, and deafening, aggressive local rap pounded out of them so loudly that Milton could feel each thudding beat in his gut. The square was packed with revellers of all ages: youngsters, middle-aged parents, and even the elderly all danced together and whooped along as an MC with a microphone led a call and response routine. Milton's Portuguese wasn't good enough to translate it, but it was evidently directed at the authorities. The music changed, and 'Fuck Tha Police' by N.W.A. roared out.

Milton stopped and looked, unable at first to see how he could make his way farther up the Hill. The space was crammed with people, and two large bonfires, one burning an effigy of the president, spilled smoke into the night sky. A firework whooshed up into the darkness and exploded, scattering colourful sparks down onto the rooftops, and, as Milton blinked the glare of its detonation from his eyes, he saw what he was looking for. There was a narrow alleyway, little more than a blade of darkness between two buildings; it would have been very easy to miss it. He turned sideways so he could slip through a gap between two women who were shaking their arms to the repetitive thud of the music and made his way to the mouth of the alley.

It became gloomy. The alley wound left and right as it traced a path away from the square. There was a little light from the bonfires that lit the way, but, as Milton took a sharp right-hand switchback, that light was extinguished and the alleyway became almost completely dark. The buildings reached higher overhead, the gap between them distinguished by a scattering of stars and the occasional flash of a firework. Milton proceeded, realised that he had taken a wrong turn, and retraced his steps to the junction where he had gone wrong. He was about to take the alternative branch when a man appeared from around a corner, his face briefly illuminated as a rocket detonated in the sky overhead. He had painted his face to look like a zombie, with pale skin and gore around his mouth. Milton stepped back; the man hooted at him before staggering away to be absorbed by the darkness.

Just a drunk.

Milton turned into the passage from which the man had emerged and continued to climb.

72

The alley narrowed the farther Milton followed it. The buildings drew closer on either side until the walls brushed his shoulders. He could see why Garanhão had chosen an area like this for his base of operations: apart from the fact that the locals were most likely on his side—because he either paid them or frightened them—the warren of narrow streets and passages, full of choke points and bottlenecks, would have been almost impossible to assault. A single operator had a chance, but a group of police or soldiers would have had to proceed with extreme caution.

The passage opened out a little so that he could walk normally again, but it remained restricted and claustrophobic. Milton gazed up and saw that he was only about two-thirds of the way up the Hill. He reached a branching point and turned left into it, following the path as it ascended a flight of uneven stone steps. Milton stopped counting at the hundredth step, his quadriceps burning as he lugged his bag of gear up and up and up. The passage wound left and right as it climbed, cleaving between the flanks of exposed brick

houses, across a tiny plaza—thankfully deserted—and back
to the steps once more.

Milton kept climbing for another five minutes until the
steps stopped and the passage emerged from between the
buildings to deposit him in another plaza. This one was
much larger than the one he had passed through earlier. He
waited in the shadows and observed his surroundings: there
was a tiny chapel across from him, a wooden cross fixed to
its roof, and a corrugated metal door standing open so that
the light from inside could spill out. The chapel was
hemmed in by houses that were distinguished by the
numbers that had been spray-painted on their sides. He saw
a large water tank made from rusted metal, with a nest of
rubber hoses emerging from an opening and snaking across
the plaza to supply the houses through doors and windows.
The plaza was atop the Hill, and, when Milton looked
through gaps between the houses, he could see the staggering vista beyond: the rump of Sugarloaf Mountain, the
statue of Christ the Redeemer with His arms spread wide
and, laid out beneath him, the lights of downtown Rio.
Volleys of fireworks were being launched from the *favela*.
One would explode, sending its colourful debris back down
to earth, and then, a moment later, the eye would be drawn
to another and then another. The booms rolled over the city,   .
a hundred different peals of thunder.

Milton turned his attention back to his immediate
surroundings. There were more people here. A group of
teenage boys came out of a brick shack with a wooden patio
that had evidently been turned into a bar. Two of them
carried four large one-litre bottles of Itaipava while the
other two carried AK-47s. Milton doubted that they were
older than fifteen. He waited in the shadows as they passed,
listening to their raucous conversation until he couldn't hear

it any longer. The bar was doing a brisk trade. The proprietor had set up a makeshift barbecue, with a metal grid laid on two brick pillars with a fire burning beneath it. A man was cooking chicken on the grid, selling the cooked meat to a loose queue of waiting customers. A half-dozen little kids gambolled across the cobbles of the plaza, dragging a kite behind them and trying to get it to take flight in the limp breeze. They whooped with pleasure as a gust of humid wind caught the kite and sent it high overhead, the string cracking as it sought to break free. Others were turned away from him, leaning on a rickety fence that marked a steep drop, watching the colourful display over the city.

Milton took out his phone and swiped across to the app he needed. It allowed him to plot his position against the GPS signals of the two others who had agreed to be added to his account. His position was represented by a solid blue dot. There were two rectangles below the map: one was labelled 'M' and the other 'P.' He tapped the rectangle for 'M' and waited as the map updated, showing a second dot that was to Milton's south, farther down the Hill. Marks hadn't moved far from where Milton had left him. It looked like he was in position for the extraction. That was good.

He tapped the rectangle that was marked with a 'P.' A third dot appeared, this one to the west of his position. Milton tapped the dot, and the phone reported that it was a quarter of a mile from his present location. Milton turned to the west and looked: a road fed into the plaza. It ran along the top of the Hill, following a ridge. There was a warehouse there, perhaps three hundred metres from the plaza. Milton recognised it from Paulo's video.

Milton heard a cry of dismay and turned to see the kite floating up into the darkness, the string snapped. The children hooted and hollered, and the men and women at the bar turned to watch them. Milton seized his opportunity, stepping out of the alley and following the shadows that gathered around the buildings to skirt the open space until he was at the road.

He walked quickly—but not too quickly—in the direction of the warehouse.

73

M ilton closed in. The warehouse was made out of bare brick that had not been well cared for: chunks of the wall were missing, and the rest had been covered in graffiti. Milton walked on. He saw an alleyway just before the building; it plunged down between two shacks made of brick and sheets of corrugated metal. Feral dogs pawed at the dirt in front of the houses, slinking out of his way as he cut between them and stepped down into the alley. The alley bent around to the west and approached the warehouse from the side facing the slope. It was the route Paulo had taken on the video.

Milton moved more slowly now. He would have had a difficult time explaining to a local why a gringo was at the summit of Rocinha, and he knew that his difficulties would be multiplied now that he was close to the seat of Garan-hão's empire. He dropped his right hand to the holster, popping the snap button and releasing the loop holder so that he could take out the SIG quickly should he need to.

The alley reached the building and opened into a road that, while wider, was still only wide enough for a car to pass with a few inches at either side. The road climbed up from the Hill, levelled out for a short stretch, and then descended to a roller door that Milton knew from the video opened into the main body of the warehouse. Milton waited in the darkness that surrounded the junction of the road and the alley. He looked back to the roller door and saw that it was closed, with a little light from the interior leaking out from beneath the bottom edge. His eye was drawn up to the roof of the building. He saw the shape of a man. The man moved, and Milton saw that he was carrying a long object: a rifle, most likely an AK.

Milton retraced his steps back to a doorway and backed into it. He laid the bag on the ground and crouched down next to it. He quietly pulled back the zip, took out the grenades, and attached them to the fabric loops that ran down the sides of his ballistic vest. He took out the HK, checked that the first magazine was properly loaded, and then shoved the second and third mags into the pouches at the bottom of the vest. He took another two magazines for the pistol and put those in his left trouser pocket so that he would be able to exchange them quickly should the gun run dry. He reached down into the bag again and took out the camo paint, daubing it across his face in broad, dark swathes. He collected the NVG monocle and the head mount, adjusting it so that the monocle was positioned over his eye. He switched the unit on and looked back at the sentry: he could see more clearly now and confirmed that he did have an AK. The glow from beneath the closed door was amplified by the monocle, a bloom of greenish-white against the otherwise green-washed building.

Milton pushed the monocle up, pressed himself back against the door, and took a moment to think. He let the HK hang loose on the strap and closed his eyes, breathing deeply, readying himself. His head was aching and he felt sluggish. He knew he was still suffering from the concussion. He wasn't even close to being at his best. He felt vulnerable, but he couldn't wait. If he didn't go now, the girl was finished.

He exhaled. He was getting too old for this.

He took the phone again and opened a message that he had already composed.

Just one word: NOW.

He pressed send.

PART VI

THE SEVENTH DAY

74

Paulo had arrived at the warehouse ten minutes earlier. He could see that the office was occupied and, aware that he had never been to see Alícia as late as this before, he found his way to the bathroom and shut himself in an empty stall. He lowered the toilet seat and sat down with his back against the cistern. He was almost rigid with fear. He had seen four different men here since he had arrived; some had left, but that was still more than he had ever seen before. Was it because of Milton and what he had done in the house in Rio Comprido? Garanhão knew that there was a threat moving against him; it looked as if he had responded by beefing up his security.

He squeezed his eyes tightly shut. What was he going to do? He didn't want to leave Alícia, but he couldn't go down to the basement without going through the office, and he was frightened that the men inside would ask him what he was doing there so late.

Paulo's phone buzzed. He was almost too scared to look at it.

NOW.

He fought back a moment of dizziness. He knew this was a moment that would determine the path his life would take. He could do what Milton had requested and pin his hopes on the fanciful notion that he would—that he *could*—do what he had promised to do. Or he could ignore him, go out the front door, and go home. But that would leave Alícia in the crawlspace. It would be her death, because Paulo knew that there was no way she was ever going to be allowed to go home. He thought of Eloá and how he would have given anything to make her well. He would have given his own life, without thinking, if his sacrifice meant that she could live a normal and happy life. But the cancer was not so accommodating; it did not make offers like that. Paulo had that choice, though: Eloá was the same age as Alícia, with so much in common save the good fortune of being born into different circumstances. He could do something right now that would offer the girl a chance of returning to her happy life. And, selfishly, it might absolve him of a little of his sin, too.

He knew that he had no choice. He opened the door of the stall and left the bathroom.

A teenager, eighteen or nineteen, was smoking a cigarette on the loading dock with his AK propped up against the rail.

"What you doing?"

"I'm here for the girl. Garanhão told me to look after her. What are you doing?"

Paulo's attitude evidently surprised the young man. He straightened up. "The boss said there might be trouble."

"So look like you're taking it seriously," Paulo snapped.

The teenager flicked his cigarette aside and, with a glare in Paulo's direction, made his way along the dock and into the corridor that serviced the main entrance on the other side of the building.

Paulo waited until he was gone and then descended the steps. He crossed the bay to the plant room with the equipment that powered the warehouse. He pushed the door and went inside. The room was full of machinery. There were large metal boxes that had been bolted to the concrete floor, with wires leading to and from them. Paulo was already sweating, and the humidity in here made it worse. The room was lit by a malfunctioning strip light overhead; the light buzzed and fizzed, strobing on and off.

Milton had told him what the box containing the circuit breakers would look like, and he squinted through the intermittent light until he found a metal box on the wall with a hinged cover that opened when Paulo pulled it back. There was a panel inside with six individual breakers and one red master switch to control them all. The switch was pushed up, with ON visible beneath it.

Paulo reached for it with a damp, trembling hand, rested his index finger on it and, closing his eyes and praying to Jesus, he pulled it down.

The flickering light went out.

75

M ilton watched and waited. He shouldered the G36 and aimed it up at the sentry on the roof. The light cut out.

He heard a muffled shout from inside the building.

Milton pulled the trigger. The rifle kicked, but Milton had anticipated it and sent another two rounds down range. At least one of the rounds found its target; the sniper stumbled forward, toppled over the parapet at the edge of the roof, and plunged to the ground below. His body hit the concrete in front of the roller door, bounced once, then lay still.

Milton moved. He led with the G36, staying in the shadows at the side of the road and descending the ramp to the small side door to the left of the roller door and the sentry's twisted body. He reached the door and paused there; he could hear the sound of raised voices from inside. He reached down with his left hand and tried the handle; the door was locked.

Milton heard the sound of a key being turned, and the

door opened. Paulo stood in the doorway and saw the sprawled-out body of the sentry.

"*Cristo*," he mumbled.

"How many inside?"

"Um... um..." He was panicking.

"How many?"

"Two in the office and one in the loading bay. He went to the front of the building, but he would have heard the shots. Those are just the ones that I saw—there might be others."

"Armed?"

"Yes."

"With what?"

"The man in the bay has an AK-47. The ones in the office —I don't know."

Milton gave a single sharp nod of understanding. "You know where you're going?"

Paulo nodded.

"Take this."

Milton held out the SIG. He would have preferred to keep it, but he didn't like the idea of sending Paulo onto the street without a means of defending himself. There was a good chance it was going to get busy.

"I can't—"

"It's ready to fire. Just point and squeeze. I—"

Milton didn't finish. He shouldered Paulo out of the way and raised the compact assault rifle. He fired a short burst, and the man with the AK who had appeared in the doorway behind Paulo fell back. The noise of the weapon was impossibly loud, rattling around the corridor. Paulo swivelled. The man toppled over, fell to the floor, and lay still. Blowback was splattered all over the bare concrete blocks.

Milton grabbed Paulo and turned him around.

"Fuck," Paulo said, his eyes wide with fear.

"Go," Milton said. "Don't stop. I'll see you at the bottom."

M ilton shouldered the rifle and aimed it ahead of him as he made his way inside. He stepped over the body of the man he had just shot. The man had seen him, and Milton had had no choice but to put him down before he could fire on them, but it had spent all of his most precious capital: the element of surprise. Milton would manage with his other advantages. He was well equipped, and this kind of closed-building assault was something that he had trained for so often it was like muscle memory. And he had the darkness. The monocle amplified the faint light that leaked in from the outside. He would be able to see the bad guys; they would struggle to see him.

How many left? Paulo had said there were three, but he wasn't convincing. Milton would anticipate more.

He followed Paulo's instructions, exiting the side corridor and coming out into the main warehouse space. He paused to check that it was empty, climbed the steps to the dock, and then crossed it to the door that Paulo had indicated.

The door was ajar; Milton nudged it with his left hand,

pushing it open just a little. He saw a flash of movement through the gap between the door and the jamb and hopped to the side a fraction of a moment before he heard the rattle of an automatic. Chunks of the door were torn out and spat into the loading bay, the bullets passing through the space that Milton had just vacated.

He let the HK hang loose on its strap, reached for a flashbang, yanked out the pin, and tossed it through the gap in the door and into the room beyond. The fuse was set on a three-second delay, and when it detonated, it lit the flash powder in the central cartridge. Milton looked down as it exploded, the flash pouring out between the gap and briefly casting his shadow behind him. The boom was deafening.

Milton had a short window of opportunity. He raised the HK and booted the door. The flash had subsided enough so that all that was left was just a faint wash on the monocle. Milton scanned the room: a table, two chairs, one of which had been overturned. He saw the shape of a man on the floor. Milton aimed and squeezed off a three-round burst. He knew he had hit his target; he didn't need to check, and he didn't have the time for it. He turned his head and saw the shape of a second man against the wall. This man was holding the rifle that had most likely been used to shoot through the door. Milton aimed into the middle of the man's torso and unloaded three more rounds.

He moved into the room, checked that the targets were down, and made sure with two further close-range shots to the head. He turned through three hundred and sixty degrees to confirm that the room was clear and found the door just as he had seen it on the video. Paulo had said there were two men in the office, and they were both accounted for, but Milton was not prepared to sacrifice caution for speed, even though he knew that he had to move quickly.

He took another flashbang, opened the door and pushed it back, pulled the pin and tossed the grenade inside.

The grenade detonated, the boom rolling up from the basement and the light flaring brightly.

Milton took the stairs, reached the bottom, and entered the room. This, too, was just as he had seen it; he saw the small door in the wall and went over to it. Milton took the key that Paulo had given him and was about to unlock the door when he remembered that he was still wearing the monocle. The girl would already have heard the sounds of gunfire, and then the boom of the flashbang at close range. She would be terrified already; he didn't want to scare her any more. He flipped the device up and away from his face and lowered the gun to his side. He took out a penlight and switched it on, turned the key in the lock, gripped the handle, and opened the door.

The space was pitch black; the glow of the penlight revealed a single bulb, but it was dead without the power. The girl had moved as far away from the door as possible, folding her body as tightly as she could and then pressing herself into a tiny space where the wall met the downward sloping ceiling. She was too far away from Milton for him to be able to reach in and grab her, and he didn't want to compromise his movement by going in after her.

"It's okay, Alícia," he said, trying to make his voice sound as calm and normal as possible. "I'm a friend. Do you remember me?"

The girl had drawn her knees up and folded her arms across them; he saw the flash of her eyes as she risked a glimpse over the top of her forearms. Still nothing.

"I came to the recital. I'm John—remember?"

She gave a hesitant nod.

"I've come to get you out."

"Paulo?" she said in a quiet voice.

"He told me where you are. I'll take you to him now."

Milton didn't think that she would respond, but, just as he had resigned himself to the fact that he was going to have to shuffle into the space to grab her, she unfolded her arms, got down on her hands and knees, and started to crawl toward him.

"Good girl," he said, backing away from the door so that she would be able to exit without feeling cramped or over-whelmed. He took a step to the side so that she wouldn't see the gun until the last moment. He couldn't afford to spook her now. He would need her to be cooperative if he was going to get her—and himself—out of the building in one piece.

She emerged from the doorway, reaching out as she stepped into the darkness. Milton crouched down, holding the HK down and reaching for her with his left hand. She didn't resist and allowed herself to be drawn closer to him.

"I'll go first," he said, speaking slowly and holding up his finger and then pointing first at himself and then the stairs. "You follow me. Okay?"

"Yes," she said.

He smiled at her, trying to be reassuring, and then made his way to the stairs. He paused at the bottom, listening intently for signs of movement in the rooms above. He thought he heard a shout, but it wasn't close at hand.

He couldn't wait to be sure. Milton killed the penlight and started slowly up the stairs, and the girl followed after him.

77

Paulo heard the sounds of the gunshots and had to fight the urge to run. He knew that the streets up here at the top of the Hill would be swarming with Garanhão's men, and he dared not bring attention to himself. The shooting had sounded loud, but the door had been open and he was close to the building. He had no idea how far the sound would carry into the nearby streets. He supposed that it might have been mistaken for fireworks. Perhaps no one would notice?

He came to the top of the slope just as a car raced around the corner. He raised his arm to shield his eyes from the glare of the headlights. The driver hit the brakes, and the car slid to a sudden stop. The car was ahead of him, blocking the way out of the narrow passage that descended to the doors of the building. There was just barely enough space for the driver and passenger to open their doors and get out; there certainly wasn't enough space for Paulo to go around the car.

He was trapped.

The lights blazed out, and Paulo couldn't make out the features of the two men who approached him.

"Hands above your head!" one of them yelled out.

Paulo put his hands up, realising, as he did, that he still had Milton's pistol in his hand.

The man who had been in the passenger seat reached him first. He had a rifle, and it was aimed right at him.

"What are you doing?"

Paulo started to feel breathless. He recognised the man; it was the man who had given him the thirty thousand. Paulo took a step away from him.

"Don't fucking move," the man said, advancing after him. "Answer the question."

"I work for the boss," Paulo said. "I've been watching the kid."

"What's that?" He nodded at the gun in Paulo's hand. The weapon suddenly felt searingly hot in his clammy palm.

Paulo tried to speak, but his mouth was too dry, and the words caught there.

"Put it on the ground," he said.

Paulo's gut shifted unpleasantly; he felt his bowels loosen as he crouched and laid the pistol on the ground.

The second man stooped down to collect the gun, then went around him and hurried toward the open door. His AK-47 was raised, and his eyes bulged with mad intensity.

"The lights are off," the second man called back.

"The circuit box is down the corridor," the first man told him. "Check it."

Paulo backed away a little more.

"Turn around."

"I didn't—" Paulo started to say, the words scraping against his dry throat.

The man didn't give him a chance to finish. He jammed the butt of the rifle against Paulo's head, a sharp and painful blow that sent him stumbling against the wall.

"Turn the fuck around," he repeated, grabbing him with his left hand and yanking him so that he was facing back down to the roller door. Paulo's head stung from the blow, and he could feel a warm trickle as blood ran down his scalp. The man shoved him between the shoulder blades. "*Move*," he spat at him.

"Where do you want me to go?"

"Inside."

Paulo went back down the slope.

"The breaker's off," the second man called back.

"Then switch it back on."

Paulo was wired with fear. He glanced back over his shoulder; the first man was close, and he knew he would have no chance of even trying to overpower him before he fired his pistol. He couldn't miss, not from there.

"I..." Paulo didn't know what to say. "I didn't do anything."

"Turn around and look at me."

Paulo did as he was told and saw that he was looking straight down the barrel of the man's gun.

"Maybe I ought to do you right now. What do you think?"

"I—"

Paulo didn't get the chance to finish the sentence. The man reversed the rifle and crashed the butt into his face. He fell forward, onto his knees, unable to defend himself as a second jarring blow connected with the side of his head. Paulo toppled over to the side, darkness rushing up to meet him.

78

Milton replaced the monocle as he climbed the stairs and looked through it with his left eye as the glowing green wash descended over everything. He reached the room at the top with the bodies of the two men that he had shot. Their bodies were where they had fallen. He hadn't noticed that there was a skylight overhead, and the clouds that had obscured the moon had passed while he had been downstairs. It was still dark, but he could tell from the way the girl gasped that there was enough dim light for her to see them. He cursed himself as the girl bumped up against his legs. He pulled the door closed a little, but he knew that it was too late.

He flipped the monocle up, turned to her, and smiled. "It's all right," he said, trying to reassure her. "They were bad men. They can't hurt you now."

She bit her lip.

"Come on," Milton said, beckoning her forward.

She shook her head.

Milton cursed himself for his own stupidity. He should

have moved the bodies out of sight, but he had wanted to move quickly.

"Shut your eyes," he said, smiling and pointing up at his own eyes as he closed them to demonstrate what he wanted her to do.

He lowered the monocle again, pushed the door with his foot, and made his way through the room. The girl was holding his hand. He couldn't see if she had her eyes closed, but there was nothing he could do about that now.

He reached the door at the other side of the room and took a moment to collect himself. The headache was worse now, and his vision flickered with distortion every now and again. He waited until it cleared, then reached down and used the heel of his right hand to push the door handle down. He nudged the door open, allowing it to swing out into the dark space beyond.

He looked through the monocle and saw two men: Paulo was on the ground with another man standing close by.

The lights came back on.

Milton was blinded. He blinked his eyes, trying to rid himself of the flare that had flashed across his retina as the monocle amplified the light.

He heard the clatter of a rifle and felt the impacts like three hard punches to his chest.

He staggered back, the wind knocked out of his lungs.

The girl screamed.

Still blind, Milton clasped Alícia tightly and bundled her back into the office.

79

P aulo groaned. His head was ringing, and he could feel the warm sensation of blood running down the side of his face. He heard a buzz of electricity and opened his eyes. The lights had come back on. The man who had struck him gaped. He raised his weapon and pulled the trigger. The gun roared, sending a fusillade across the loading bay.

Paulo blinked furiously until he could see a little better. The second man came out of the door. "What the fuck?"

"There's someone in the office. They came for the kid."

"You get him?"

"I think so. Go over there and cover the door. We need to check."

The man raised his rifle and scuttled around the wall. They were both aiming at the door; if Milton and Alícia were in there, they were trapped.

"Come out," the man called in Portuguese. "You're hurt. You got nowhere to go."

Paulo couldn't see Milton. Had he been shot? He

thought of Alícia. The girl was in that room; maybe she was on her own.

The first man was creeping ahead, his attention fixed on the office door. There was a crowbar resting against the wall a few paces to Paulo's right. He pushed himself up and took a step, fighting back the dizziness. He took another, reaching down and lacing his fingers around the cold iron.

"Come out!" the man yelled across the room.

He didn't notice Paulo as he took an uncertain step toward him, nor did he see as he gripped the crowbar in both hands. Paulo drew the bar back and—like a batter taking a swipe at an inbound fastball—he stepped into a swing that terminated against the side of the man's head. He was unconscious before he hit the floor, his body sprawling out limply across the concrete and his AK slipping from his grip. Paulo grabbed the rifle. He had never held one before, let alone fired one, but he had seen how the others held theirs; it couldn't be that difficult. He cupped his left hand beneath the forestock, slid the index finger of his right hand through the trigger guard, aimed at the second man, and pulled the trigger. The rounds sailed high above the head of his target, drilling the concrete wall.

The man ducked down instinctively, then spun in Paulo's direction, bringing his own AK to bear.

He saw the blur of movement in the doorway to the office. Milton was there, stepping out of cover, his rifle raised as he took aim at the second man. The two of them fired at almost the same time: Milton was a fraction earlier, two rounds slamming into the man's chest a moment before he pulled the trigger. Paulo flinched as a volley of bullets streaked just to the side of his head, cracking into the wall behind him and sprinkling him with brick dust.

Milton stepped out of the office, his rifle aimed at the man he had just shot.

"Paulo," he called out, "are you okay?"

"Yes," he said. "I'm all right. What about you?"

"All good," he said, and Paulo saw the black sleeveless ballistic jacket that Milton was wearing.

Alícia came out of the office behind Milton. She saw Paulo and, before Milton could stop her, she sprinted toward him. Paulo picked her up in his arms and lifted her off the floor. She burrowed her head into the notch between his shoulder and chin and held on as tightly as she could.

"Your head," she said. "You're bleeding."

"It's okay," Paulo whispered to her. "I'm fine. Are you all right?"

"I'm scared."

"I'm scared, too. But that's okay. We're going to get you out of here."

80

M ilton checked that Paulo was okay; he had received a nasty blow to the side of the head and was unsteady on his feet. Milton would have preferred to give him a moment to get his balance back, but they didn't have the luxury of time; they had to get on the move. Milton could have carried the girl, but she would have slowed him down, and it would have made him a sitting duck. He was happy to hand her over to Paulo, and he could see that she was happier that way, too. That suited him very well.

He went outside first, telling Paulo to stay back with the girl until he was happy that the way ahead was clear. There was enough light from the moon and stars in the clear sky overhead that he didn't need the monocle, and he removed it and put it in the pack. Paulo found the SIG that Milton had given him and, at Milton's request, he picked it up and handed it back. Milton put the assault rifle back into his pack, too, put his arms through the straps, and adjusted it so that it was comfortable. He checked that the SIG was ready to fire.

There was no indication that there were any other *trafi-cantes* in the neighbourhood, although Milton was acutely aware that there were plenty of places where it would have been easy enough to hide. He had already been luckier than he deserved; the vest had stopped the three rounds that had found their mark, arresting their momentum before they could blast into his chest. His ribs and sternum were sore from the impacts, and he knew from experience that he was going to have another collection of bruises to commemorate his good fortune.

"Come on," Milton said. "We need to hurry."

Paulo moved forward with him, carrying Alícia in his arms. The girl wrapped her arms around his neck and locked her legs around his waist, her head buried in Paulo's neck. She had seen things that a child should never see; it had given Milton fresh motivation to get her as far away from this place as possible.

"Stay close behind me," Milton said.

"You don't know the way as well as I do," Paulo said.

"You guide me. But stay back."

Paulo nodded. Milton saw the young man in a different light now. He had been fearful before, and, while Milton could see that he was still afraid, he also showed resilience. He had shown selflessness beyond what Milton had expected, and Milton might never have made it out of the warehouse if it hadn't been for Paulo's bravery in taking the crowbar to the shooter. He could have made a run for it, and he had not. Milton wouldn't forget that.

"Ready?"

Paulo put his arm around the girl's shoulders and held her a little more tightly. He inclined his head.

Another fusillade of fireworks shot up from halfway down the Hill and exploded high overhead. The distraction that the celebrations provided might have been fortunate, Milton thought; the gunshots could easily be mistaken for firecrackers. It might be the reason why they had not seen any more *traficantes*. It didn't matter; Milton was not interested in analysing his good fortune, only in taking full advantage of it. He set off, the SIG held in both hands, the muzzle angled down to the ground, ready to bring it up and fire should the need present itself.

He started by retracing his steps. The passages and alleyways were quiet, but they were also very similar to one another, and Milton was quickly unsure if he had drifted away from his previous route. It was easy enough to know that they were going in the right direction—they just needed to make their way down the Hill—but Milton knew that there would be areas that it was best to avoid. They turned into a narrow alley that descended by way of a flight of stone steps. A lattice of electrical cables had been strung above, and one of the walls was painted with graffiti in support of the Brazilian football team. The steps were slick with grime, and Milton proceeded carefully, the muzzle of the SIG pointing ahead.

The steps levelled out and deposited them at a junction where two other alleys joined this one.

"Go right," Paulo said.

Milton waited a moment, confirmed that the other two passages were clear, and then made his way into the alley on the right. It continued on a downward slope and quickly passed between the flanks of more substantial buildings than the shacks that they had passed nearer to the top of the Hill. They passed a church, with a colourful mural of Jesus with a dove perched on his outstretched hand. There was trash everywhere, and a trench along the wall ran with sewage that the residents had poured out of buckets from the windows above.

Milton saw the shape of a person coming toward them. It was a middle-aged man wearing a T-shirt and shorts, weaving left and right as he slowly climbed the Hill. He was drunk, but Milton hid the pistol against his leg until the man had navigated around them and continued on his way. Milton waited. He could hear the sound of a crowd from not too far ahead and, over that, the throb of bass.

"Where are we?" Milton asked.

"Halfway down. Rua Um is ahead. We have to take it."

Milton remembered the *baile funk* that he had passed through on his way up the Hill. The crowd might not be such a bad thing now.

Milton took off the ballistic vest and dumped it into the industrial bin that they had just passed. There was a bottle of water in the pack; he poured it over his face and scrubbed as much of the paint away as he could. He shoved the SIG into the waistband of his jeans and arranged his jacket so that it fell over the butt of the pistol, hiding it from sight.

"Nice and close," he said.

Milton took a breath, clenched and unclenched fingers that itched with tension and latent violence, and continued toward the sound of the music.

81

The crowds were as thick as when Milton had climbed the Hill, and they provided excellent cover as they followed the road back to its base. They reached the junction with Estrada da Gávea where Milton had arranged to meet Marks, but there was no sign of the old man's BMW.

Milton took out his phone and dialled Marks's number.

It rang and rang, but Marks didn't pick up.

"Shit," Milton said under his breath.

"What is it?" Paulo asked.

Milton ignored him. He activated the tracking app. The dot that represented Marks's phone was moving away from them, heading west. Milton cursed again. He was beginning to get a very bad feeling about this.

"We can't wait here," Paulo said. "We're too close."

Marks wouldn't have left them. There was no way, and that left only one possibility: he had been compromised.

"Milton," Paulo hissed urgently, "look."

Milton turned and looked up the Estrada da Gávea. There was a large blue-painted building just before the road turned left, and there were two cars just in front of it. They were bullying their way through the crowds, and, as the lead car made its way down the slope and drew a little closer, Milton could see that there were shirtless men leaning out of the windows hooting and hollering for the men and women slowing their passage to clear the road. The men were wielding rifles and, as Milton watched, the man leaning out of the passenger window fired a round into the air to encourage the crowd to part a little more quickly.

"That's them," Paulo said.

Milton made a quick assessment. If the *traficantes* had taken Marks, it was possible that they had come to the conclusion that he was there to make a rendezvous with Milton. The thought occurred to Milton just before he noticed a man with a white T-shirt loom out of the crowd around them and reach for the butt of the pistol he had pushed into the waistband of his dirty jeans. Milton leapt for him, grabbed the man's wrist, and bent it up. The man was strong, but Milton had leverage on him and, with a firm yank, he pulled back on the man's fingers and heard the snap as he broke them. The man yelped with pain and hopped back; Milton let go of his mangled hand, reached around for the SIG, and shot him point blank in the chest.

The man's shirt was suffused with blood as he stumbled back into a group of men and women who were queuing for food from a mobile cart. He toppled into the cart, over-turning it. A woman screamed, and the crowd scattered in sudden terror.

Milton spun. There was a Renault behind them, the driver penned in by the panicking crowd. He raised the SIG and aimed it at the driver, skirting the car until he was able to open the door. He reached in, grabbed the driver, hauled him out, and dumped him on the asphalt.

There was a loud blare as the *traficantes* sounded the horn of their car, and then another rattle of automatic gunfire.

Milton opened the rear door and reached for Alícia. The girl was rigid with fear.

"You drive," Milton yelled to Paulo. "Get us out of here."

82

Paulo didn't need to be asked twice. He shoved the Renault into reverse, spun the wheel all the way around, and stamped down on the accelerator. The people who had been gathered around the food cart had scattered, spooked after watching Milton shoot the *traficante* and then fleeing out of the path of the fast-approaching cars with the gun-toting hoodlums hanging out of the windows. The car juddered as the rear wheel ran over the torso of the man Milton had shot, and then bumped into the raised wall that demarked the left-hand side of the road. Paulo changed into first, and the car shot forward, racing down the Hill toward a sharp left-hand turn. Paulo kept the accelerator pressed down to the floor, the car just holding its line and narrowly avoiding a parked truck.

They completed the turn and raced toward a parked bus that was pointed down the Hill and another truck headed in the opposite direction.

"Hold on," Paulo yelled.

There was a narrow gap between the bus and the truck. Paulo nudged the wheel, changing course just a fraction and sending them straight down the middle of the road. It didn't look as if there would be enough space for the three vehicles to fit on the road, but Paulo was confident in his judgement. The Renault raced ahead, the right wing mirror striking the side of the bus and the denuded stump drawing sparks as it carved a track down the flank of the vehicle. The gap narrowed, and the other mirror was knocked off, the mount scratching against the truck and the metallic scrape competing with the roar of the engine.

Paulo glanced in the rear-view mirror and saw that the *traficante's* car had also forced its way through the gap. Milton was looking back through the window, too. He had his arm around Alícia, holding her close to his body.

"Faster, Paulo," he yelled out.

This part of the road was straight and reasonably quiet save for the men and women who idled along the sidewalk. Paulo changed up to second and then third, the speedometer showing fifty as he shot around the left-hand side of a slow-moving bus and then swerved back again just in time to avoid the moped that was struggling up the Hill.

The road was jammed up ahead. Paulo stomped on the brakes but, just as he thought that they were trapped, he saw that the sidewalk to the left was clear. There was a stall selling T-shirts beneath a green awning, but there were no customers, and the owner was leaning back against the wall as she stared at the phone in her hand. Paulo turned the wheel to the left, mounted the pavement and then straightened out. The car careened through the wooden pillar that supported the awning and slammed through the table that held a selection of flip-flops. The tarpaulin and the disturbed T-shirts fell on the windscreen, blinding Paulo as he yanked the wheel and left the sidewalk just before he would have struck the group of men in Flamengo tops who were walking up the Hill. They regaled him with furious hoots and hollers as he straightened up, the tarpaulin catching the breeze and sailing away from the car to drift back down to earth behind them.

Paulo looked up into the mirror again; he couldn't see the *traficantes*.

"Go!" Milton yelled. "Go, go, go!"

Paulo swerved left into Avenida Niemeyer, leaving the clutter of the *favela* for the wider, emptier streets that he knew from racing. He changed up to fourth, the car racing up to sixty as he headed east toward Vidigal.

83

Milton looked behind them; Paulo had lost the pursuit, and the road was clear. He turned his attention to the girl sitting on the seat next to him.

"Are you okay, Alícia?"

She was pale, but she looked up at him and gave him a timid nod.

Milton's phone buzzed. He took it out and checked the display.

Marks.

He accepted the call and put it to his ear. "Yes?"

"Mr. Milton." It was a man. He spoke English with a heavy accent.

"Who is this?"

"You know, I think."

"Rodrigues?"

The man didn't answer. "Your friend was picked up by the police. I have him here with me. Would you like to speak to him?"

Milton gripped the phone tight. The next voice was
Marks's.

"I'm sorry."

"Are you okay?"

"I feel a bit stupid."

"Have they hurt you?"

"Just my pride. They must've seen my car."

"I'm coming to get you."

"Don't—"

The phone was taken away before Marks could finish
what he was going to say.

"Please do," Rodrigues said. "Please do come and get
him. I'd like to meet you. You've caused me a lot of trouble,
one way or another."

"Let him go."

"Or?"

"You think *this* is trouble? I can make it get a lot worse."

Garanhão chuckled. "You are a confident man, Mr.
Milton. But I know about you now. Your other friend, Mr.
Drake, he tells me all about you. He says you were a soldier?
Special Forces. He said you were a drunk, but I think he
underestimated you. I won't make that mistake."

"Let him go."

"I don't think so. Watch. I want to show you something."

Milton pulled the phone away from his ear; the display
asked whether he would accept a video call. He pressed
accept, and, after a moment, the display changed to show a
live shot. He saw a road, part of a car, and a fringe of vegetation. The lights of the city twinkled in the background. A
firework bloomed. Wherever it was, it was high up.

Milton felt his throat tighten. He turned the phone away
so that only he could see it and thumbed the volume down.

There was movement in the shot, and then a man was

dragged into view. It was Marks. The old man was pushed down onto his knees and turned so that he was looking up into the camera. Whoever was holding the phone switched it to his left hand so that he could aim a pistol with his right.

"Rodrigues—" Milton began, but his warning was cut short.

There was a single bang and the pistol jerked up; Marks's body fell to the left. The camera pulled back so that Milton could see the old man's body lying across the road, and then the feed was interrupted as the shot switched between the phone's forward- and backward-facing cameras.

Milton saw a man: young, smooth-skinned, a glint from a gold tooth catching the light. It was Rodrigues.

"Don't think this makes us even, Mr. Milton," he said. "We're not even."

Milton wanted to tell him that he had just made a bad mistake, that he might as well put the gun to his head and pull the trigger because that would be easier than what he was going to do to him, but Alícia was looking across at him, and he bit down on his tongue hard enough to draw blood.

He kept his voice neutral and said, instead, "Why don't we meet and talk about that?"

"I'd like that very much. I'm sure you could find me, but I'll save you the effort. I'm at the top of the Hill. Come and see me. I'll be expecting you this time." He looked as if he was about to end the call, but he didn't. "Are you with Paulo?"

Milton didn't answer; Paulo stiffened in the driver's seat.

"Tell him I'm disappointed. After everything I did to help him and his daughter, he treats me like this. Tell him he has been foolish, please, Mr. Milton. He'll know what that means."

The screen went to black.

"My family," Paulo said at once. "I have to go to them."

"Where are they?"

Paulo swore in Portuguese; his voice was taut with fear.

"Paulo," Milton said sternly, "where is your family?"

"In a hotel," he said. "I told them they needed to get out of the apartment. But he'll find them. He'll find them and... and..."

"Go there now," Milton said.

Paulo drove them into Vidigal, a neighbourhood that was close to Rocinha. He followed Avenida Niemeyer to the Shalimar, a hotel that proudly advertised rooms starting at just fifty-nine *reais*.

"There," Paulo said. "They're in there."

"Drive on," Milton said.

Paulo did, and Milton examined the hotel and the surrounding streets for anything that appeared out of the ordinary. He saw nothing.

"Park," Milton said, pointing to a bay at the side of the road.

Paulo slid the car into the bay and flicked off the lights.

Milton took another moment to look around: the hotel was on a cliff, separated from the ocean by the road, a wide sidewalk, and a stand of palm trees. There was a bus stop on the sidewalk with a number of men and women gathered there; Milton stared at them, but it would have been impossible to say whether any of them were more than they appeared to be. Probably not, but he would be careful.

"How much does your wife know?" he asked.

"Not much."

"How did you explain why they needed to move into a hotel?"

"I said I was in trouble. I said the man I borrowed money from was coming after me. That's true," he added, as if he needed to justify it to himself.

To a point, thought Milton. He didn't say that, though, telling him instead to call his wife, to tell her that Milton was coming to collect them, and to describe him to her.

"It's one in the morning," he said. "She'll panic. What do I say to her?"

"She's your wife. Think of something. What's her name?"

"Rafaela. And my daughter is Eloá."

Milton looked at Alícia, sitting quietly in the back next to him, and decided that more caution was required.

"Drive up the road a little and then call her," he said. "Tell her I'm coming to collect her and Eloá and describe what I look like."

"She doesn't speak English," Paulo said.

"So tell her what to do."

Milton didn't wait for Paulo to say that he understood. He opened the door and stepped out into the heat of the night.

THE SHALIMAR WAS EVEN MORE DOWN-AT-HEEL than it had appeared from the road. It was separated from the sidewalk by a ten-foot-high wall that was ugly and utilitarian, with the only means of access through a gap marked ENTRADA.

The entrance was across a small courtyard and beneath a large awning with a cheap vinyl sign that proclaimed the price of their rooms.

Milton eyed the men and women waiting at the bus shelter, but, as had been the case before, none of them arrested his attention. Satisfied but far from complacent, he passed through the opening and approached the entrance. He felt the comforting weight of the SIG against his leg, brushing his fingers against its cold edges as he pushed open the door to reception and went inside.

The desk was unmanned, and Milton could hear the sound of a television in the office behind it. He didn't wait, crossing the lobby and taking the stairs to the third floor. Paulo had told him that his wife and daughter were in room 311, and Milton followed the corridor until he reached the right door.

He knocked on it gently and waited in the corridor until he heard the sound of footsteps. The door opened; a woman stood there with a young girl half-hiding behind her legs.

"I'm John," Milton said.

The woman paused, looking intently into his face. Milton hoped that Paulo had told her what he looked like, and that she was just comparing him to his description. She bit her lip, unable to hide the trepidation that Milton guessed she must be feeling.

"Rafaela?" he said.

She nodded.

He gestured to the girl. "And this is Eloá?"

She nodded for a second time.

"We need to go," Milton said firmly. "Okay? I'll take you to Paulo."

She swallowed and, for a moment, Milton thought that

she was going to close the door. But, instead, she stooped down and picked up a bag that Milton hadn't noticed. With the bag in one hand and her daughter's hand in the other, the woman stepped into the corridor and let the door swing shut behind them.

Milton led the way to the stairs.

85

Milton waited in the lobby of the hotel until he saw the Renault. He opened the door, letting the humid air wash inside, and hurried Rafaela and Eloá across the courtyard to the entrance. He stepped out first, checking left and right, and then, with his hand close to the SIG, he crossed the sidewalk, opened the car's rear door, and beckoned Rafaela to follow. They got into the back of the car next to Alícia. Paulo must have explained at least some of what was happening when they spoke on the phone because she sat quietly and said nothing about what they were doing, nor did she enquire as to the identity of the young girl who was on the back seat with them.

Milton shut the door and went around to get into the front passenger seat. He closed the door, and Paulo pulled away.

Milton glanced over and noticed Paulo exchange a look in the mirror with his wife. He saw that Milton was watching and looked back to the road. "Where now?" he asked.

"Somewhere outside the city," Milton said. "A hotel. Somewhere no one would look to find you."

Paulo exchanged words with his wife. "We know a place," he said. "Rafaela's mother is in Campo Grande."

"No," Milton said. "That'll be one of the first places they look. Somewhere else."

Paulo and his wife spoke again, and, when Paulo turned back to Milton, there was certainty in his answer. "There's a hotel in Grumari. We've been there before."

"So you go there," Milton said. "You don't stop. Understand?"

Paulo nodded. "Yes."

"And I want you to take a picture of Alícia when you get there and send it to me."

Paulo nodded.

"You're responsible for Alícia," Milton said a little more quietly. "Make it right."

Paulo didn't answer, but he set his jaw and gave a determined nod.

Milton turned around to the girl in the back of the car. She was pressed up against the door, her knees drawn up to her chin. She looked so small and fragile, and Milton couldn't help the fresh doubt about whether he was doing the right thing. He wondered, again, whether he should stay with her until she had been safely handed over. He knew that what he had decided to do could be considered selfish. And then he thought of Marks, and he knew that he had no other choice. He had a code, and there were certain crimes that could not go unpunished. Rodrigues had crossed a line —*several* lines—and that had consequences.

The doubt was still there, but then he thought of Paulo and the way the girl had clung to him as soon as Milton had fought his way out of the building, and his fears receded just a little.

They passed a nightclub with a rank of taxis outside it.

"Pull over," Milton said.

Paulo slid over to the kerb and stopped. "What's the matter?"

"Remember," Milton said. "Don't stop. Not for anything. Just drive."

He reached for the door handle and opened the door.

"You're not coming?"

"I have something I need to do."

To Milton's surprise, Paulo reached over and snagged his arm. "No," he said. "That's crazy."

"Paulo..."

"You want Garanhão?" Paulo said in an urgent whisper. "There's nothing you can do. Forget him—just be thankful you can still get away."

Milton gently removed Paulo's hand. "I can't do that."

"He *wants* you to go up there," Paulo protested, "and he knows you're coming this time."

"I'm not going back. He's coming to me." Milton opened the door and stepped out. "Good luck."

Paulo reached his hand across the cabin again and offered it. "Thank you," the younger man said.

Milton shook his hand. "Be careful."

Milton released his hand, closed the door, and watched the car drive away.

PART VII

THE EIGHTH DAY

86

Milton stole a car from a quiet side street near the Sheraton and drove it across the city to the cache for the things that he thought he might need for the rest of the night. The gate to the yard was closed, but Milton was able to scale it without being seen. He jogged to the garage and opened the door with the key that Marks had given him. He picked out the things that he wanted and left the garage as he had found it; he wondered how long it would take for Marks's store to be discovered. Months, probably. He doubted that he himself would ever return.

He drove south and parked the car two blocks north of the apartment block in Ipanema, grabbing his bag of gear and making his way to the twenty-four-hour McDonald's on Rua Visconde de Pirajá. He had called Felipe Saverin earlier. He had arranged to meet the judge here and, as he approached, he saw that Saverin was waiting for him. Milton paused on the other side of the street and observed. Saverin was sitting in the window with a cup in front of him. He was picking at the cup, peeling pieces of Styrofoam away from it and discarding them on the table. Milton was not surprised that he was anxious. He waited on the street for another minute, checking for any sign that Saverin had been followed. Nothing stood out.

Milton crossed the street and went inside the restaurant. Saverin was the only customer there, and he turned at the sound of the door. Milton made his way to a table away from the window and beckoned Saverin over. The judge left his empty cup, came across, and took the seat opposite Milton.

He spared the pleasantries. "Where is she?"

Milton took out his phone.

"What happened?" Saverin pressed. "What happened, Smith? Where is my daughter?"

"You can speak to her."

Milton dialled Paulo's number. The call connected.

"Hello?" Paulo said.

"Where are you?" Milton asked.

"We're here."

"In the hotel?"

"Yes. Everything's fine."

"I'm with *senhor* Saverin," Milton said. "Could you pass the phone to Alícia, please?"

Milton handed the phone to Saverin and watched.

"Alícia?" the judge said tentatively.

And then his expression melted, replaced by one of joy. Saverin spoke quickly. Milton didn't understand the Portuguese, but his reaction was just as Milton would have expected: there was a catch in his throat, and his eyes filled with tears. Milton let him speak for as long as he wanted; Saverin's hand was shaking when he finally handed the phone back again.

"Where is she?" he asked, his eyes red and damp.

"A hotel in Grumari. I'll give you the address and you can go and get her."

"Who is she with?"

"A man I trust. Paulo de Almeida—she's with him, his wife and his daughter."

"Who is he?"

"He's going to need your help," Milton said. "Antonio Rodrigues was extorting him. He made Paulo drive the car the day they took Alícia. He had no idea what he was being asked to do, and then they threatened his family unless he agreed to guard Alícia. He helped me to get her out tonight —I wouldn't have been able to do it without him."

Saverin's brows clenched angrily. "He worked with Garanhão? And Alícia is still with him? Are you *crazy?*"

"You're not listening to me, *senhor* Saverin. Paulo was desperate and naïve. But he's more than made up for it since then. You need to look after him and his family. They're in danger."

"We will put them in protective custody until I work out—"

"No," Milton cut him off firmly. "No custody. No investigation. He's the only reason your daughter is still alive. I wouldn't have been able to find her without him, and then he stopped us both from being shot when I was bringing her out. There's no case to make against him. He deserves your gratitude, not your suspicion. That part of this is non-negotiable—please don't push me on it."

Saverin stared at Milton, but Milton did not look away; instead, he fixed the full focus of his cold eyes on him. Eventually, the prosecutor nodded his head. "Fine. He will be protected. Him and his family."

"Thank you."

"Where is Rodrigues?" Saverin asked. His relief had been replaced by the steel that Milton remembered.

"I don't know," Milton said. "He wasn't there when I got her out. But I want to find him."

"That's easier said than done."

Milton rested his forearms on the table and leaned a little closer. He stared at Saverin again. "Someone hired him to take Alícia," he said. "I want to know who it was."

The judge paused; Milton could tell that he knew who was responsible, but he didn't immediately say.

"Who paid him?" Milton pressed.

"He wasn't being paid," Saverin said. "At least I doubt that he was."

"So why would he take her?"

"There is a man—a businessman—called Andreas Lima. I arrested him last week for corruption and fraud. When you said Rodrigues was involved, I knew it had to be him. But the relationship between Lima and Rodrigues isn't commercial. It's nothing to do with money."

"So what is it?"

"It's family. They're brothers. Well, half brothers," he qualified. "They were both born in Rocinha. Same mother —Meleni. Meleni married a man who ran a store, and Andreas was their child. The marriage broke up, and Meleni started a relationship with a crook who was with one of the gangs. Antonio was born a year later. Lima has always made a big show of how he made his way out of the gutter. Rags to riches. He's been in magazines about it." Saverin shook his head derisively. "But he's a charlatan. He keeps his relationship with his brother quiet, as you might imagine, but he goes to him whenever he needs something done. I guessed this was him when it happened. I should have been more careful."

"Where is Lima now?"

"Under house arrest," Saverin replied. "I would have preferred to have moved him to Curitiba, but he is a rich man—he can afford the best lawyers in Brazil."

Milton stared at Saverin. "I need you to take me to him."

The judge shook his head. "I can't do that."

Milton stared at him hard. "Rodrigues murdered an old friend of mine tonight. My friend helped me to find your daughter, and Rodrigues shot him while I was watching. Think about what he's done: he took your daughter, he killed two of the guards you paid to protect her, and now this. Tell me honestly—will you be able to prosecute him?"

Saverin glanced down, then looked back up at Milton again. "Not easily," he admitted. "Rodrigues would deny it. And I have only your word of what happened."

"And Paulo's," Milton added.

"Would you both give evidence against him?"

Milton certainly wasn't prepared to do that, and it would be unfair to ask Paulo. "Probably not."

"No, of course not. And even if I could build a case against him, prosecuting it would be difficult. We would have to arrest him first, and Rocinha..." He spread his arms helplessly. "Well, they would have to send the military police in, and the government is not ready to do that yet. There would be bloodshed."

"So Rodrigues goes free? Unpunished?"

"I didn't say that," Saverin began. "Eventually—"

"Eventually isn't good enough," Milton cut in, struggling to keep the irritation from his voice. "The longer you wait, the more difficult it will be. There's another way. A better one."

"You will go back into the *favela*? You know how stupid that would be?"

"No," Milton said. "That *would* be stupid. I wouldn't be able to get near him."

"So?"

"You take me to his brother."

"So that you can threaten him? Beat him up? Please, *senhor* Smith. I can't do that. I have Lima by the balls—if he gets hurt because of something I've done, his lawyers piss all over my case and he walks free. It's taken me six months to reel him in. I can't risk that now."

"I'm not going to hurt him," Milton said. "I just want to speak to him."

"Really," Saverin said sternly. "I can't do it."

Milton was not about to give up. "I want to talk to Lima. That's it. He can tell me about Rodrigues—where I can find him, how I can get to him. No one needs to know that I spoke to him. Nothing will happen to him. And you can be there the whole time." Milton looked at Saverin; he could see that he was wavering. "Think of your daughter. He kept her in a basement for a week. She was locked in a crawl-space with nothing. Think of how scared she was. They did that to her—Lima and Rodrigues. Are you going to let that go?"

Milton watched his face and saw that he was winning: the visceral anger of the father whose daughter had been kidnapped was overcoming the resistance of the lawyer who wanted to do things by the book.

"Do you believe in justice?" Milton asked him.

"Of course."

"You'll get justice against Lima. You'll win your case, and then you can punish him for what he did, lock him up for years. But if you don't work with me, you don't get justice against Rodrigues. He goes unpunished. If he had taken my daughter..." Milton let that drift.

Saverin looked away and bit down on his lip. "Okay," he said, speaking quickly, as if that might prevent him from changing his mind. "This is the only way it happens: we go and *talk* to Lima. We get proof that Rodrigues was involved. If we get the evidence, then we can think about what to do next. Maybe I can take it to the governor, and then we can go and get him. They won't be able to say no—he can't be allowed to attack a judge like this."

Milton had no intention of letting things go down like that, but Saverin's concession was enough for him. There was no need to ask for more. "Fine."

"You don't hurt Lima. No violence. There's been enough of that already. Maybe... maybe you frighten him a little."

"That's what I had in mind."

Saverin sighed; he looked tired. "Okay," he said. "I'll take you."

87

Milton took Saverin to the stolen car and drove him across the city. It was three in the morning, and the streets, while far from empty, were much quieter than they had been earlier. They didn't speak. Saverin had called his wife before they set off and told her what had happened with their daughter. Milton had urged the judge not to send his wife to the hotel in Grumari on the off chance that Garanhão had their apartment in Ipanema under surveillance, and he had agreed on the basis that they would collect the girl as soon as they were done with Lima.

Saverin told Milton that Lima lived in Jardim Botânico, and directed him there. He seemed to be wrestling with the good sense of going along with Milton's plan; Milton, for his part, was trying to find an alternative to the only course of action that was open to him. He was reluctant to follow through with what he had in mind, but, much as he tried, he was unable to come up with another way to reach the same ends. He had already concluded that they justified the means.

Jardim Botânico was one of the city's higher-end

districts. It was surrounded on three sides by a nature reserve and, high up, it offered a spectacular view of the statue of Christ the Redeemer standing tall atop the summit of Corcovado Mountain.

"This is a bad idea," Saverin said as Milton parked next to a hillside. "If he says that I came here…"

"It'll be his word against yours," Milton said. "And he's not going to want to give me a reason to come and see him again."

Saverin looked over at him anxiously. "You said you wouldn't hurt him."

"I won't," Milton said. "I give you my word."

Saverin looked up, and Milton followed his gaze; there was a line of big villas at the top of the rise.

"What is it you think you might find?" Saverin asked.

"There are two people you won't be able to reach: Lima's brother and Shawn Drake. There'll be something that links Lima to at least one of them: a bank statement, an email, a message on his phone. You speak to him, and I'll have a look around."

Saverin looked far from convinced, but he exhaled and gestured up to the villa nearest to the car. "This is it," he said. "First on the right. You want to know how much it costs? Eight million dollars. Who said crime doesn't pay?" It was rhetorical, and the judge laughed bitterly as he reached for the door handle. "We couldn't keep him locked up, but we managed to get a curfew. He should be inside."

88

S averin led the way, following a neat path up the flank of the hillside. The villa at the top was constructed from glass and steel, with tall windows designed to offer up as much of the stunning view as possible. There was an infinity pool, lit from beneath the water, and two stands of perfectly kept palm trees that swayed gently in the breeze. Saverin made his way to the door.

"Who does he live with?" Milton asked.

"He lives alone," Saverin said as he held his finger against the doorbell. "He's a..." The judge searched for the word. "A bachelor."

Milton noticed that there was a camera set above the door, and put himself out of view by standing beneath it. It took several minutes before they heard the sound of footsteps approaching the door from the inside.

An intercom crackled into life. Milton heard a voice, gruff and raspy with sleep. The voice spoke in Portuguese; Milton guessed Lima was asking what Saverin could possibly want at this time of night. The judge leaned closer to the microphone and told Lima to open the door. Milton didn't understand the response save that Lima was evidently irritated to be disturbed. The conversation continued for another few exchanges, and then Saverin raised his voice and banged a fist against the wood.

There was a moment of silence, and then Milton heard the sound of the door being unlocked. It swung open. Milton was at the side of the door and waited as Saverin went inside. He heard the sound of Lima's voice, angry and declarative, and Saverin's snapped retort.

Milton reached down, pulled the SIG from the back of his jeans, and went through the door before it could close.

He took it all in quickly: marble flooring, huge cream settees, a well-stocked bar, spotlights illuminating pieces of modern art. Saverin was two steps inside, to Milton's left. Lima was next to the door, caught in the act of closing it. The businessman was wearing an expensive pair of silk pyjamas and, around his left ankle, a bulky monitoring bracelet.

"Que merda é essa?" Lima exclaimed.

Milton raised the gun and aimed it at the businessman.

Saverin turned and saw the weapon. His mouth fell open. "What are you doing?"

Lima was close to Milton, close enough for Milton to turn the pistol around and crack the butt down against the top of his head. Lima fell to his knees, knocking over the lamp as he reached down in an attempt to prevent himself from falling flat on his face.

"Don't!" Saverin called out. "Smith—*don't!*"

Milton moved inside and closed the door behind him. "I'm sorry," he said to Saverin. "This will only work my way."

"Put the gun down."

"I can't do that."

"Put the gun *down!*"

Saverin took a step forward as if he might try to force Milton to comply; Milton straightened his arm, aiming the weapon at the judge's head, and froze him to the spot.

"Please don't come any closer," Milton said calmly. "I'd rather we could part on good terms."

Saverin's face deformed into an angry scowl. "I don't care what you've done to help me. I'll send the police after you, just the same as I would if you were Garanhão. I can't allow violence. You're as bad as them."

Milton almost said that he was worse, but he held his tongue. "Give me your phone," he said to the judge.

Saverin looked as if he was about to resist, but he looked at Milton and then at the gun that was still pointed at his head. He reached into his pocket and took out his phone. Milton pocketed it.

"This isn't justice."

"You can't guarantee that Garanhão will get what he deserves. I can. He will. I *promise* you that he will."

"You're a vigilante."

"Perhaps. Now—sit down over there, please."

Milton indicated the chair on the other side of the room. Saverin backed away and lowered himself to the chair. Milton waited until he had sat down and then stepped closer to Lima. The businessman was woozy, and his head was bleeding from where Milton had pistol-whipped him.

"Do you have a safe?"

"What?" Lima said.

"What?" Saverin exclaimed. "Now you're a thief as well?"

Milton ignored the judge and aimed the gun directly at Lima's head. "Your safe," he said calmly. "Where do you keep your valuables?"

Lima pointed to a cupboard beneath the stairs.

"Open it for me, please."

Milton followed Lima as the businessman opened the cupboard to reveal a small freestanding safe. He spun the combination dial, pulled down on the handle, and opened the unit. Milton came closer and saw bricks of banknotes and a stack of loose papers. He had noticed a paper take-away bag on the kitchen counter; he backed up to collect it and gave it to Lima.

"Put everything inside, please."

Lima swore under his breath, but put the money into the bag.

"Everything," Milton insisted.

Lima turned. "Come on," he protested.

"And the papers. Don't make me hit you again."

Lima swore again, but reached for the papers and slid them into the paper bag, too. Milton took it from him and moved him away from the cupboard.

"This is wrong," Saverin said. "You can't do this."

Milton tuned him out, knelt down and inspected the bracelet around Lima's ankle. It was of standard design. They were not designed to stay on at all costs; a device that could not be removed without special tools would pose a health risk to its wearer. This one even came with a dotted line on the fabric sheath that told him where to cut. He reached into his pocket and took out the Aircrew knife that he had taken from the assault vest and sliced through the material. Milton saw the two pieces of the wire that were sewn into the sheath and knew, now that he had severed it, that an anti-tamper alarm would have been transmitted and that the police would soon be on their way.

It didn't matter. Milton didn't plan on being here for long.

He reached down, grabbed the collar of Lima's pyjama top, and hauled him up to his knees. Milton had cable ties from the cache, and he took one and secured Lima's hands behind his back. He dragged the trussed-up businessman to his feet and shoved him toward the door.

"Smith," Saverin protested, "please."

"The police will be on the way now," Milton said, gesturing down at the two pieces of the severed bracelet. "I'll call Paulo and tell him to call so you can go and collect your daughter. Please just focus on her. Don't try to follow me. It wouldn't be a good idea."

There was a set of keys on a table near the door. Milton took them, opened the door and pushed Lima through, and then, without looking back at Saverin, closed the door and locked it from the outside. He had no doubt that the judge would call the police—he suspected that he was probably searching for a phone right now—but at least the door would keep him inside long enough that Milton could get Lima away from the area. He didn't want a confrontation with him. On the other hand, Milton knew that there was only one way to play this—*his* way—and, although he didn't want to incapacitate the judge, he would have done just that if Saverin had tried to stop him. As he led Lima down the steps to the car, he was thankful that violence would not be necessary.

At least not for a little while.

89

Milton's phone buzzed with a picture message as he drove to Jacarepaguá. He checked it, opening the message and confirming it was what he needed, then put the phone away again.

He pulled into the Joy Motel. Marks had rented the room for a week, and the place had not been busy on the previous occasions that Milton had been there. He suspected that it would normally be quiet, frequented, perhaps, by prostitutes and addicts and other itinerant dregs who wouldn't pay attention to another late arrival. He arrived in the lot, noting with satisfaction that it was almost empty, and reversed the car so that the trunk was closest to the door to the room. He switched off the engine and waited for a moment, opening his window and listening to the sounds of the city. He heard the hum of traffic, a muffled TV, a jetliner's engines overhead, but that was the sum of it. The forecourt was peaceful, and Milton was satisfied that he wouldn't be seen.

He took the bag from the passenger seat and looked inside: the banknotes were all high denomination, fifties and hundreds, and there were lots of them. The papers looked to be bank statements. Milton took those out and left them on the seat. He put the notes back into the bag and stuffed it in the glovebox.

He got out, crossed the lot to the veranda, and knelt down in front of the door to the room. It was a simple lock, and it took him less than fifteen seconds to pick it. He pushed the door back, went back to the car, and opened the trunk. Lima was lying there, his hands still fastened behind his back. Milton reached down for the cable tie. He used it to haul Lima out of the trunk and then dragged him backwards across the veranda and into the room. He closed the door, locked it, and turned Lima around so that he was facing him. The man's face was deathly pale, and his eyes darted left and right, perhaps looking for a way out that he wouldn't find. Milton shoved Lima in the chest, and he toppled back onto the bed.

Milton had been responsible for interrogating men and women for the information they held, and there had been many occasions when the means necessary for extracting that information had diverged from what was legal. Some of those sessions had involved techniques that Milton was not proud of, but he had always told himself that he could justify the means by reference to the ends. It was dissembling, of course, and the things that he had done had been added to the catalogue of indiscretions for which he was now seeking to make amends.

That did not mean that he would shy away from his full playbook today. He thought of what had happened to Alícia, and then what had happened to Marks, and he knew that nothing would be off the menu if Lima chose to be uncooperative. He would do whatever it took.

Lima said something in Portuguese.

"English," Milton said.

His eyes flashed with fear and anger. "Who are you?"

Milton was silent, aware that each second that passed without an answer would increase the tension in the room, tighten the sense of foreboding that Lima must surely have been feeling.

"Do you know who I am?" Lima said.

Milton ignored him again.

Lima swallowed down his fear. "Do you work for Saverin?" he said. "I'm going to fucking ruin him, and then, when I've—"

Milton interrupted him, taking two fistfuls of his pyjama jacket and yanking him off the bed. He swung him across the room and sent him stumbling backwards. Milton followed him; he grabbed him again and dumped him into the wooden chair with his wrists still behind his back. The chair tipped and bounced against the wall. Milton righted it.

"It doesn't matter who I am," Milton said. "I'm not a friend. And I'm definitely not someone you want to have as an enemy."

"You're out of your mind—"

Milton reached around and took the SIG from the back of his jeans. He pressed it against Lima's forehead. "Be quiet, please."

Milton sat down on the edge of the bed, the pistol aimed squarely at Lima's chest. "I know what you've been doing."

"With what?"

"Saverin's got you for corruption."

"Nothing about what he says is true, and, when my lawyers have finished with him, there'll be a different story to tell."

Milton smiled at him. "You can't kid a kidder, *senhor* Lima. I'm going to ignore your bullshit and cut straight to it

—I don't have the patience to play games. I have a lot to do tonight."

"I don't know—"

"Antonio Rodrigues is your brother, isn't he?"

Milton saw Lima's larynx bob up and down.

"They call him Garanhão in Rocinha, don't they? The Womanizer. The Stallion."

"You crazy? I don't..."

Milton stared at Lima, let the businessman look into his eyes for a moment, and waited as his protests died in his throat.

"Your brother helped you out," Milton went on. "You asked him to put pressure on Saverin, so he kidnapped his daughter. Am I getting warm?"

"You're crazy," he repeated, although he spoke with much less conviction.

"Spoken to him recently? Antonio?"

Lima didn't reply; Milton could see the blood slowly draining out of his cheeks.

"Probably not," Milton said. He took out his phone, woke it, and navigated to his photographs, selecting the one that Paulo had sent of him with Alícia in the Grumari hotel room. He held the phone up so that Lima could see it.

Lima stared.

"That was taken this morning," Milton said. "Doesn't look like your brother has kept you up to speed. Let me help you out with that. I went up the Hill and got her. She's safe now—once the judge gets over what happened at your villa, he'll go and see her. I expect he'll take his family to Curitiba, where you won't be able to get to them. No more leverage for you, *senhor* Lima. You've played your cards. And you lost."

Milton took out the knife, making sure that Lima could

see it. "The best case for you now is that I give you back to Saverin. He'll add kidnapping and conspiracy to murder to your charges, and then you'll go to prison for a long time. It won't be pleasant, but you should look on the bright side: there's no death penalty here, is there? At least you'll still be alive."

Lima bit down on his lip and his fists clenched and unclenched. He couldn't take his eyes off the blade.

"Nasty, isn't it?" Milton said. "The RAF give them to pilots. It's for cutting parachute shroud lines after a bail-out." Milton held the blade closer. "See the curved end? It's not made for stabbing, but it's all I've got. I won't lie. It'll hurt like hell."

Milton leaned forward; Lima flinched and leaned back, but there was nowhere for him to go.

"Like I said," Milton continued, "prison is your best-case scenario. The alternative is much worse: I cut your throat and toss your body in the ocean." Milton held up his hand, forestalling Lima's retort. "I know, I know... You might be thinking that that's a bluff."

There was a towel on the edge of the bed. Milton took it, forced Lima's mouth open, and shoved the fabric inside. He leaned down, putting all of his weight on Lima's left knee so that the leg was immobilised, and then pressed the tip of the knife against his thigh. He held it there, just enough for Lima to feel the prick of the blade. All Milton needed to do now was push down, and the tip would slide into the flesh. Lima was anticipating the pain, mumbling into the towel. Milton knew that Lima wouldn't call his bluff. The fear would be too much for him.

"I'm your worst nightmare," Milton said. "I have nothing to lose. And I'll be honest with you: you and your brother have been unlucky. If you'd pulled this off two weeks ago, or if you'd waited a week, I wouldn't even have been here. But you didn't—you took that little girl when I was responsible for her. And the man I thought was my friend was stupid enough to ask me to come along to help him out, and now he's on my list along with your brother. The only question is whether you get out of here alive. I'd say it's fifty-fifty at the moment. It's down to you, really."

Lima was trying to speak.

"What's that? Are you going to cooperate?"

Lima nodded; fear blazed out of his eyes.

"I'm going to ask you one question," he said. "It's a simple question. If you answer it honestly, and if I believe you, you'll live. You have my word."

Milton pulled the towel out of his mouth.

"You want me to trust you?" Lima stammered.

"I don't care," Milton said. "But if you don't answer honestly, I promise you'll leave this room in a box. I'll chop you into little pieces."

Lima gritted his teeth and looked up at Milton. "*Filho da puta*."

"I know," Milton said. "It's been said before." He raised the knife and held it against Lima's throat, the blade catching against the bristles on his skin. "Ready for the question?"

Lima blinked, his face crumpled with terror.

Milton took him by the chin again and tilted his head up so that he could look down into his eyes. "Where is your brother?"

90

The convoy rolled into the compound at four in the morning. They rode in two Escalades and a Hummer, each equipped with privacy glass to hide the occupants. Antonio Rodrigues rode in the Hummer, with armed outriders in the Escalades ahead and behind. It was a two-hour drive from the city, heading almost due north through the Parque Nacional de Serra dos Orgãos. His bodyguards had called ahead, and they were met by a second armed detail as they rolled inside the perimeter. The gates—ten feet high and tipped with razor wire—rolled shut as soon as the last car was clear.

Rodrigues had been persuaded that he should leave for Itaipava after he had killed the old man at the top of the Hill. It had become obvious that John Milton was rather more dangerous than Shawn Drake had suggested. The man was far from his description as an 'old drunk.' Instead, he had single-handedly mounted an attack on the heart of Red Command territory, killing even more of his men before swiping the Saverin girl from the basement and then escaping in one piece. The feat was as unprecedented as it was alarming, and Rodrigues had agreed with his guards that it made sense for him to retreat to his farmhouse until the threat that Milton posed had been neutralised.

He felt the same sense of pride as he always did as he got out of the car and looked around. To call this retreat a farmhouse was seriously underselling it. There had been a single building on the site when the previous owner had purchased it, but it had been renovated and extended in the years that had followed, and Rodrigues had added a number of other buildings to form a U-shaped collection. The compound sat on a picturesque hill surrounded by mountains and was encircled on three sides by a moat. The interior of the main house had none of the froideur that marked the architecturally designed residences in the city, the sort of places that his half brother and the political class would pay millions of *reais* to buy. Instead, Antonio had insisted that the building should retain the exposed beams and hardwood panels that had been included when it was first constructed. There were some luxuries: a dining table that could seat eighteen, a secluded spa room where a masseuse was kept on twenty-four-hour call, an infinity pool that offered a beautiful view of the national park. The new buildings provided accommodation for his guests and for the three bodyguards that stayed by his side at all times. There was a six-car garage, too, carpeted and climate controlled to provide the perfect environment for his collection: a Ferrari F50, a Honda NSX, a Bentley Continental GT, and a Maybach Landaulet.

The building still retained its farmlands, too, and was surrounded by five hundred hectares of forest and pasture. It was secluded and easy to defend. Rodrigues had always felt safe here.

Lucas Peres got out of the lead car and came back to

open the door of the Hummer. Peres had a gold-plated 9mm in a holster attached to his belt, but he was a lot more relaxed than he had been as they had left Rocinha. Antonio stepped outside and allowed Peres to close the door after him.

"Don Rodrigues," Peres said, "I have bad news."

"Go on."

"I sent Luis and Branco to your brother's villa, just as you said. They have just called me. Something is wrong."

"What do you mean?"

"The police were outside. Two cars. The door to the villa was open, and they saw Saverin inside."

Antonio had called his half brother as soon as he had realised that Milton had taken the girl. He had told Andreas that he should come to the compound, too, but Andreas had said that he could not. Antonio had forgotten about the curfew and the radio bracelet that the court had made him wear. Antonio had no reason to believe that Andreas was in any more danger than he had been the day before, but events were changing fast, and he did not want to be caught out. How much did Paulo de Almeida know? Not much, surely, but he couldn't be certain. Shawn Drake was more concerning; he knew plenty, and Antonio had been unable to find him since he had come to apologise for the fuck-up at de Oliveira's house when Milton had killed Alessandro and Junior.

"What do you want me to do, Don Rodrigues?" Peres said.

"Speak to Barbantinho. He needs to find out what the police are doing there and where my brother is. And send a car back to the city. He is not brave. He's probably on his way here now." He flicked his hand, exasperated. "Whatever. Just find him and keep him safe."

Rodrigues stalked across the courtyard toward the main house. They were miles from anyone, but it was far from quiet: cicadas chirped, and he heard the moan of a potoo and then an answer from somewhere in the fringe of forest to the south of the house. He paused to look into the darkness that gathered between the trees. He knew that he was safe here, but the news that his brother was not where he was supposed to be had unsettled him. He wanted to get inside.

91

Milton had been driving for two hours, the last ten minutes with the lights off. Lima had provided a detailed description of the security at Rodrigues's compound, including that there would likely be sentries posted on the road half a mile out from the gates. Milton did not intend to announce his arrival to them and had decided that he would travel the rest of the way on foot.

There was a dirt track leading away from the main road, and Milton took it, rolling around a bend so that the car was out of sight behind a stand of rubber trees. He brought it to a halt and opened the door, but then stayed where he was for a moment and filled his lungs with clean, cool air. His head was still sore, his chest was bruised from the three rounds that had struck him earlier, and there had been moments during the drive when he would have liked nothing better than to pull over and sleep, but he knew that would have to wait. He had a brief window where he held the advantage over his prey; he would seize it. Rest would come later.

He collected his bag of equipment from the passenger

seat and set it down on the baked, rutted track. He took out the G36 and slipped his head through the strap, adjusting it so that he could hold the stock in his right hand. He collected the spare ammunition and shoved it into his pockets. He took the SIG, screwed on a suppressor, and pushed it into the waistband of his trousers. He would have liked the security of the ballistic vest, but that was in an industrial bin somewhere on the Hill. Never mind. He still had the stick of camo paint, and he reapplied it, checking in the mirror until his face was black save for the whites of his eyes. He took out the head mount and positioned it on his forehead again, testing the monocle and then pushing it up so that it was out of the way.

His muscles were stiff and sore. He pushed his shoulders back and felt the cracks as his spine realigned. He was as ready as he would ever be.

Milton went around to the back of the car and popped the trunk. Andreas Lima was curled up inside. Milton had secured his wrists and ankles with cable ties and had wrapped tape around his mouth, making sure that he could breathe through his nostrils.

Milton had decided to spare Lima for two reasons: first, because he didn't want to rob Saverin of his prize, and, second, because he had promised that the businessman would be unharmed and Milton's word meant something to him. Milton might have chosen to hand Lima over to the judge, but that didn't mean that the next few hours of Lima's life had to be pleasant. Milton intended to see to it that they were not.

"Uncomfortable?"

Lima's response was muffled by the tape.

"Never mind," Milton said. "You don't need to say anything. We're here. I'm going to go and see Antonio now.

Is there anything you want me to say to him before I kill him?"

Lima moaned again, the words indistinguishable.

"I'll be off, then. We're in the middle of nowhere. Make as much noise as you want. No one will hear you."

Milton slammed the lid of the trunk and turned away from the car. The track continued ahead, mirroring the road as it climbed into the foothills to the north. It was dark; he wouldn't be seen, especially not in the shelter of the undergrowth.

He set off.

MILTON SETTLED into the cover provided by a stand of palm trees. He glanced up into the canopy; the tree was laden with hard fruits that had attracted the attention of a family of spider monkeys. They chattered irritably at Milton's incursion and scurried higher into the branches with their prizes.

It was five in the morning. Milton had taken his time covering the approach to the compound, but he was here now. The land dipped down into a wide bowl with a collection of buildings at its centre. The buildings were enclosed within a brick wall. A dirt track wound its way between the trees before making its final approach through a section that had been cleared to offer better visibility to the guards on the gate. Milton watched the scene through the monocle. He counted three men: one on the gate and two leaning against a big Escalade. None of them looked particularly vigilant. Why would they? The compound sheltered behind its walls, and only a madman would consider going up against someone like Antonio Rodrigues here, on his own turf.

They probably thought the risk had passed as soon as the gates rolled shut behind them.

They would have been wrong.

Milton scoped out the last section of the approach. The vegetation had been kept down at the front of the facility, but it had been allowed to grow back around the sides. There was a margin of ten metres that he would have to cross where he would not be able to rely upon the cover afforded by the ferns and palms, but he could see no guards at that side who might otherwise spot him.

Garanhão had allowed his power to go to his head. Milton had seen his type before. The Don knew that people feared him. He revelled in that fear and assumed that it would protect him. And that was enough to keep most of his adversaries in line. But Milton was not most adversaries. Garanhão was arrogant and lackadaisical, and it was going to kill him.

Milton scoped the compound through the monocle once more and, satisfied that he was clear, passed through the fringe of overgrowth so that he could get around to the unattended stretch of wall. He paused at the edge of the vegetation, took a breath, scoped left and right one final time and, after confirming that he was clear, he sprinted for the wall and hauled himself up.

92

Antonio Rodrigues had only been asleep for a few hours before he awoke. Something had disturbed him, and, as he lay in his expensively upholstered bed, he couldn't quite put his finger on what it was. He opened his eyes and looked around the room. It was dark, with the curtains still drawn; everything was just as he would have expected it to be. He fumbled across the bedside table for the Rolex President and blinked his eyes until he could make out the time. It was six. He had only been in bed for a couple of hours. He closed his eyes again, running his finger against the links of the watch's yellow gold bracelet. He had bought the watch after he had made his first big score. He had stolen a backpack of coca paste from a *matuto* who had brought it over the border from Bolivia, and sold it to one of the entrepreneurial chemists who would turn it into powder and then sell it to local *cariocas*. Antonio had made ten thousand and had haggled with the thief who was selling the stolen watch until he had accepted four. Antonio had split the remainder three ways: he'd kept two for himself and given two each to his half brother and father. He had been twelve years old.

He often remembered that first score, thinking about how far he had travelled since then. It was one of the memories that he played back before he settled into sleep, but, try as he might, it didn't have its usual soothing effect this morning. He gave up and, cursing at the thought of how tired he was going to be today, he sat up, swung his legs out of bed, stood and padded across the room to the window.

He parted the drapes and looked outside. His bedroom was in the central portion of the house, with two stubby wings extending out to form an enclosed courtyard. The two Escalades and the Hummer were parked in the same spots as last night. There was something, though, out beyond them, past the courtyard and out to the garage where he kept his cars.

He blinked, then rubbed his eyes.

A man was lying spread-eagled across the gravel.

He rubbed his eyes again.

He looked over to the accommodation block and saw another body leaning back against the wall as if resting. It was a man, and he was wearing a red, white and green Fluminense jersey, the same as Lucas Peres had been wearing last night.

Rodrigues felt sick.

He turned away from the window, and, in the second before the drapes came together, in the moment before the light that fell into the room was closed out, he saw that someone was sitting in the armchair on the other side of the room.

Rodrigues froze.

"You wanted to meet me, Antonio. Here I am."

Rodrigues fought back the fear. "*Senhor* Milton," he said, "you've gone to a lot of trouble. It really isn't necessary."

"You made it necessary."

The voice was blank, emotionless, calm. Rodrigues remembered it from the phone call that he had made on the top of the Hill last night.

Rodrigues saw that the man was holding something in his lap.

"What do you want?"

"There's a cancer in Rocinha. It needs to be cut out."

Milton moved his hand, and a thin shaft of light sparked against the gun in his hand.

"No," Rodrigues said, "this really isn't necessary, not like this. Perhaps we can reach an arrangement. Look around you. I am a rich man. What is your price?"

Milton did not answer; instead, he shook his head.

"Everyone has a price, *senhor* Milton."

Milton still did not speak.

"Fine—perhaps something else. It is revenge that you want?"

"You can call it that if you like. I prefer justice."

"You want to settle a score. I can understand that. You could kill me, but then what about the man who betrayed you? *Senhor* Drake. I expect you would like to see him again."

"I would," Milton said.

"Then you will need me to help you do that. He has gone to ground. You won't be able to find him."

"You have a very low opinion of me."

"Not at all, *senhor*. You are an impressive man. But your friend—he is frightened."

"He should be. He knows what I'm going to do to him."

The shadow shifted in the chair. "But you're right—I am interested in him. You know where he is?"

"Of course. If I tell you, we can part on friendly terms?"

"Him and half a million dollars. No negotiation. You asked my price—that's it."

Relief. Perhaps he could be bargained with. "Fine. *Senhor* Drake and half a million. You walk away, and you give me my brother—I am assuming you have him?"

"He's in the trunk of my car. He's fine. I'll hang onto him until I'm away from here, just to make sure you don't get ideas when you don't have a gun pointed at you. I'll dump him at the side of the road when I'm safe."

"Then we have a deal."

Rodrigues was too wise to be reassured, but he allowed himself to entertain the notion that he might walk away from this after all.

Milton raised a hand. "There is one more thing. We can treat it as a sign of your good faith. The girl that Drake is with—Sophia Lopes. Is she involved?"

"Involved?"

"Does she work for you?"

"No," he said. "She has nothing to do with me." He shrugged.

"Thank you."

Milton stood.

Rodrigues took a step back. "Are we good?"

"We're good."

"What about your money? How do you want to get paid?"

Milton aimed the pistol at Rodrigues.

"In kind," he said.

93

Paulo de Almeida leaned back and scrubbed his tired eyes. It had been quite a day.

Milton had called him again after Saverin had spoken with his daughter and had provided him with clear instructions: he was to telephone the judge and give him the address of the hotel. Milton had explained what would happen next, and had been largely proven right. Saverin himself had driven out to Grumari with six policemen and had taken custody of Alícia. The officers had said that Paulo, Rafaela and Eloá would have to come with them, too. Paulo had not resisted. Milton had predicted that, too.

They had been taken to the main Polícia Federal building in Centro and, after being given food and drink, they had been questioned. Paulo had explained that Rafaela knew very little, and, after satisfying themselves that that was the case, the officers had taken her and Eloá to a room with a bed where they could rest. Paulo had not been extended the same offer, and a succession of different officers had asked him the same questions with minor variations. He answered them honestly, as Milton had said that he should, and eventually they had left him alone. He had been in the room for hours, and he wanted to see his family. He got to his feet and was about to go and try the door when it opened and Saverin came inside and made his way over to the table.

"Sit down," he said firmly.

Paulo did. The judge was quite different now to how he had been this morning; then, he had barely acknowledged Paulo and his family in his hurry to get to his daughter. Now, though, he was all business. He wore the stern countenance that was so well known from his appearances on the television news, his brows knitted together in a heavy frown and his eyes sharp and piercing.

"I haven't thanked you yet," he said. "Smith said he wouldn't have been able to get my daughter without the risks you took. I'm grateful."

"I'm glad I could help," Paulo replied a little nervously; it was obvious that the judge's expression of gratitude was a formality, and that it would soon be replaced with something else entirely.

"But that's not what I want to talk to you about," Saverin said. "It's John Smith. I want to know who he is."

"Who?" *John Smith?* Paulo assumed that Saverin meant Milton, and caught himself before he could say anything else, but Saverin was sharp. He leaned forward.

"Smith isn't his real name, is it?"

"I don't know," Paulo said.

"Yes, you do, Paulo. You know. You need to give me everything. *Everything.* He assaulted and then abducted a federal suspect yesterday evening. We still don't know where he is. We found three dead bodies in a house in Santa Teresa. We think he was involved with that, too." Saverin leaned back and managed a smile. "Look, Paulo—I know you were implicated in what happened to my daughter, but I want you to know that I'm working on an amnesty. You have my word that you'll be looked after if you cooperate. You and your family. No charges. We'll get you out of the city if you want, and I'll make sure that your daughter gets the treatment that she needs." The smile disappeared, and he leaned forward again, avid, like an eagle addressing a mouse. "But if I think you're lying to me... If I think that, then we're not going to be friends. There'll be no deal, and I'll bring charges against you. Understand?"

"Yes, sir."

"Good. Now—what is his name?"

"Milton," Paulo said reluctantly. "John Milton. But I know very little about him."

"What *do* you know?" Saverin gestured impatiently with his hand. "Everything."

Milton had told him that he could tell Saverin everything, even if Saverin were to ask about Milton himself, because, in fact, Paulo really did know very little about the man who had saved his life.

"He speaks English," Paulo said. "He's medium height and build. Middle aged. Blue eyes."

"I know all that," Saverin said impatiently. "What about his background?"

"Probably military."

"Why do you say that?"

"He was very good with guns."

"What else? Where was he staying?"

"He had a room at a hotel in Jacarepaguá."

"You went there?"

Paulo said that he had. Saverin asked for the details and wrote down the address in a notebook.

"More."

Paulo shrugged helplessly. "I don't know what else to tell you."

Saverin stared at him, drumming his fingers on the table, and then took a photograph out of the notebook and slid it across the table. "You know him?"

Paulo looked down; the photograph was of the old man who had been working with Milton, the man who had fitted him with the camera. "Yes," he said. "He was working with Milton. They were friends."

"You know his name?"

"No," he said.

"I do," Saverin said. "His name was Harry Marks. He was English—he came to Rio years ago, had a place in Laranjeiras. Past tense. His body was found at the top of the Hill this morning. He'd been shot in the head and left at the side of the road."

Paulo remembered the video call that Milton had received from Garanhão as they had driven away from the Hill. He hadn't seen what had happened, but it was easy enough to guess.

Saverin was about to ask another question when the door opened and a uniformed policeman hurried inside.

"What is it?" Saverin snapped.

"Judge," the officer said, "we got a call ten minutes ago. A man said there was a car parked outside and we should go and check it out. It was the car that Smith was driving last night."

Saverin stood. "And?"

"You have to come and see."

Saverin hurried out of the room, leaving the door open behind him. Paulo waited for a moment and then got up. He wasn't under arrest; no one had said anything about staying in the room. He looked left and right outside the door and then walked down the corridor in the direction Saverin had gone.

The lobby of the station was thronged with officers and other men and women who worked for the department. A path had opened up at the door to the street, and a man was being brought inside. Paulo recognised Andreas Lima from the news: he was the businessman that Saverin had arrested at the airport just over a week ago. He looked different to how he had looked on the television. Instead of the expensive suit that he had been wearing then, now he was dressed in pyjamas. And rather than the haughty expression that he had managed to put on his face as he had been led away from the airport, now he looked frightened. His hands and feet were secured with cable ties, and two officers had to half-carry and half-drag him inside. Paulo stood with the officers and staff and heard the same question over and over again.

What had happened to him?

Paulo knew what had happened.

John Milton had happened.

"Clear the room," Saverin called out, making his way to Lima. "And get those restraints off him."

Paulo returned to the peace and quiet of the interview room and half closed the door.

Milton.

He remembered what the Englishman had told him as they had spoken earlier that morning. Milton had given him an address in Parada de Lucas and told him to remember it. He had explained it all: Paulo was to go to the address once things had quietened down and find the lock-up garage that he described to him. Milton told him where to find the key and what to look for once he was inside. He said that he had left something there that would help with Eloá's treatment.

Paulo went back to the chair and lowered himself into it again. He hadn't slept for over a day, and he was suffering because of it. He wanted to see his wife and daughter again, to be alone with them, to hug them and tell them that everything would all be all right. They were caught in the eye of the storm, but Paulo knew that things were going to work out for the best.

Paulo thought of Milton and everything that he had done for him. He knew so little about him. He didn't understand why he had risked his life for the life of the girl, and why he was working so hard to make things right for Paulo and his family, too. Paulo had told the truth to Saverin. He knew almost nothing about Milton, apart from one thing about which he was certain: he would never see the Englishman again.

Paulo wondered where he was now.

EPILOGUE

Dawn broke over the city. Milton was starting to feel tired: his eyes were gritty and uncomfortable, and his muscles and joints ached like they always did when he hadn't had enough sleep. He never used to feel that way when he was in the army. He could go forty-eight hours without sleep back then and still feel reasonable; it was different now, just another sign that he was getting older.

He leaned down again and put his eye to the optical scope. He was in the unfinished house on the other side of the road from Drake's place in Santa Teresa. He could see the villa poking through the dense vegetation as the road curled up and around ahead of him. He had remembered this spot from his previous visits: Drake had mentioned that the developer had gone bust and that the villa had been left unattended. Milton had sliced a hole in the plastic sheeting that covered the open window frames and set up his equipment in the upstairs bedroom that faced the road. The wall had big spaces where floor-to-ceiling windows would be installed, and Milton had cut another slice in the sheeting through which he inserted the barrel of the Galil assault rifle that he had taken from the cache. The scope was excellent and provided a clear visual of Drake's villa and the garden in front of it.

There had been a lot of time to plot and then perfect what he proposed to do. He had been here for almost two days and was prepared to be as patient as necessary. He was as sure as he could be that Drake's house was empty.

He had seen Sophia on the first day of his watch. She had been driven to the house by an older man who looked like he might be her father. The man had wheeled a suitcase into the house, and Milton had watched through the scope as the two of them had gone from room to room packing things into it. They were inside for no longer than half an hour and had left without a backward glance. Milton had let her go. He had already satisfied himself that she was not involved, and Rodrigues had confirmed it. Sophia hadn't sold him out to Drake; rather, either Rodrigues or Drake had put Xavier de Oliveira's house under surveillance, knowing that Milton would go there eventually.

Drake and Milton had been hunter and hunted then, but the roles were reversed now.

Milton had brought a bedroll and a blanket and had set those up next to the rifle, snatching an hour or two of uncomfortable and fitful sleep where he could. He had military rations, MREs that he warmed up with the supplied flameless ration heater, and two big bottles of water.

He had been awake for most of the time and had distracted himself with two stories that had quickly appeared on Brazilian websites. The main sites—*O Dia, O Fluminense, Meia Hora* and *O Globo*—all led with the same image: a lucky photographer had snapped the moment that Andreas Lima had been found in the trunk of a stolen car in a lot near the police building in Centro. Two officers were photographed helping him out of the car.

There was a stock picture of Felipe Saverin in the *O Globo* story. There was a quote, too, and Milton had pasted it into Google Translate: Saverin said that Andreas Lima and Antonio Rodrigues were half brothers, and that the abduction of his daughter had been carried out by Rodrigues at Lima's request. Kidnapping and murder would now be added to the businessman's already extensive charge sheet.

The competing story was the murder of Rodrigues at his compound in Itaipava. Garanhão, and six of his men, had been found by a delivery driver. The don's men had been stabbed and strangled, while Rodrigues had been shot in his bedroom. There was speculation about who had killed them, with the most popular theory implicating the military police. The body of an ex-BOPE policeman—Xavier de Oliveira—had been discovered at his home in Santa Teresa, and Red Command were suspected of his murder. A Reddit thread that Milton scanned suggested that Rodrigues and the others had been executed by the military police as a warning to the gangs that they would not win in a direct battle with the state.

Milton had been busy. He had driven back to the city from the compound, had dumped the stolen car in Centro, then called the police and told them who they would find in the trunk. Then he had made his way to the cache. He had opened the garage for the final time, collecting the sniper rifle, bedroll and rations. He had taken one of Marks's junk televisions, kicked out the screen, and hidden Lima's money and the Rolex that he had taken from Rodrigues inside the cabinet. Milton had counted the cash: there was two hundred and fifty thousand *reais*, and the watch would be worth another fifty thousand on top of that. Enough to make a difference to a family who needed a break. Milton had moved the set to the front of the line so that it would be easy for Paulo to find, had gone outside, pulled down the door and hid the key where Paulo could find it. Then he had made his way here. He had been in place ever since.

Milton snapped back to attention as he heard a beep from the portable receiver that he had placed on the floor next to the rifle. The beep was from a motion detector connected to one of the bugs that Milton had hidden in Shawn Drake's villa. Milton picked up the receiver and turned the volume all the way up.

He heard the sound of footsteps and then a door opening. He used the scope to check the front of the house. Nothing. Whoever was inside had gone in through the back. He heard more footsteps and then caught a flash of movement in the bedroom window. He nudged the rifle down and stared through the scope until he saw the movement again.

It was Drake. He was putting clothes into a bag that he had dumped on the bed. He was moving quickly, without discretion. He was bugging out.

Milton settled down on the floor, ensuring that his body was in line with the Galil and not canted out to the side. He made sure the rifle's stock was against his shoulder and then grabbed as much floor as he could.

Milton took out his phone, put it on speaker, and dialled Drake's number.

He relaxed his body, nudging the bipod legs forward until the muzzle was back on target and he had forward pressure against the bipod.

The call connected. "Hello?"

Milton slid his finger through the guard and curled it around the trigger.

"Hello?"

Milton watched through the scope as Drake froze.

"Hello? Who is this?"

"It's me," Milton said.

"John?"

"Surprised? Did you think I'd just disappear?"

"Where are you?"

Drake turned to the window and gazed out. Milton could see the wary expression on his face.

"How much did Rodrigues pay you?"

"Don't be sanctimonious, John. You would've done the same thing."

"You don't know me very well at all, Shawn."

Milton shifted an inch to his left, pressing his cheek closer against the rifle.

"You want to settle this?" Drake said. "Tell me where you are. I'll come to you."

Milton ignored the offer. "You're all on your own now."

"How do you work that out?"

"Rodrigues is dead."

"So I heard. I underestimated you."

"And Sophia's gone."

"Yeah? You speak to her?"

"Didn't need to. I watched her pack up and leave. Just like you're doing now."

The scope was powerful. Milton could see Drake's horrified reaction as he realised the danger he was in.

Too late.

Milton emptied his lungs with a long, even breath and squeezed the trigger.

A WORD FROM MARK

I hope you enjoyed 'Redeemer.' It was great fun to write, but then all of Milton's adventures are like that. There's something about finding an interesting place in the world, with issues that interest me, and then dropping him right into the middle of it. And, after writing about Milton for a few years now, every new novel is like meeting an old friend again.

John will be back again soon with a novel that will see him investigate a pair of assassins who have murdered a defector in a sleepy English seaside town. And, yes, before you ask, it *is* influenced by current events. I live in Salisbury in the southwest of England and, not that long ago, a spy and his daughter were attacked here with a nerve agent. They were found by two people that I know on a park bench five minutes from where I'm writing this. It has been impossible not to be influenced by those events, and they will provide a backdrop for what will be an exciting and topical read.

Building a relationship with my readers is the very best thing about writing. I occasionally send newsletters with details on new releases, special offers and other bits of news relating to the Milton, Beatrix and Isabella Rose and Soho Noir series.

If you join my Readers' Club I'll send you this free Milton content:

1. A free copy of Milton's adventure in North Korea - '1000 Yards.'

2. A free copy of Milton's tussle with a Mafia assassin in 'Tarantula.'

3. An eyes-only profile of Milton from a Group Fifteen psychologist.

You can get your free content by visiting my website at markjdawson.com. I'll look forward to seeing you there.

ALSO BY MARK DAWSON

IN THE JOHN MILTON SERIES

The Cleaner

Sharon Warriner is a single mother in the East End of
London, fearful that she's lost her young son to a life in the
gangs. After John Milton saves her life, he promises to help.
But the gang, and the charismatic rapper who leads it, is not
about to cooperate with him.

Buy The Cleaner

Saint Death

John Milton has been off the grid for six months. He
surfaces in Ciudad Juárez, Mexico, and immediately finds
himself drawn into a vicious battle with the narco-gangs
that control the borderlands.

Buy Saint Death

The Driver

When a girl he drives to a party goes missing, John Milton is worried. Especially when two dead bodies are discovered and the police start treating him as their prime suspect.

Buy The Driver

Ghosts

John Milton is blackmailed into finding his predecessor as Number One. But she's a ghost, too, and just as dangerous as him. He finds himself in deep trouble, playing the Russians against the British in a desperate attempt to save the life of his oldest friend.

Buy Ghosts

The Sword of God

On the run from his own demons, John Milton treks through the Michigan wilderness into the town of Truth. He's not looking for trouble, but trouble's looking for him. He finds himself up against a small-town cop who has no idea with whom he is dealing, and no idea how dangerous he is.

Buy The Sword of God

Salvation Row

Milton finds himself in New Orleans, returning a favour that saved his life during Katrina. When a lethal adversary from his past takes an interest in his business, there's going to be hell to pay.

Buy Salvation Row

Headhunters

Milton barely escaped from Avi Bachman with his life. But when the Mossad's most dangerous renegade agent breaks out of a maximum security prison, their second fight will be to the finish.

Buy Headhunters

The Ninth Step

Milton's attempted good deed becomes a quest to unveil corruption at the highest levels of government and murder at the dark heart of the criminal underworld. Milton is pulled back into the game, and that's going to have serious consequences for everyone who crosses his path.

Buy The Ninth Step

The Jungle

John Milton is no stranger to the world's seedy underbelly. But when the former British Secret Service agent comes up against a ruthless human trafficking ring, he'll have to fight harder than ever to conquer the evil in his path.

Buy The Jungle

Blackout

A message from Milton's past leads him to Manila and a

confrontation with an adversary he thought he would never meet again. Milton finds himself accused of murder and imprisoned inside a brutal Filipino jail - can he escape, uncover the truth and gain vengeance for his friend?

Buy Blackout

The Alamo

A young boy witnesses a murder in a New York subway restroom. Milton finds him, and protects him from corrupt cops and the ruthless boss of a local gang.

Buy The Alamo

IN THE BEATRIX ROSE SERIES

In Cold Blood

Beatrix Rose was the most dangerous assassin in an off-the-books government kill squad until her former boss betrayed her. A decade later, she emerges from the Hong Kong underworld with payback on her mind. They gunned down her husband and kidnapped her daughter, and now the debt needs to be repaid. It's a blood feud she didn't start but she is going to finish.

Buy In Cold Blood

Blood Moon Rising

There were six names on Beatrix's Death List and now there are four. She's going to account for the others, one by one, even if it kills her. She has returned from Somalia with another target in her sights. Bryan Duffy is in Iraq, surrounded by mercenaries, with no easy way to get to him and no easy way to get out. And Beatrix has other issues that need to be addressed. Will Duffy prove to be one kill too far?

Buy Blood Moon Rising

Blood and Roses

Beatrix Rose has worked her way through her Kill List. Four are dead, just two are left. But now her foes know she has them in her sights and the hunter has become the hunted.

Buy Blood and Roses

Hong Kong Stories, Vol. 1

Beatrix Rose flees to Hong Kong after the murder of her husband and the kidnapping of her child. She needs money. The local triads have it. What could possibly go wrong?

Buy Hong Kong Stories

Phoenix

She does Britain's dirty work, but this time she needs help. Beatrix Rose, meet John Milton...

Buy Phoenix

IN THE ISABELLA ROSE SERIES

The Angel

Isabella Rose is recruited by British intelligence after a terrorist attack on Westminster.

Buy The Angel

The Asset

Isabella Rose, the Angel, is used to surprises, but being abducted is an unwelcome novelty. She's relying on Michael Pope, the head of the top-secret Group Fifteen, to get her back.

Buy The Asset

The Agent

Isabella Rose is on the run, hunted by the very people she had been hired to work for. Trained killer Isabella and former handler Michael Pope are forced into hiding in India and, when a mysterious informer passes them clues on the whereabouts of Pope's family, the prey see an opportunity to become the predators.

Buy The Asset

The Assassin

Ciudad Juárez, Mexico, is the most dangerous city in the world. And when a mission to break the local cartel's grip goes wrong, Isabella Rose, the Angel, finds herself on the wrong side of prison bars. Fearing the worst, Isabella plays her only remaining card...

Buy The Assassin

IN THE SOHO NOIR SERIES

Gaslight

When Harry and his brother Frank are blackmailed into paying off a local hood they decide to take care of the problem themselves. But when all of London's underworld is in thrall to the man's boss, was their plan audacious or the most foolish thing that they could possibly have done?

Free Download

The Black Mile

London, 1940: the Luftwaffe blitzes London every night for fifty-seven nights. Houses, shops and entire streets are wiped from the map. The underworld is in flux: the Italian criminals who dominated the West End have been interned and now their rivals are fighting to replace them. Meanwhile, hidden in the shadows, the Black-Out Ripper sharpens his knife and sets to his grisly work.

Get The Black Mile

The Imposter

War hero Edward Fabian finds himself drawn into a criminal family's web of vice and soon he is an accomplice to their scheming. But he's not the man they think he is - he's far more dangerous than they could possibly imagine.

Get The Imposter

ABOUT THE AUTHOR

Mark Dawson is the author of the breakout John Milton, Beatrix and Isabella Rose and Soho Noir series.

For more information:
www.markjdawson.com
mark@markjdawson.com

ACKNOWLEDGMENTS

To all the members of Team Milton for their amazing insight and support. And also to Rafael Aymone, Sergio Petejo and Daniel Davidsohn for assistance on Rio de Janeiro and Portuguese. I'm grateful to them all.

AN UNPUTDOWNABLE ebook.
First published in Great Britain in 2013 by UNPUTDOWNABLE LIMITED
Ebook first published in 2013 by UNPUTDOWNABLE LIMITED

Copyright © UNPUTDOWNABLE LIMITED 2013-2014 v2

94818180R00259

Made in the USA
Columbia, SC
01 May 2018